"I'M SORRY," CRAIG SAID

Jennifer crossed her arms over her chest. "What for?"

"For coming here without finding some way to warn you . . . for leaving the way I did seven years ago."

"What happened before is history. Something both of us would be better off forgetting."

"Can we at least be friends?" he asked gently.

"I don't know if that's possible," she admitted. "I've spent too much time hating you. There's no way I can make those feelings disappear overnight." When she saw the flash of pain her words provoked, she was surprised it brought her no satisfaction.

"Jennifer . . . you have to realize by now that I had no choice."

"You used me."

"I loved you." And he still loved her, but he had lost the right to tell her so.

ABOUT THE AUTHOR

Georgia Bockoven, a Sacramento, California resident, found herself falling in love with Kentucky when she visited the state to do research for her fifth Superromance. She was also exhilarated closer to home, when, for the first time, she had the opportunity to address three hundred members of her public at a recent Harlequin Reader Party in her hometown!

We are delighted to announce that Georgia's last Superromance, *Today, Tomorrow, Always*, has recently won the Romance Writers of America Golden Medallion Award.

Books by Georgia Bockoven

HARLEQUIN SUPERROMANCE
82–RESTLESS TIDE
102–AFTER THE LIGHTNING
138–LITTLE BY LITTLE
179–TODAY, TOMORROW, ALWAYS

HARLEQUIN TEMPTATION
14–TRACINGS ON A WINDOW
57–A GIFT OF WILD FLOWERS
94–A WEEK FROM FRIDAY

These books may be available at your local bookseller.

Don't miss any of our special offers. Write to us at the following address for information on our newest releases.

Harlequin Reader Service
901 Fuhrmann Blvd., P.O. Box 1397, Buffalo, NY 14240
Canadian address: P.O. Box 603,
Fort Erie, Ont. L2A 9Z9

Georgia Bockoven

THE LONG ROAD HOME

Harlequin Books

TORONTO • NEW YORK • LONDON
AMSTERDAM • PARIS • SYDNEY • HAMBURG
STOCKHOLM • ATHENS • TOKYO • MILAN

Published August 1986

First printing June 1986

ISBN 0-373-70222-1

Printed in Canada

For the men in my life—John, Shawn, and Paul.

With special thanks to Linda Serafin,
and Liz and Dick Brahams.

CHAPTER ONE

THE YELLOWED NEWSPAPER CLIPPING slipped from Craig Templeton's numbed grasp. For an instant it hung suspended above the rolltop desk, caught by the early morning summer wind that swept through the open window behind him. Then, as if somehow weighted by the staggering information it contained, the paper fell to rejoin the other dozen or so sheets that lay scattered across the green ink blotter.

After a moment his gaze focused once more on the bold headlines. "Ransom Note Yields No Clues In Mitchell Kidnapping." Despite a desperate internal struggle to deny what lay before him, the words, written almost twenty-five years earlier, were impossible to ignore. Slowly his long fingers nudged the clippings until he had once again exposed them and forced himself to read the headlines on each. It wasn't until he had reached the last that his chest tightened as he held his breath against the agony of knowing. He stared at the photograph of a child less than a year old, with softly curling black hair and large dark eyes. And he knew as surely as he had ever known anything—he was that child.

All that he was, all that he had believed in, was based on a lie. The bloodline that bound him to the land he called home had in actuality stopped with the man whom he had called father. He had always been told that his love for Oklahoma was something passed on to him, his birthright as the fifth generation of Templeton men to wrest their living from the unyielding soil.

Dammit! How was it possible for him to have felt that bonding when it wasn't really there? The newspapers were wrong—they had to be.

Searching for a reason, for the smallest grain of evidence that would allow him to disbelieve the facts in front of him, he reread the article that accompanied the photograph of the infant.

Lexington, Kentucky—Federal investigators are following up on dozens of possible leads in the Mitchell kidnapping. When asked for a statement about the chances of finding the Mitchell baby alive after two weeks without word from the kidnappers, Felix Dempster, chief investigator on the case, replied, "We have no reason to believe the child is not alive; therefore, we are continuing the investigation as if he were."

Asked about a possible alternative motive for the crime, Dempster disagreed with the suggestion that the kidnapping might be the work of black-market baby merchants. "This crime simply does not fit the standard method of operation for those people," he said. "They prey on a different socio-economic group." When reminded that the child had been taken from the home of a relative who lived in a less than affluent area of Lexington, Dempster had no comment.

Earlier this morning it was announced that the parents had gone into seclusion at their home on Mitchell Farm and would not hold another press conference unless further news was received. Agnes Mitchell, the infant's mother, is currently under the care of the family physician after collapsing yesterday during an emotional plea she had made to the kidnappers, carried on national radio.

Craig's gaze shifted to the people in the photograph above the child's. Even with their faces lined with grief, their eyes sunken from lack of sleep, he could see a piece of himself in them—something he had never been able to do with the man and woman who had claimed him as their own.

Abruptly he turned from the evidence of deception and walked to the window. He brushed aside the lace curtain to stare at the horizon, now grown purple with the false dawn. Without conscious effort he could feel the pressure of his "father's" arm resting across his shoulders and hear his "mother's" lilting voice. *How could he accuse them of something as heinous as stealing someone else's child when they were no longer alive to defend themselves?*

Why had she kept them? What perverse instinct had made his mother keep the clippings when she must have known he would find them someday? Or had that been her intention all along?

His gaze swept over his inheritance—thousands of acres of soil, good for little more than grazing cattle and sinking natural gas wells. It was land, he had believed until that morning, that provided enough money to keep things going comfortably around the ranch on a year-to-year basis with little left over for luxuries. Never had he imagined there was any real wealth that would someday be his. But it hadn't taken long for the lists of stocks and bonds and their worth to become almost incomprehensible as they were enumerated that morning by the attorney in his low droning voice. *Why had they always lived as if money was a rare and precious commodity?*

Craig's hand closed into a fist, crushing the delicate lace curtain. What good would it do to relive the past now? Even if he found answers, they wouldn't change anything. For all that he had obviously received from his biological parents—his lankiness, height and angular features—his adoptive parents were the ones who had left the deeper etchings on who and what he was.

He returned to the desk. Carefully he gathered the fragile papers, folding them at their original creases and fitting them into the envelope he had found at the back of the ranch safe. The small package felt heavy in his hand as he carried it to its previous resting place. When he closed the safe's door, his hand lingered on the dial. Suddenly the grainy photograph of a grief-stricken man and woman flashed through his mind. He swore softly. It seemed the ghosts from his past would not be denied so easily.

CHAPTER TWO

WITH THE GENTLE URGING of shorter, cooler days and the insistent demands of nature, the Kentucky bluegrass region had reluctantly but flagrantly announced autumn with brilliant splashes of scarlet and gold. The frantic pace of the racing season, early- and late-summer yearling sales and the rounds of parties for any and all conceivable reasons, had begun its ritual wind down toward the near-hibernation of winter. Anxious owners watched their prized covered mares grow heavy with what they hoped would be multimillion dollar foals, while the current year's crop of colts romped on legs still spindly with youth.

While most welcomed the slower pace, Jennifer Langley dreaded the season because of the months that would necessarily follow. After nature's showy striptease came the gentle, transitory blanketing snows of winter. And with winter came the memories that were tied with bright shiny ribbons of pain to snowflakes and holidays.

Alone in the offices of Mitchell Farm while Lynn, her secretary, ran errands in town, Jennifer felt oppressed by the quiet of a Thoroughbred farm preparing for winter. It allowed her far too much time to think. She leaned her elbows on the insurance forms in front of her and rubbed her temples, her fingers automatically stopping just short of the raised line that marked the place where broken bone had mended.

Learning precisely where her touch would not spark a memory was something she had discovered after she had left the hospital for the first time. To avoid looking at herself directly in a mirror was a habit that came later, after the final surgery and the acceptance that she would look as she did for the rest of her life. Even after two years there was always an instant of shock when the image reflected was not the one she remembered. It took so little to make a difference—the arch of an eyebrow, the length of a nose.

It wasn't that she felt the surgeons had failed. After all, putting back together pieces of bone that offered fewer clues than a jigsaw puzzle had been the critical objective. If the nose happened to be more perfect than before, or the cheeks a little on the hollow side or the eyes infinitesimally farther apart, surely those were minor faults when considering what a miracle it was that she had a face at all. Besides, how could she complain when the look she had been given was the very one most women supposedly strived to achieve? She was pretty—some even said beautiful. But because her face wasn't the one she remembered, she didn't feel at home or even comfortable in her own body.

Being able to use the skills she had learned in college to run the bookkeeping end of Mitchell Farm had been a godsend. For the past year she had eagerly put in long hours, relishing the work that was usually complex enough to require her full concentration. The room she had been given to work in was separated from the foyer and Lynn's desk by a solid ash door with a large sign that said Private. The isolation easily allowed her to avoid the flow of visitors who came to the farm throughout the summer. Only the men and women who actually worked and lived on the farm, her family or longtime friends were ever invited inside her office. It was easier that way. Sooner or later, no matter how well-intentioned, strangers asked questions.

Since she had moved into one of the farm's homes for employees, she rarely left the grounds anymore. Even the trips into Lexington to the plastic surgeon had ceased when he informed her that there was nothing he could do for her headaches unless she consented to another operation—something she had vowed never to go through again. At twenty-three, she had learned to mark her days with the cynical acceptance of a prison inmate. Today, tomorrow, the next day, none were regarded as anything more or less than periods of time she managed to get through.

A car, its approach heralded by the crackle of dry leaves that covered the roadway, caught her attention. She raised her head to glance at the clock on the opposite wall. Twelve-thirty...too early for the courier from the accountant's office or the delivery Lynn said she was expecting from the stationery store. She reached into the left-hand drawer of her desk and withdrew a half-empty economy-size bottle of aspirins. With deft, well-practiced movements she shook out three of the white tablets, then reached for the cup of tepid coffee sitting beside her partially eaten sandwich. She grimaced as she swallowed the unpalatable combination.

The grimace became a puzzled frown when she heard the car pull into the parking space outside her window. A door squeaked open, then shut. Boot heels sounded a light tapping as they struck the concrete walkway in a decidedly masculine stride. She mentally pictured the visitor's progress as she heard him round the building. She imagined his steps as he traveled the chrysanthemum-lined walkway to the small porch...gave him time to read the notice that said the office was closed until three o'clock... pictured him turning—

She blinked in surprise as the bell on the outer door sounded, announcing that someone had entered. Lynn must have forgotten to lock up when she left, or perhaps she had figured that because of the season there wasn't any need.

With a resigned sigh she pushed herself away from her desk, got up and went to the door. She had been right; it was a man. He stood with his back to her, studying the trophy case. Dressed in jeans and a tweed jacket and wearing well-broken-in lizard-skin boots, he looked comfortable and natural in clothing that had become an affectation on many. "Can I help you?"

He turned at the sound of her voice, and she pulled back in surprise. She knew him... and yet she knew just as strongly that she had never seen him before. There was something hauntingly familiar about him—from his thick black hair to his square jaw, to his deep set, almost black eyes.

"I'm here for the tour," he said, his voice a compelling, resonant bass.

"The tour?" she repeated inanely, her concentration captured by an overwhelming feeling of déjà vu.

"...of the farm. I was told to be here at one." He glanced at his watch. "I'm a little early."

Because of the amount of business the farm did each day, the ornate iron gates at the main entrance to the property were always left open and, for some reason that Jennifer could never understand, an open gate was as good as an invitation for Lexington tourists. "I'm afraid there has been a mistake. Mitchell Farm doesn't give tours except by special arrangement. And then, only in summer."

Subtly, stubbornly, his posture changed as he shoved his hands into his pockets. "So I understand. However, when I explained to Ms Colson that my sole purpose for coming to Lexington was to visit Mitchell Farm—you see, I have several mares I would like covered by quality stallions next year—she said she would bend the rules a little."

"Today was the first time you'd made contact with the farm?" His answer would tell her how serious he was about using Mitchell stallions for breeding. The usual procedure was to make arrangements far ahead of time. That way, one of the men who normally handled the breeding program would have been available to answer questions and to give a proper tour of the facilities.

He nodded. "I know I should have written to make an appointment before I came, but I was on my way home from purchasing three of the mares I would like bred and decided to chance dropping by." He glanced at her to see if she bought his explanation, trying to decide whether or not he should embellish the lie in order to convince her. Satisfied, he let well enough alone.

Jennifer studied him. She could easily imagine her secretary succumbing to the coaxing sound of his voice and arranging a private tour, but she couldn't believe Lynn would make such an obvious mistake with the scheduling. "Are you sure you have the right day?" Not waiting for a reply, she went over to the appointment calendar on the desk. There it was, written in red pencil, slanted across the time period of one o'clock to two-thirty: Craig Templeton—tour. She looked up. "You're Craig Templeton?"

"In the flesh."

So much for positive statements about Lynn's scheduling. Jennifer went over the names of the people who normally conducted tours for tourists. With the end of the summer, most of them had been transferred to work in other sections of the farm. And she wasn't about to call on one of the men who ran the breeding program for a "walk-in" customer.

She decided to go ahead and check the stallion barns on the off chance someone was available. Sitting on the corner of the desk, she reached for the phone. "I'll see if I can find a groom to show you around."

"I'd appreciate that," he answered.

After the eighth ring and no answer, she hung up. "I'm sure Lynn explained that we're not geared for visitors during this time of year." The aspirins had done absolutely nothing to relieve her headache, but they made her stomach feel as if she had swallowed ipecac. The rest of the day would be a lost cause if she didn't do something to control the pain in her head. "Since I don't know what arrangements Lynn had in mind, and this is not my area of expertise, I'm sure you'd get a much better understanding of the farm if you could come back tomorrow. I personally promise there will be someone here to meet you who will be able to answer all of your questions." Fully expecting him to agree to the arrangement, she gave him an automatic dismissive smile.

"If it's all the same to you," he said amicably but with unmistakable determination, "I'd just as soon wait around to see if someone becomes available after lunch."

In a gesture filled with frustration, she crossed her arms over her chest and gave him a look that was meant to intimidate. Since he'd decided not to play by the rules neither would she. "Why? Just what's so special about today?"

Her bluntness threw him for a second. He hesitated before answering, giving her a slow half smile. "I guess you could say I'm a product of the television generation—incapable of patience.''

Jennifer mentally groaned. One way or another, it seemed she was stuck with him. She let out a resigned sigh. ''Wait a minute... I'll get my sweater and take you around myself.'' She slid off the desk and stood. Immediately huge black waves of pain flung themselves against her temples and behind her eyes, stealing her vision and balance. She reached for the desk. Craig's hand came forward to grasp her arm.

''Are you all right?'' he demanded.

''I will be... in a minute.'' Slowly her vision returned, and she attempted a reassuring smile. ''I must have stood up too fast,'' she said, trying to hide the familiar pain that sliced through the top half of her head like surgical blades. Involuntarily her free hand went to her forehead.

''Here, sit down.'' Craig led her to a chair. He crouched in front of her and caught her chin with his hand. ''You're lying,'' he said, studying her face. ''No one looks like you do because she stood up too fast.''

''I have a headache—that's all. It's no big deal. I get them all the time.'' She winced when she twisted her neck to remove her chin from his grasp.

''Where do you keep your aspirins? I'll get them for you.''

Her stomach threatened to convulse. ''I've already taken some.''

''How long ago?''

''About fifteen minutes.''

He peered at her for a moment longer, put his hands on her knees for balance and stood. Stepping behind her, he began massaging her shoulders.

''I'm all right,'' she said, making a half-hearted attempt to stand.

"For Pete's sake, sit still. I'm not going to attack you."

"Easy for you to say. You're not the one with a strange man's hands around your throat."

"Strange?" he echoed. "And here I thought I was being my charming best." Gently, insistently, he worked the muscles that ran across her shoulders. He glanced down at his hands; they seemed large and awkward against the delicate fabric of her blouse, analogous to the way he felt about being in Kentucky. The gently undulating hills and lush green of the countryside he had visited during the past two days were a vivid contrast to the austere plains of home.

It had taken months of sorting through his continued denial and then a time of intense soul-searching before he had reached a compromise with the emotions that tore at him. It was that compromise that had brought him to Kentucky surreptitiously. He had decided that before he contacted them he would learn everything he could about the people whom he had finally accepted as his true parents. That way he could determine how disruptive, and possibly destructive, his reappearance might be to them and as well protect himself from people whom possibly he was better off not knowing.

It had sounded so simple. Go up to Lexington, ask a few questions, decide. But the only things he had been able to find out about Frank and Agnes Mitchell since his arrival had to do with the horses they raised, not the people themselves. It was as if a conspiracy of silence surrounded them. Finally, frustration had made him decide to risk a chance meeting by going to the farm himself.

"I can't believe I'm letting you do this," Jennifer murmured, tilting her head forward in response to pressure at the back of her neck.

Her words snapped him out of his musing. "You mean this isn't part of the tour?"

She laughed lightly. "After today, it very well might be."

Craig ran his thumbs along the length of her neck and then into her hair. Slowly he worked his way across her scalp, his fingers making small circular movements. When he reached for her temples, she jerked away. "Don't touch my face." The words were as much a plea as a demand.

"All right," he answered, confused but not inclined to pursue it. He let his hands drop back to her shoulders.

After another minute she stood and ran her fingers through her short brown hair, coaxing the strands back into place. "I'm feeling much better now." Her tone betrayed none of the earlier panic. "Thank you." She offered a smile filled with genuine warmth. In answer to the skeptical look he gave her in return, she said, "Really, my head doesn't hurt nearly as much as it did."

"Does that mean the tour's still on?" He was there for only one reason, he reminded himself. If she had some hang-up about having her face touched, it certainly wasn't any of his business.

"After what you just did for me, how could I say no?" She disappeared into her office. When she returned, she was wearing a bright red sweater that matched the red in her tartan plaid skirt.

He liked the way she looked and told her so, surprising himself as much as her. The people who lived where he grew up considered casual compliments, and those who gave them, a little suspect.

"Thank you . . . again," she said, and dropped a set of keys into her pocket. "Ready?"

When they were outside, Jennifer directed Craig to the path that led to the barns where the farm's most famous stallions were kept. They walked together in an easy silence, listening to the soft sounds of the leaves that whispered in the trees and to the loud crackling of those that had fallen beneath their feet. The crisp air caressed them as they passed; the sun warmed their faces.

Although he itched to get to his real reason for coming, Craig watched and waited. He commented on the uncommon beauty of Kentucky in the autumn, pointing out the tree-lined road, the white fences and the deep green of the manicured grass. Jennifer told him that a visitor to the farm had once asked her what it felt like to live in a place where every view was postcard perfect.

"And?" he prodded, his gaze drawn to the way the sun created streaks of gold in her shiny brown hair.

"I told him that since I've never lived anywhere else, I had always assumed the entire world looked this way."

"It must take a small army just to keep the fences painted," he said, using her statement to begin the questioning.

She took a comically exaggerated breath before she rattled off the information, "There are 147 year-round employees, with an additional 30 hired each summer. The farm consists of 3,900 acres; there are 38 homes for employees on the property and 12 more in town. It takes 93 miles of fencing and 32 miles of blacktop to get around the farm." She tilted her head sideways and looked up at him, a self-satisfied smile on her mouth. "Didn't think I would know all that 'guide' stuff, did you?"

He met her gaze with a quick, lopsided grin. "I learned at a very tender age that it doesn't pay to answer questions like that one."

"Go ahead then. Ask me something else." She stepped off the path to shuffle playfully through a windswept pile of leaves, but stopped midway through, taken aback at the spontaneity of her actions. Carefree behavior had not been a part of her makeup for such a long time that she had almost forgotten how good it could feel.

"How many horses are housed here?"

She groaned. "Come on . . . something hard."

Suddenly he didn't care for the role of spy. Subterfuge had never been his style, nor did he like using people. Forcefully he buried his reluctance to continue, reminding himself that there was no other way. "Tell me something about the Mitchells. What kind of people own something like this?" He tried to make the question sound offhanded, no more or less than the sharing of a bit of gossip.

"They're . . ." She struggled for the right word. "They're wonderful—plain and simple." She shrugged. "I admit I'm prejudiced, but I can't think of another word more appropriate. They're kind and thoughtful and considerate—"

He laughed. "I think you just described the perfect Boy Scout."

"Well, how would you describe two people paying the salaries of doctors and nurses who are willing to spend a year in the backwoods and coal towns of Western Virgina and Kentucky to take care of people who otherwise couldn't afford their services? Or how about someone who sets up college scholarships with need as the only criterion? They believe so strongly that education is the road out of poverty that each year they buy tons of supplies for primary and secondary schools in impoverished areas of the state. When there was a federal cutback on the school lunch program—"

"Whoa—I believe you." Her words stirred a peculiar sense of pride in Craig.

"I guess for me it isn't so much what they do, anyway, but how they do it. Not many people know what I just told you. The Mitchells do their charity work quietly so that the recipients can maintain their dignity. I only know about their philanthropy because I'm doing the book-keeping now." She hugged herself against a sudden burst of cold air. "Which is a job I won't have too much longer if I keep shooting my mouth off like this."

He was filled with questions, but he knew it would be a tactical error to pursue personal information about the Mitchells too enthusiastically when he was supposedly there to find out about stallions. "Now it's your turn," he said. "Tell me something about you." It was intended as a temporary detour in their conversation, a diversion until he felt it safe to return once again to the Mitchells.

She stopped, pulled her sweater up to her chin then folded her arms across her chest and stared down at the ground. "There's something you should understand before we go any farther." All the warmth had left her voice. "*I'm* not a part of this tour."

Her abrupt coldness surprised and then intrigued him. If he had given her the slightest indication that he might be coming on to her, he could have understood her reaction. But he had purposely done nothing that she might misinterpret. It was important that he put her at ease so that his questions would seem to come from idle curiosity. With studied detachment he reached over to remove a leaf that had landed on her shoulder. They started walking again. "I can appreciate your not wanting to fill me in on your childhood. I can even understand your reluctance to discuss your high school years on such short acquaintance," he said, injecting a gently teasing quality into his voice and expression. "But I think it's downright unfriendly not to at least tell me your name. What if I should need to get your attention later? 'Hey you' is so impersonal, and somehow 'ma'am' seems kinda stuffy. And—''

"Jennifer Langley."

He held out his hand. "I'm pleased to meet you, Jennifer Langley."

She walked several more steps before glancing back at him over her shoulder. His mouth was turned up in an engaging grin which, in spite of herself, she responded to. Her statement had obviously sounded as supercilious to him as it had to her. *God, would she never return to normal behavior around strangers?* She came back to where he stood and put her hand in his. "I'm pleased to meet you too, Craig." When the handshake lasted longer than she had intended and thus became far more intimate, she tugged her hand free. "Now can we get on with the tour? I have a ton of work to do this afternoon." Actually there was very little left for her to do that day, but it was as good an excuse as any to get them going again.

He continued to stare at her. "I could come back tomorrow," he offered, hoping as he said it that she would refuse.

"That's all right," she answered, surprising herself even more than him. And then, as if an explanation for her reversal were necessary, she added, "My work will still be there in the morning. It always is."

They started walking again, continuing along the same path until they came to a gate. Here the walkway divided; one direction paralleled the fence, the other traveled beyond the gate to a stable. Jennifer hesitated, her gaze automatically sweeping the paddocks around the stable. The nine horses kept there were the stallions the tourists came to see. They were the showpieces of the farm—Derby and stakes winners that had been retired from racing and syndicated. These horses commanded stud fees that ranged from sixty thousand to a half-million dollars. No one who worked on the farm ever passed this area without at least a quick look to make sure everything was as it should be.

"Isn't that Morgan's Pride?" Craig asked, recognizing the roan Thoroughbred from ads he had seen in racing magazines.

She followed him over to the fence. "And that's Lady's Man in the paddock behind him. His two-year-olds have had a magnificent summer." Her voice held a distinct note of pride. "If next year's crop of colts is anywhere near as good as this year's, he could easily command the largest stud fee in the farm's history."

"I didn't know Lady's Man was a Mitchell Farm horse."

"He wasn't until two years ago. When we bought into the syndicate, it was decided to board him here."

A man driving a pickup truck with Mitchell Farm painted on the side drove by and honked. Jennifer smiled and waved to him. "We almost lost Lady's Man last winter when he had a bad reaction to a medication we were giving him for a hoof problem," she said, returning to her role of guide, relaying the kind of inside story she had been told visitors to the farm liked to hear. "One of the owners flew in from Florida, set up a cot in the adjoining stall and didn't leave until he was convinced his investment was going to survive. He damn near drove the vet crazy."

Craig tried to imagine himself as part of a world where one animal was worth more than the hospital the townspeople in Colby Station, Oklahoma, were still trying to fund. His gaze swept the rolling acres, the miles of painted fences, the stable, the ribbon of asphalt that disappeared over the hill. He sought an affinity, a sense of homecoming, but found only awe and wonder at the richness, the lushness. "How long have the Mitchells owned this place?"

"For six generations—since 1853."

One more generation of Mitchells in Kentucky than of Templetons in Oklahoma. A by now familiar ache returned. No, it wasn't five generations of Templetons, it was four. "It's still family owned, then?"

"Uh-huh. And if Frank has anything to say about it, it always will be."

Craig took a deep breath. He could hear his heart pounding in his ears. "That must mean there are children to take over eventually?" How often he had wished for brothers and sisters as a child. What would it be like to find them now?

"Three." She leaned her back against the railing and looked down the road. "As a matter of fact, Andrew should be arriving any time now. He's supposed to be bringing in a yearling we bought this summer that's been in quarantine in Maryland. By tradition the running of the farm passes on to the oldest son, so he'll be the one who eventually takes over the job. I'll introduce you, if you like."

Following her gaze down the road, Craig willed the truck not to arrive. He wasn't ready to meet his brother yet. He needed time to adjust. More importantly, he needed time to decide whether or not he ever wanted to meet Andrew Mitchell. "If you don't mind, I think I'd just as soon get on with the tour. I'm sure I'll have plenty of opportunity to meet everyone later if I decide to use Mitchell Farm."

His answer surprised her. He sounded more serious about using the farm than she had thought he was. "Why don't we go directly to the main stallion barns, then? If you'd like to see any of the horses up here more closely, we can stop on the way back." She glanced at her watch and then down the road, looking for one of the Mitchell Farm trucks that might be coming their way so they could hitch a ride. "If you're in a hurry, we could go back to the office and pick up a car."

"Would that be more convenient for you?"

At first she didn't understand, then realized he was referring to the "ton" of work she had waiting for her at the office that afternoon. "Actually, I think I would enjoy the walk. It feels good to get outside once in a while."

Once in a while? He would have guessed she was the type who was hard to keep inside. But then, what Jennifer Langley did on a day-to-day basis had nothing to do with the reason he was there. With single-mindedness he brought the conversation back to the true purpose of his visit. "As you've undoubtedly figured out by now, I'm a little green when it comes to this business. Mitchell Farm is the first place I've gone to find quality stallions. Maybe you could tell me what I should be looking for."

She gave him a "you've-got-to-be-kidding" look. He was either incredibly rich or incredibly stupid. She sincerely doubted the latter, but the absence of the usual telltale signs of money wouldn't let her accept the former, either. What was he really after? "First of all, why don't you tell me what made you decide to start your search for stallions at Mitchel Farm?"

He hadn't expected to be put on the defensive so soon. "I read a couple of articles and liked what I read."

"Which was?"

He hesitated while he shoved his hands into his back pockets. When he answered, he lowered his voice and spoke slowly, pretending to suppress a flash of anger in an attempt to intimidate her. "I'm afraid I can't answer you on that one. You see, I didn't realize when I was reading the magazines that I'd be quizzed about their contents later."

"I'm sorry. I didn't mean to sound—"

"Don't apologize," he said, purposely softening his tone. "I think I can understand your reluctance to take me seriously. After all, why should you, when you know nothing about me?" *Dammit!* He hadn't meant to give her such a broad opening.

But she didn't pursue the opening—his private life was his own affair. All she cared about was the business he might bring to the farm. "You must admit that your approach hasn't been exactly orthodox." She offered a tentative smile. "Why don't you tell me about the mares you bought." It would be insanity to pay Mitchell Farm prices to cover anything but the finest mares.

Craig had anticipated he would be questioned about the mares and had spent time that morning researching credible answers. He named two fairly well-known farms in Maryland and one in California, where he said he had purchased a total of seven mares. Before Jennifer had a chance to ask him about their bloodlines, he mentioned the price he had supposedly paid, hoping she would use the figure and the reputation of the farms to judge the quality. Apparently it worked, because the next question she asked had nothing to do with horses.

"Why don't you tell me something about your background?"

He smiled purposely to try to soften the words he would say next. "Let me get this straight," he said slowly. "*You're* not a part of the tour, but *I* am?" It was the perfect reply to throw her off personal questions, but he regretted its necessity. When all of this was over, he was going to owe her one hell of an explanation and apology for his peculiar behavior.

She could feel a flush of embarrassment warm her neck and was grateful the crisp air had already reddened her cheeks. She considered telling him that her question had been professional and she was only interested in knowing his background as it applied to horses, but she let it drop. "Touché," she said, forcing a light tone.

"Why don't we go back to neutral territory and talk about the Mitchells," he said. "You were telling me that Andrew was the firstborn son."

"Not the firstborn, the eldest. There was another son, Eric."

He waited for her to go on, and when she didn't, he gently prodded, "What happened to this Eric?" He struggled to make the question sound like any other.

"He died when he was just a baby," she said softly. "Sometimes I think the Mitchells have never truly accepted his death. But then, considering the circumstances, I don't know if I blame them."

How strange it felt to hear someone say they believed him dead and to learn that his mother and father still grieved for him. What would they say, how would they feel, if they knew he had not died?

Or had he? The child they'd lost had been an infant. Would they—could they—accept the man he had become?

CHAPTER THREE

JENNIFER STROLLED over to the paddock that held the stallion, Winsome, while she waited for John Wilkins, the head groom, to finish telling Craig about the arrangements that could be made to board his mares when they came into season. She leaned against the railing to watch the chestnut horse that was focusing all his attention on the stallion in the next paddock. Reaching for the chain that held the gate closed, she rapped it against the wooden post. Winsome looked up at the sound. When he saw who was calling him, he trotted over to her. He pressed his nose against her outstretched hand and, after exhaling an audible greeting, raised his head in welcome. He turned sideways to give Jennifer ready access to his back.

"I had a dog just like that when I was growing up," Craig said, joining her. "When he got old and couldn't reach the middle of his back, he'd do the craziest things to get someone to scratch it for him."

Jennifer gave the stallion a final pat before turning her full attention to Craig. "Did you find out everything you wanted to know?"

"And then some," he answered warmly, feeling grateful for her eagerness to be helpful and an increasing sense of unease for lying to her about his reasons for being there. "It's going to take me awhile to sort through it all."

"Then you're ready to go back to the office now?"

He glanced at his watch. "I suppose we should. I've already taken up the better part of your afternoon with a tour that was only supposed to last an hour and a half." Although there were hundreds of questions he still wanted to ask, he felt he had pursued the subject of the Mitchells just about as far as he could in one day without creating suspicion. Perhaps Jennifer would volunteer information on their way back to the office, but he had sense enough not to bring up the subject himself. Especially after the way the people in town had acted whenever he asked anything personal about the Mitchells. He could just imagine what the employees would be like if they thought he was getting a little too inquisitive.

"I enjoyed getting out," she admitted. "If you hadn't come along, I would have been stuck in the office all day and never smelled this glorious autumn air. And I certainly wouldn't want Winsome to have to go through another day without getting his back scratched."

They had started down the path when a pickup pulled to a stop beside them, and a man whom Craig judged to be near his own age leaned out the window. "Need a lift?" he said to Jennifer, giving Craig a quick but thorough once-over.

"Yes, as a matter of fact, we do," Jennifer replied, smiling. "When did you get back?"

"About an hour ago."

"How does the filly look?"

"Fantastic. Someday she's going to drop dynamite colts."

Jennifer turned to Craig. "This fellow, who looks like a cat that got into the cream, is the heir apparent to Mitchell Farm I told you about earlier," she said. "Craig Templeton . . . Andrew Mitchell."

It took a moment for Craig to regain his emotional balance. When he did, he stepped up to the truck to take his brother's outstretched hand. Although Andrew was near Craig's own build and coloring, there were few other similarities. Craig felt a peculiar surge of disappointment that they weren't more alike. But then, what had he expected? The newspaper hadn't said he was a twin. "I'm pleased to meet you," he said, his voice betraying none of his inner turmoil.

"Just visiting... or are you thinking of doing some business with the farm?" Andrew asked.

Jennifer laughed lightly and started around the truck. "I forgot to tell you, Craig, Andrew is the pragmatic member of the Mitchell family. If he has his way, this place will be the General Motors of Thoroughbred breeding someday." Her voice held a teasing quality, but there was also a thread of seriousness woven into the words.

"Right now I'm visiting," Craig answered Andrew. "But if things work out as I'm hoping they will, it's likely we'll be seeing more of each other in the future."

Andrew carefully studied Craig, as if he could understand the hidden meaning behind Craig's answer. "You seem familiar. Have we met before?"

"I doubt it. This is my first trip to Kentucky."

He studied Craig for a moment longer before shifting his gaze to the roadway in front of him. "Well, I hope it's a good one for you."

"Thanks." Craig followed Jennifer around the truck and climbed in beside her.

What had taken them a half hour on foot took less than five minutes' driving. During the trip Craig found it difficult not to stare at Andrew as he searched for points of commonality, things that would irrefutably stamp them as brothers, a mannerism, a turn of phrase. He was disappointed that he could see nothing of himself in his brother, even though reason told him it would be improbable that two men raised in different parts of the country by different parents would be anything alike.

After Andrew dropped them off, Craig watched the truck until it disappeared over the hill. He struggled with conflicting emotions; a part of him ached to call his newly discovered brother back and a part equally as compelling wished they had never met.

Craig's turmoil was reflected on his face and in his stance, making Jennifer wonder at its cause. "Is something wrong?" she asked.

He jerked his head around to look at her. "What?" He only knew she'd spoken. What she'd said had been lost.

"Did Andrew say something that bothered you?"

Noting the concern in her eyes as well as in her voice, he realized he'd let down his guard and quickly tried to cover himself. "I think I'm just a little overwhelmed by everything I've seen today. I had no idea Mitchell Farm was this big." He knew his defense made little sense, but caught by surprise, it was the best he could do.

She considered his curious answer. One of the Maryland farms he'd said he bought mares from was as large as Mitchell's, and the farm he'd gone to in California was larger. Why would what he'd seen today overwhelm him? "I guess growing up here has made me take the farm for granted," she said. She stepped onto the porch of the cottage that had been transformed into the business office and reached into her pocket for the key. "It's hard for me to imagine what someone seeing all of this for the first time would feel." She opened the door, turned and extended her hand to him. "I hope you'll be doing business with Mitchell Farm. I've enjoyed our afternoon together.'' Not until she'd said the words did she realize how true they were. Even though she'd spent several hours in Craig's company and had found out little about him, she knew she liked him too much not to worry that he might get tied up with the wrong farm when he chose a place to service his mares.

As he listened to Jennifer tell him goodbye, it occurred to Craig that his only real link to Mitchell Farm was ending, and there were still hundreds of unanswered questions tearing at him. ''I'm the worst person in the world when it comes to picking good places to eat,'' he said, reaching behind her to take hold of the doorknob and effectively block her entrance to the office. ''Do you suppose you could you give me the name of a restaurant where I might get a good steak?''

It had been so long since Jennifer had gone in to Lexington for dinner that she was reluctant to suggest a restaurant. ''I'm afraid I couldn't. You should have said something earlier. Lynn is the farm's resident gourmet, and she's gone home for the day.'' She thought for a moment. ''If you want to come inside, I could call her. I'm sure she'd be home by now.''

''It isn't so much where I go, anyway,'' he said, leaning slightly closer, his voice low and coaxing. ''It's eating alone that I don't like. What do you say we take our chances together? Would you go out to dinner with me?''

Jennifer moved away from him until her back was pressing against the door. His actions had taken her completely by surprise. Not once during all the time they had been together had he given her the impression he intended to make a pass. ''No...I mean, I can't. I don't go out on dates.''

''Surely you go out with friends. Just because we've only known each other a few hours doesn't mean we can't consider ourselves friends, does it?'' Under normal circumstances he would never push this hard. If his only interest had been to date her, then he would come back tomorrow and try again, and if necessary, he would even come back a third time, working on her until she gave in. Never would he have put this kind of pressure on her in the beginning. But these weren't normal circumstances. With her openness and intimate knowledge of the Mitchells, she had become an important link in the chain leading him to a family he found he was steadily becoming more and more anxious to know.

"No, I don't . . . go out with friends, I mean."

Suddenly he became aware of her as a person and realized she had given an almost panicky reaction to his simple request that she go out with him. What kind of person went out with no one? Was she lying? He purposely fixed his gaze on her. She was young, with a startling beauty, but he had also thought he'd noticed a fleeting look in her eyes he had seen only one other time in his life. It had been on a hunting trip with his father when he was eight years old. They had spent an entire day stalking a stag before finally cornering it. Sheer terror had radiated from the stag's eyes when the regal deer realized he was trapped. The moment was indelibly printed on Craig's mind, and he would swear he had just seen the same look in Jennifer's eyes.

He moved away from her so that he no longer had her backed into a corner. "Then how about making an exception," he said gently. "I would consider it an honor and a privilege if you would have dinner with me. Also, you'd be doing me a big favor."

Nervously she smoothed her hair, tucking a wayward curl behind her ear. It immediately returned to its former position. After surgery had restored her face to the point where strangers no longer stared, she had agreed to date again in order to please her friends and family, who insisted it would help her to put the tragedy behind her and get on with her life. But each date was worse than the last as she struggled to return to a "normal" life and succeeded only in making herself miserable.

Finally, realizing what was happening, her mother stepped in. She told Jennifer it was useless to try to pretend nothing had changed in her life and that, from then on, she would act as a buffer between Jennifer and her friends and family until they understood there were times when the mind needed more time to heal than the flesh. After that Jennifer had been allowed to progress at her own pace and in her own way. "I'm sorry..." Jennifer finally said, the words little more than a whisper, "but I can't go out with you."

"Please..." he answered as softly. The more she resisted, the more important it became. "Tonight of all nights, I don't want to be alone."

Something about the way he asked made her realize he wasn't just handing her a line. He really didn't want to be alone and was reaching out to her. She understood that kind of need. "All right," she said, feeling as if she'd left the safety of her familiar shelter to step into a storm.

"I'll pick you up at seven," he answered, heading down the walkway to his car. He was afraid that if he lingered she would change her mind.

"Don't you want to know where?" She'd told him that her home was on the farm but hadn't mentioned its location.

He stopped and looked at her, a crooked grin creating a dimple in one cheek. "It might help get me there on time if I didn't have to knock on thirty-eight doors to find you."

She gave him the directions to her cottage, but even as she spoke, she told herself she was making a terrible mistake. He didn't write them down, just repeated the time he would pick her up, got in his car and drove away. She watched him leave, trying to convince herself that the knot in her stomach was from the aspirins she'd taken earlier. She needed to believe she really wasn't the timid soul her behavior indicated she had become.

JENNIFER LEANED HER FOREHEAD against the narrow window beside the front door and stared out into the darkness. It was ten minutes before seven, and she was a nervous wreck, torn between hope that Craig would forget all about their date and fear that he might. She'd decided she wasn't ready to start going out again, even though logic told her she had been a recluse far too long. Desperate for something to do to consume time, she wandered over to the fireplace and adjusted a log that had already caught fire.

She put the poker back in its stand, leaned her elbow on the mantel and stared into the hearth. If it was indeed time for her to integrate herself back into society, at least Craig was a perfect starting point. He would be gone in a few days and, if need be, she could go back to her normal routine without anyone knowing she had deviated from it. That reasoning was precisely why she had decided to fix dinner herself rather than go out to a restaurant. If anyone should see her with Craig, the questions and suppositions would be endless.

Lost in her thoughts, she didn't hear Craig's car approach and was startled by his knock. She cast a quick look in the antique gilt-edged mirror that hung over the sofa, took a steadying breath and went to the door. "Right on time," she said, forcing a cheerfulness she didn't feel and looking to see if he'd parked behind the hedge so his car wouldn't be visible from the road. He had traded the urban cowboy look for a sport coat, slacks, tie and sweater and carried it off with the same natural ease. She had a feeling he would look as handsome and comfortable in a tuxedo as he would in cutoffs and ragged tennis shoes.

"And it only took three trips around the block to arrange my perfect timing." He handed her a bouquet of mixed flowers as he came in. Wynona's influence had been deeply ingrained: "Never go calling empty-handed," she'd admonished the sixteen-year-old headed for his first date. The lesson had been a wise one, and he had lived by it since.

"You didn't have—" She stopped, embarrassed by her clichéd acceptance of his gift. "No, of course you didn't have to bring flowers, but I'm glad you did. They're beautiful. Thank you."

Her graciousness made him especially glad he had made the effort, and he noted that his pleasure had nothing to do with his hope that she would be comfortable enough with him later to talk openly about the Mitchells. "Are you ready? I made reservations for seven forty-five at a restaurant the desk clerk assured me was one of the best in Lexington."

"Would you mind terribly if we ate here instead?"

"I don't understand."

"You said you wanted a really good steak, and I just happened to have two in my freezer, so I thought we might as well use them rather than trust our luck to a restaurant."

"I don't know what to say."

"Yes would be good for starters."

Except for the meals he'd shared with Bill and Cloris Mason, Templeton Ranch's foreman and his wife, he'd been cooking for himself, with a modicum of skill and predictability of menu, since the accident that had killed his parents. A meal prepared by Jennifer and the opportunity to spend an evening with her in her home was too good an offer to refuse. "Yes it is then."

"Wonderful. After you call to cancel the reservation, why don't you open the wine?" She pointed to an end table beside the sofa where she had put a bottle of Cabernet Sauvignon on a tray with two glasses. "I'll be back as soon as I put the flowers in water."

Craig watched her leave before going over to the phone. He was dumbfounded by the change in plans for the evening. After her reluctance to go out with him at all, he wasn't sure what he'd expected to find when he arrived that night, but the possibility of a home-cooked meal eaten beside a crackling fire hadn't even crossed his mind.

After calling the restaurant, he tackled the wine. Giving the corkscrew a final turn, he popped the cork and poured a finger of wine into a glass. He held the stem between his fingers and took a sip of the deep burgundy liquid. Too bad he hadn't had an audience. His performance had been perfect. The only problem was that he had no idea whether the wine caressing his palate was exceptional or a short step away from vinegar. Hoping for the best, he filled the two glasses and started for the kitchen.

Jennifer jumped when he came through the door. "You startled me," she said, picking up the bright yellow mum she had dropped. Her hand trembled so violently that she dropped the flower again. To hide the trembling she leaned against the counter, using her hands for support.

"Is there anything I can do to help?" Craig held a glass of wine out to her.

"Would you please put it on the counter? My hands are all wet." She couldn't let him see her like this, but then she couldn't spend the evening sitting on her hands, either.

Craig put both glasses down and reached for the yellow flower, which he slipped into the vase. "Have I done something to make you nervous?"

He'd seen how her hands shook. She felt like a spineless imitation of a Southern belle. Next would come an attack of the vapors. "It isn't you: it's me. I get the shakes whenever I forget to eat properly, and I've been doing a lot of that lately."

"Then it seems to me we should get this meal going as soon as possible. Tell me what to do." He shrugged out of his jacket and hung it over the back of one of the kitchen chairs.

Unbuttoning his shirt sleeves and pushing his sweater up to his elbows, he obviously intended to help whether she wanted him to or not. "If you don't mind the smell on your hands, you can rub the wooden bowl over there with the garlic clove I left on the bottom."

When he finished that task and demanded another, she led him, step by step, through the making of Caesar salad while she finished the flowers and prepared the steaks for the broiler.

Carrying the teak salad bowl in one hand, their glasses precariously balanced in the other, Craig nudged the swinging kitchen door with his hip and headed back into the living room, where a small round table for two had been set by the fire. He filled their plates with salad before going back into the kitchen to get Jennifer. He refused to listen to her protests that the steaks must be watched and insisted she come with him and start eating.

She was sitting across from him with a forkful of salad poised in midair, ready to be eaten, when Craig proposed a toast. "To this wonderful meal, the romantic setting and the woman who conceived it all."

Jennifer's jaw dropped. "But I didn't mean..." She had only thought to provide a pleasant place for their dinner. How could he think... She looked at the table with its white Irish linen, at the delicate china and hand-cut crystal, at the fire in the fireplace, and she chastized herself. Of course he had thought the setting romantic. It looked like a desperate woman's trap to snare an unsuspecting man. She cringed.

"Are you trying to tell me I've misinterpreted your intentions?" he asked gently, never having misinterpreted them at all.

"I'm so embarrassed."

"Don't be." He smiled. "I'm not. And if I understand this correctly, I'm the one who's being rejected." For some unfathomable reason, he couldn't resist teasing her.

"No, you're not," she rushed to explain. "It's just that I'm not interested in getting involved with anyone right now. I certainly never intended to arrange a romantic evening with you." She made a face. "I'm not explaining this very well." She looked down at her plate and remembered the steaks. "I'll be right back," she told him, grateful for an excuse to leave the room.

Craig leaned back in his chair, trying to understand what was happening between him and Jennifer. The signals she had been sending were about as clear as the air in a summer dust storm. The scene might be perfect for seduction, but the participants were all wrong. Jennifer was trembling with nerves, or was it fright? And he had come to gather information, not to make a conquest.

When it became evident that Jennifer was not going to return immediately and he was not going to figure out what was going on, he killed time by looking around the room. His gaze settled on a photograph in a silver frame standing between two stacks of books in the wall unit opposite him. It was the only highly personal thing in the room. He went over to take a closer look.

The photograph was of a plain but not unattractive young woman in a wedding dress and a smiling young man in a tuxedo. They were standing with their arms around each other's waists, their eyes radiating happiness. As in every other wedding picture he had ever seen, there seemed to be an almost visible aura of promise surrounding them.

Jennifer came back into the room just as he was returning the photograph. "Are they friends or relatives?" he asked conversationally, going over to rejoin her at the table.

"Neither," she answered, trying to sound normal despite the lump that had suddenly appeared in her throat. She struggled with an urge to return the photograph to its exact former resting place. "That's me."

"You're married?" He was startled to discover how much he cared about her answer.

"Not anymore. David is dead."

"I'm sorry," he answered automatically, taking a minute to assimilate the information. When he had, he understood much of what had happened between them that day.

Jennifer watched Craig, curious about his reaction. "It was a long time ago," she said, dropping her gaze to the plate she carried, satisfied that "I'm sorry" did not mean he *felt* sorry for her.

He glanced back at the photograph, trying to recognize her as the smiling young woman in white. "You've changed."

Methodically she put the steaks and baked potatoes on their plates. "I'm living proof of the miracles of modern medicine."

He waited for her to go on, afraid to break the spell by speaking.

"David and I were married less than a week. We were on our honeymoon in Switzerland and were walking back to our hotel after a day of skiing when a car skidded out of control and hit us. David died instantly. It took almost two years for the plastic surgeons to put my face back together. They did the best they could, but I don't look much like I did before."

She had spoken in an emotionless monotone that was more heartrending than tears. Craig wanted to reach out to comfort her but sensed she would not welcome the gesture. "Jennifer, would you like me to leave?"

She looked up at him and saw the concern in his eyes. He was offering her friendship, and in so doing, made it possible for her to admit she was desperately in need of a friend. "No...don't go." She gave him a tentative smile. "There's no way I can eat all this by myself."

He hadn't realized how much he wanted to stay until she told him he could. He reached across the table to take her hand and gave it a gentle, reassuring squeeze. "Do you want to talk about him?"

Automatically she shook her head, even though she really would have liked to talk to him about David. She had stopped mentioning David to her family and friends a long time ago because she could see how uncomfortable it made them. She knew they loved her and only wanted what they thought was best, but their reactions had forced her to keep emotions hidden that needed openness in order to be put to rest. No one seemed to understand that David was as much a part of her as the years she had spent in competitive show jumping or the time she had passed in school. She had as much need to talk freely about David as she had to talk about every other part of her life.

Craig let go of her hand and refilled their wine glasses. "Would you mind if I asked questions?" Because there were times when he ached to talk to someone about all that had happened to him, he thought that perhaps, despite her denial, she did, too.

"Not if you don't mind when I don't answer."

"Fair enough. But first, let's eat." He wasn't sure how much of her nervousness was due to lack of food and how much was caused by his presence, but getting a meal into her couldn't hurt.

"While we're eating, why don't you tell me about the mares you bought," she said, filling her potato with sour cream and sprinkling fresh chives across the top.

Craig almost choked on a piece of lettuce. "Mix business and pleasure? Why don't we leave that for another time?"

"What should we talk about, then?" she asked.

He thought a moment. It was a perfect opening to ask her about the Mitchells. "Tell me about your tomboy years," he said instead.

She smiled. "They never really ended. The love of my life before I met David was show jumping. It was my dream to make the Olympic team someday."

"That must take up a lot of your time."

"It did once, but not anymore. I haven't been on a horse for three years." She took a bite of steak. It tasted wonderful, which surprised her; food hadn't tasted good in a long time. "I'll go back to it eventually."

They ate in silence for a while. Finally it was Craig who broke the silence. "I don't think I've ever ridden a horse just for the fun of it."

"Oh?"

He smiled. "Ranch work isn't fun too often."

"You own a ranch? Where?" All afternoon, whenever she had asked him about himself, he had sidestepped her questions.

"Oklahoma."

"I've never known anyone from Oklahoma. What's it like there?"

"Nothing like here. If Lexington has a corner on green, we've got one on brown."

"What do you raise on your ranch?"

"Cattle, and a few gas wells . . . not much more."

"And you want to bring in Thoroughbreds to change all that."

"It seemed like a good idea at the time." He finished his steak and poured the last of the wine. "How old are you, Jennifer?" he asked, steering the conversation away from himself.

"Twenty-three."

"You were married young."

Unable to finish what had been a piece of meat big enough for two, Jennifer stood to clear the table. "It seemed like a good idea at the time," she echoed.

Craig got up to help her. They went into the kitchen where he made coffee and Jennifer loaded the dishwasher. When the coffee was ready, they went back into the living room to sit by the fire. Again they slipped into a comfortable silence. This time it was Jennifer who spoke first.

"I met David in college," she began, her voice soft, her manner hesitant. "We had gone together two years when he was accepted for graduate work at Georgetown University, and we were faced with a long separation. Our families asked us to wait until we were both through school, but we decided to get married rather than try to maintain a long-distance relationship.''

''What was David studying?''

''Political science. He wanted to work in the foreign service, with the idea that someday he'd be an ambassador. His family had strong political ties with Washington.''

''It must have been a devastating blow for them to lose him.''

''Especially since he was their only child.'' For the first time she felt a sorrow for David's parents more powerful than any she had ever felt for him or herself. David was gone. Any anger or hurt or frustration she might have felt about what had happened to him had dissipated, and somehow somewhere, she had come to the realization that eventually, she would recover. But his parents were alone and would live with the loss of their only child every day for the rest of their lives.

It grew late without either of them noticing as Jennifer shared a part of herself with Craig that she had shared with no one in a long time. At first he thought it sad that she was still living in the past, but slowly, he came to realize she was simply laying old ghosts to rest. Beneath the exterior of a woman who had withdrawn from life was one who was ready to embrace it with arms flung wide. She was on the threshold of returning to the living but unsure how to take the first step.

Almost from the moment when she had opened up to him, she had changed. The trembling and hesitancy disappeared; her hands moved expressively and with confidence as she talked. There were times when her wondrously deep blue eyes grew moist with unshed tears, but there were also moments when they sparkled with merriment.

The fire they had refueled three times was down to embers when they agreed it was time for him to go. Jennifer walked him to the door. As he put on his jacket, she stared at him and then playfully reached up to touch his ear. He gave her a questioning look.

"I was checking to see how far I'd bent it tonight," she said, skirting an open apology for the one-sided conversation but wanting him to know that she was aware of how patient he had been in listening to her.

"And?"

She looked from one side of his head to the other. "The left one seems a little the worse for wear."

His hand rested on the doorknob. "Since I prefer having a matched set, how about doing this again tomorrow night?" Perhaps he would find a way to ask her about the Mitchells then. He was reluctant to give up the possibility.

As usual, whenever asked to do anything, her first reaction was to say no, but this time she caught herself before the word had a chance to tumble out. "And I suppose you'd want to have steaks again, too?" Was she really agreeing to see him again?

"We could go out," he offered without much enthusiasm.

"Or I could fix something different."

"Seven o'clock?"

She nodded.

Craig hesitated, thought better of saying anything more, opened the door and left.

Jennifer went to the window to watch him leave. A pleasant numbness sheltered her from the full realization that her life had been irrevocably changed by the simple act of sharing her past with a man she had known for less than a day.

CHAPTER FOUR

UNABLE TO SLEEP, Craig listened to the rain as it rushed through the drainpipe outside his motel room. The storm clouds had moved in while he was at Jennifer's and had started dropping their burden as he drove through the streets of Lexington. He had been listening to the resulting sounds since. He rolled to his side to look at the glowing red numbers on the digital clock radio that had been glued to the nightstand. Four twenty-five—too early to get up and too late to get a decent night's sleep.

Turning onto his back, he tucked his hands behind his head and stared up at the faintly lit ceiling. Lately he had come to hate times like these. He had nowhere to go and no one to see to keep him busy enough to escape knowing that he was scared and uncertain about what he was doing. Alone, with only his thoughts for company, he was forced to face his fears head-on.

Why had Wynona kept the clippings? He had been content—no, *proud*—to think himself a Templeton. Why would the woman who had reared him with such devotion and love want to take away a heritage that she had helped to instill in him? Was it possible that she hadn't realized what it would do to him if he found out he wasn't a Templeton? Did she think the environment in which he had spent his first twenty-six years had so thoroughly molded him that when everything else was taken away he would still feel bound to the land?

Had Max known she had kept the clippings? Craig thought about his father, a man as suited to his name as he had been to the land. Short and powerful and normally taciturn, Max could turn lyrical when talking about the generations of Templetons born on the ranch. And in the end, he would always tell Craig that someday the land would be Craig's, to be given to his own child. Templeton Ranch had been everything to Max. It was the enduring legacy that had passed from father to son for five generations.

Craig's throat tightened against a futile cry of injustice. If his mother had thought to give him back his true heritage, she had sadly misjudged the man he had become. He didn't belong in a place where the land was divided and fenced in tidy little plots, where men were hired to do nothing but trim grass from around fenceposts and where horses were worth more than hospitals. Life was simpler in Oklahoma, more direct. And the people who lived there reflected their uncomplicated lifestyle.

But that had been the way things were before. A part of his life, he now knew, had been an illusion. In the four months since his parents' death, he'd spent more time in town at the lawyer's and accountant's offices than he had at the ranch. Before the one-car accident that had taken Max and Wynona's life, Craig had never picked up the financial section of a newspaper, let alone read the stock market page. He still lacked a clear picture of how much he had inherited and hadn't begun to try to decide what he would do with the millions the lawyer claimed were his. The transition from average to monied would have been hard enough on its own, but the establishment of ties to a family that had long thought him dead still seemed more than he could, or perhaps even wanted, to handle.

Until . . . the times when he was filled with such bone-deep loneliness that fear and hesitation were buried under its weight. He had found a brother yesterday, had even shaken his hand. The feeling was indescribable. What would it be like to look into the eyes of the woman who had given him life? And his father, what would he be like? Would Frank Mitchell express the same passion for his three-thousand-acre Thoroughbred farm that Max had for the rolling miles of grassland on Templeton Ranch? Craig felt confident he would, and the feeling created a bond of understanding.

So where did that leave him? Jennifer had said the farm traditionally moved from father to oldest son. Craig knew nothing about Thoroughbred breeding and didn't think he cared to learn. Then there was Andrew. Where would he fit in once the firstborn Mitchell son rose from the dead? Each new question bred another, and answers eluded him. Perhaps Jennifer would provide the key later that night. If he could get a real sense of the kind of people the Mitchells were, it would help him decide whether to make contact or to go home and forget he had ever come. A twinge of guilt about using Jennifer surfaced. Life had already used her enough. But then the force of his own needs shoved the guilt aside. When the time came, he would make sure she understood why he had had no other choice. Somehow he would make it up to her.

Craig sat up, swung his legs over the side of the bed and headed for the shower, abandoning all attempt at sleep. He would get dressed and find an all-night restaurant to wait for the coming day, a place filled with people and noise where he would have more than his thoughts for company.

THE RESTAURANT CRAIG FOUND was near the interstate. Two sleepy truckers, a middle-aged couple anxious to get an early start on their cross-country trip and a young male hitchhiker nursing a cup of coffee while he waited out the rain were the only customers. Noise was limited to cups clicking against saucers and an occasional exchange between the dark-haired curvacious waitress and the ancient-looking cook.

Craig slipped into a booth and pulled the menu from behind the metal napkin holder. After a few minutes the waitress ambled over, carrying a steaming glass pot filled with coffee.

"Ready to order?" she said, turning over the cup in front of Craig with the automatic assumption he would want coffee at that hour in the morning.

"I'll take a number five with the eggs over easy."

She pulled her order book from her apron pocket. "Whole wheat or white toast?"

"Whole wheat."

"Orange, grapefruit—" she looked up from her book and smiled "—or prune juice?"

Craig returned her smile, glad for the innocent conversation and company. "Orange juice will be fine."

"Anything else?" She picked up the menu and tucked it back behind the napkin holder.

Craig shook his head. "But before you leave...if someone wanted to learn more about this area, where would you suggest he go?"

She set the coffeepot on the table and tucked her pencil behind her ear. "What'cha got in mind to learn?"

"A little history...something about the farms that are around here...what it takes to make one successful... who owns them...that kind of thing."

She thought for a minute. "Some of the bigger farms are still open to tourists, but most of 'em have stopped letting people visit. You could call around and check. For the history thing, your best bet would probably be the Horse Park out on Iron Works Pike. I've never been there myself, but lots of the people who come in here have, and I never heard any of them say they didn't think they got their money's worth."

"How do I get to this Iron Works Pike?"

"Highway 75 north. It'll take you right to it."

"Thanks."

She picked up the coffee. "Don't mention it." She was several feet away when she turned, a puzzled expression on her face. "How come you're so interested in the history around here?"

Craig glanced down at his hands, curled around the white ceramic cup. Several seconds passed before he looked up again. She would never understand the real answer—that he thought his father would be pleased if Craig knew something about the place where he had been born—so he smiled and shrugged and said, "I've got this thing about knowing the history of the places I visit."

JENNIFER YANKED HER HAND AWAY from the casserole lid and stuck her finger into her mouth. She was in a hurry, and every time she was in a hurry, she did something dumb—like forgetting to use a pot holder when reaching for a lid that had been in a 350 degree oven for fifteen minutes. If she had more time, she would have stuck the throbbing appendage in cold water, but Craig was due in half an hour and she hadn't even changed clothes.

How had her mother managed to cook and serve six-course meals to a dozen guests and to make it seem effortless? She glanced around the room, taking in the array of pots and pans and general clutter, trying to decide which she should clean first, herself or the kitchen. The decision was momentarily delayed when the doorbell rang. Her gaze fixed on the oven clock. It *couldn't* be Craig—it was barely six-thirty. She whipped her apron off, flung it on the counter and headed for the door, saying a silent prayer that none of her family had picked tonight to come by to try to talk her into going out. She'd never be able to convince any of them that the meal simmering in the kitchen was something she'd whipped up for herself for a quiet dinner alone.

She took a second to compose herself, finger-combed her hair and opened the door. "*Craig...*" she groaned. "What are you doing here?"

The smile left his face. "I thought we—"

"What are you doing here *now*?" she corrected. "You weren't supposed to arrive until seven."

He shrugged helplessly. "I finished my work and didn't think you'd mind if I came over early." Actually, he'd been glancing at his watch all afternoon, willing the hands to move faster, anxious to return to the farm. He'd convinced himself the reason was his growing need to make a decision about contacting the Mitchells and that Jennifer was the one person who could help him. But now that he was with her again, his reasons for being there no longer seemed so cut-and-dried. He realized he was drawn to her. She had shared a part of herself with him last night that he had a feeling she'd shared with few others. By listening, he had given a tacit promise that he would not betray her trust. The understanding sent a sobering chill down his spine. *If he knew all he claimed to know, what was he doing there?* He should have called and canceled. If he had any sense, he would back out now.

She had planned to greet him wearing something soft and pretty, not a three-year-old pair of tweed slacks and an oxford shirt more suited to a football game than entertaining guests at home. "No, of course I don't mind," she said, stepping aside to let him enter.

"I could go away and come back later, and we could pretend this never happened." *What in the hell was he doing there?*

She reached for his arm to pull him inside. "I would take you up on that if I thought we could pull it off." She couldn't believe how good seeing him again made her feel. She had missed having friends over to visit far more than she had realized.

"At least now there's time to chill the champagne."

"We're not having—"

He took his other arm from behind his back and handed her a paper bag. "Oh, yes we are."

Jennifer took the bottle from the bag. "I'm impressed," she said, looking at the label. "What are we celebrating?"

The champagne had simply been a last minute purchase to avoid arriving empty-handed. "*I'm* celebrating having met you," he said, because it was the first thing that came to mind. "*You* can celebrate anything you like." He was taken aback by the flash of panic he saw in her eyes.

"Craig...just because I let you come here again tonight, I don't want you to think—"

"Stop right there. Let me rephrase what I just said." How could he have forgotten how vulnerable she was? "What I wanted to say was that I brought champagne tonight to celebrate a wonderful new friendship—nothing more."

Not once in all the scenarios she had created that day had she imagined she would make such an idiot out of herself. She gave him an embarrassed smile. "I think I could drink to that. Now why don't you make yourself comfortable while I put this on ice?"

"I'd rather go with you. Surely there's something I could do to keep myself busy." He didn't want her to have time alone to reconsider the panic his words had created. They needed to put the evening on solid ground again.

"As soon as I've taken care of the champagne, I'm going to my bedroom to change clothes."

A mischievous twinkle lit his eyes. "Does that mean no?"

"Most emphatically." Now her smile was one of pleasure as she responded to their easy repartee. She went into the kitchen, put the bottle in the freezer to get a head start on the cooling process and bent down to rummage through the cupboard for the champagne bucket—a wedding present she had never used. Her thoughts were on Craig as she moved the toaster and peered past the blender. She felt as if she had known him for years. And yet there was a sense of excitement about having him waiting for her that she hadn't experienced since…when? Her heart gave a funny little beat when she recognized what was happening to her. She was reacting to Craig as she'd reacted to no one since David—as a woman to a man.

The champagne bucket forgotten, Jennifer sat down on the cool linoleum floor and leaned her back against the cupboard. Why had she been so slow to realize what should have been obvious? She looked around the kitchen. The signs were everywhere—a meal meant to tempt and please, a feeling of frustration that she hadn't had time to change her clothes, an inability to concentrate on anything at the office that day. She drew her legs up to her chest and put her forehead against her knees.

Now what? Fall for a guy who lived a thousand miles away? Someone who didn't know as much about Thoroughbreds as her three-year-old cousin Amelia? *No way!* If and when she fell for anyone, it was going to be a born and bred Kentuckian, someone who shared her passion for horses and who intended to spend the rest of his life in Lexington.

Jennifer heard the door open and looked up to see Craig staring at her.

"You don't have another headache, do you?" he asked.

She shook her head.

He came over and crouched down beside her. "Then what's wrong?" he asked gently.

She folded her arms across her knees and propped her chin on them. "I realize it's a little strange to come into a room and find your hostess sitting on the floor, and I wish I could give you a logical explanation, but I can't."

"It's been one of those days for me, too," he said, sitting down beside her.

"Somehow, I don't think it's been quite the same." Now that she understood what was happening to her, having him sit so close was unnerving. She was confused and ill at ease and wished there was a convenient dark hole she could crawl into and hide until she had a better grip on her emotions.

"Why don't you tell me about your day, and then I'll tell you about mine."

"You go first." She needed time to come up with a believable explanation for her peculiar behavior. "As I recall, it's your turn to spill your guts. I had mine last night."

He settled into a more comfortable position, moving so that his back rested against the cupboard, only inches from hers. "I spent my morning driving around Lexington looking at the different farms, and then went over to the Horse Park and wandered around for a few hours."

"Why?" She was surprised and intrigued. Could it be his desire to get into breeding Thoroughbreds really was more than a whim?

"Curiosity, I guess." While driving the narrow country roads surrounding Lexington, Craig had searched for a sense of belonging. He had also thought about Jennifer, the tragedy she had experienced in her twenty-three years, and how he planned to return to her house that night with every intention of using her for his own purpose. Acknowledging his reason for seeing her again had made him uncomfortable, but it hadn't made him stay away.

"Did something happen?"

He shot her a questioning look.

"You implied you'd had a bad day."

"Not bad," he said softly. "Just thoughtful." He had a sudden, compelling desire to tell her what had brought him to Lexington. He had talked to no one about the clippings he'd found in the safe almost four months ago, and the desire to do so now was powerful. But it would be unfair to tell her who he was and expect her to keep his secret. Then there was always the possibility that he would decide to return to Oklahoma without contacting his parents. Where would that leave Jennifer?

Craig touched her hand. It created an unexpected appealing blanket of warmth against his callused palm. "Now it's your turn," he said.

There was no way she could withdraw her hand without being obvious, so she remained precisely as she was, careful not to move in any way that would seem encouraging. Her concentration was so completely focused on the contact that she had to struggle for an answer. "I, uh, I . . . It's been so long since I've entertained that I seem to have forgotten how. Even though I took off from work an hour early, I'm an hour behind schedule. My casserole is going to be ready before my vegetables, and I don't think the lemon pie I made earlier is going to set up, and I'm still wearing the clothes I've worn all day and—"

"And you have flour on the end of your nose."

"I do not." She reached up to wipe her nose despite her denial. Looking at her hand, she grinned sheepishly. "Well, maybe just a little bit."

"Certainly no more than if you'd actually dipped your nose in the bin." He reached up to wipe the last traces of the white powder away. "Surely that can't be all that has got you down."

She wished she knew him better. How was she ever going to get through an entire evening with him? She needed time alone to think, to rationalize her out-of-control emotions. She needed a calmer head to prevail, to tell her that what she was feeling was no more than a long-delayed rebound syndrome. Craig had happened along precisely when she was most vulnerable. It should have come as no great shock that she was reacting accordingly. "Let's just leave it at my clumsy reentry into society, okay?"

He studied her, wondering what she was keeping from him. "All right." He stood and held out his hand to help her up. "If we're not going to share deep dark secrets, let's get this show on the road. I skipped lunch and I'm starved."

"I'll go in and change—"

"You look fine the way you are."

"Is that your mind or your stomach talking?"

"Turn around."

"What?"

"Turn around—I want to see all of you before I answer."

Reluctantly she complied, turning with the graceful athletic movements her years of riding had ingrained.

Craig openly and intentionally looked at her, from the flush coloring her neck where her button-down collar stood open to the rigid way she held her back. His gaze swept the lush fullness of her breasts, noting the way they pressed against her blouse and how they yielded when she turned and her arm brushed against them. He took in the narrowness of her waist and the incredibly seductive way her hips flared from that narrowness. Beyond her hips the slacks were loose and hid the contour of her buttocks and thighs, but by then his imagination had taken over. "Like I said before, you look fine," he repeated, fighting to emit the words from a throat suddenly gone dry.

What a stupid-ass thing to do, he mentally railed. The last thing either of them wanted or needed was to further complicate their lives by getting involved with each other. And one thing he knew for sure—if he were to do anything about the way looking at her had made him feel, their lives would become one giant mass of complications.

Jennifer made herself breathe normally, but there was nothing she could do about her erratically beating heart. "Do you realize what this means?" she said lightly, forcing a teasing quality into her voice. "You will undoubtedly never get to see me in mauve. However, since you probably won't starve as a consequence, I guess the trade-off might seem equitable."

Craig smiled. He wondered what Jennifer had been like before the accident. He guessed she'd been the type who was seldom down, someone who brought sparkle and exuberance wherever she went and to whatever she did. David must have been special to attract someone like her, and she must have loved him very much. Now all she had were memories. Not only of David, but of the person she had been. Even her image of herself had been taken from her and replaced by a beautiful, hesitant stranger.

And after all she had been through already, he had come back that evening for no reason other than to use her. The thought made him sick. She trusted him, and he no more deserved her trust than a fox sunbathing inside a chicken coop.

"If you bought something special for tonight, I think you should wear it."

She couldn't let him believe that. She let out a tiny laugh. "I haven't bought anything new for myself in years. Between Christmas and my birthday, my family makes sure I wind up with enough clothes for three women." She shrugged dismissively. "I just thought this might be a good time to rotate something in my closet."

Why didn't he believe her? "If that's really all it was, let's get going on this meal."

Craig discovered that beyond cleaning and setting the table there was very little left to do. The meal was ready so quickly that the champagne didn't have time to cool, so they decided to wait until later to open it. At Craig's insistence they ate in the kitchen at a table that sat in a tiny alcove, almost completely surrounded by mullioned windows. It was the spot where Jennifer normally had all her meals. Lights from other homes on the farm shone in the distance, but there was a sense of cozy isolation as they consumed their dinner.

Because he had finally looked at Jennifer as a woman instead of just as a source of information, Craig found himself watching and listening to her differently than he had before. He noticed things as inconsequential as the elegant way she served the meal—as if her table manners had been inbred—and the small scar at the base of her neck where he could see her pulse. He became aware of the artful way she turned the conversation from herself and concentrated on him, making him feel important, the center of her attention. And that knack caused him to wonder about her background. He suspected she was more than a young woman whom the Mitchells had hired for her bookkeeping skills.

They were finished with the meal and clearing the table when Craig asked, "Have you always lived in Lexington?"

"Born and raised." She tossed him a mischievous smile. "And convinced anyone who wasn't deserves sympathy."

"Funny..." He nudged her out of the way to stack some plates in the dishwasher. "That's the way native Oklahomans feel about anyone not born there."

"Obviously few of them have had the chance to visit Kentucky."

"One or two of us have managed the trip."

She turned to face him, leaning her hip against the counter. "And?"

Craig felt the question in the pit of his stomach. "And I have to admit, there are some things to like here."

"But?" she prodded. Jennifer had purposely kept the conversation on a superficial level throughout dinner, sidestepping anything personal, evading direct questions and trying to ignore her no longer deniable attraction to the man who had been sitting across from her. While listening to him talk about the museum at the Horse Park, she had mentally listed a dozen reasons to distrust her wildly fluctuating emotions. She was lonely, and he had come along when she was most vulnerable. He was handsome in a way that had always appealed to her—a face that wasn't movie-star pretty, but etched with character and strength. And he made her smile and laugh, and it seemed such a long time since she had done either. Even the headache that had struck earlier that day had impressed her as less severe than usual when she had concentrated on her plans for that evening.

Craig pulled out the top rack of the dishwasher and loaded two glasses into it. "But you people aren't much for open spaces," he went on with his appraisal. "And I'm not sure I could get over the feeling of being closed in."

"I've never experienced that feeling," she said. "Personally, I like the orderliness and the sense of family that develops when people work closely together. We've created our own little community at Mitchell Farm."

"In other words, it's a world of its own. One you never have to leave," he said softly.

She shot him a defensive, angry look. "What's that supposed to mean?"

"It was just an observation."

"I suppose it's different in Oklahoma? There's no closeness among the people who work on your ranch?"

"Cowboys are an independent breed. Some have been with us since before I was born. Others have disappeared after one season and not come back for years, if ever."

"Well, I'm glad it's not that way here."

He tucked his fist under her chin, forcing her to look at him. "Makes life interesting, doesn't it?"

No, she thought sadly, not interesting, complicated. Suddenly, more than anything, she wanted him to leave. If he left now, and she never saw him again, she could step back into her normal routine and go on with her life. In a few weeks she would begin to forget the tall, hauntingly familiar stranger who had magically appeared in her office one day. If he stayed, she feared there was nothing but grief in store for both of them. Then why couldn't she ask him to go? "Would you like some coffee?"

"Just coffee? Didn't I see a lemon pie somewhere around here?"

"I don't think...oh, what the heck. Grab a knife out of that drawer over there, and we'll see whether we need plates or bowls."

They took their dessert and coffee into the living room. After a hesitant taste Jennifer decided the pie was the best she had ever made, tart without being bitter, and with just the right amount of sweetness to balance the flavor. Craig heaped effusive compliments on her, and she flushed with pleasure.

When they were finished and the fire had been refueled, they sat back with second cups of coffee and continued the conversation they had started in the kitchen.

"Tell me what it was like being raised on a ranch," Jennifer said.

His first thought was to turn the conversation away from himself because he was worried that it would be too easy to let something slip if he didn't. But then he realized how much he ached to share that part of himself with her, and he ignored the warning sounding inside him. "It's a different kind of life," he began. "If you're not born to it, or don't have a streak of it somewhere in your makeup, the isolation would probably get to you after a while. I never knew what it was to be around kids my own age until I started school.''

"That must mean you were an only child.''

"My parents were in their forties when they had...when I was born. And since there weren't any relatives, there weren't even any cousins.''

"Who did you play with, then? Who were your friends?''

"In the summer between third and fourth grade, I discovered a kid named Henry Keily had moved in a few miles down the road from our place. We became friends and rode our bikes over to see each other whenever we could. Henry stuck around until we were juniors in high school and then took off to Texas with his parents.''

"Do you ever see him anymore?''

"Not much. He went to UCLA on a football scholarship, got injured and decided he'd better do some studying if he was ever going to make a living for himself. Last I heard he was working for a computer company up near San Francisco.''

Jennifer mentally compared her life—the hundreds of friends she had had while growing up, the parties she had attended and the big family celebrations that accompanied every holdiay—to the life Craig had lived, and her heart went out to him. "I don't think I would be the same person I am if I had been raised the way you were.''

"How's that?''

She answered before she had time to think. "I'd probably be a recluse and...'' She stopped in midsentence, struck by what she had said. "What I mean is that I'd probably find all the activity that goes on around here nerve-racking and try to find a way to avoid it.''

"Nerve-racking isn't the way I would have put it, but I have to admit that I think it would be hard to adjust.''

"Why would you even want to try?" she asked, suddenly wanting very much to know.

He took his time answering, looking for a way to avoid lying to her. "The thought occurred to me that it might be a good idea to find a way to at least feel comfortable in a place I might be visiting from time to time on business."

She considered his answer. "Finish telling me what it's like to live on a ranch," she said, kicking off her shoes and tucking her legs beneath her.

He laughed. "In fifty words or less?"

"Take as many as you need. After all, we've got all night."

He, too, settled more comfortably into the couch. "It's dogs and chickens and horses and weeding the garden when you're still too little to be chasing cattle, and privately wishing you could be back weeding when you're big enough to fall out of the saddle. It's a hundred chores that never stay done." His words brought poignant memories. "It's the smell of homemade bread and tart apple pies and being so tired you don't remember falling into bed at night. My father—" his mind stumbled over the words as conflicting emotions of betrayal and loyalty assailed him. "—my father insisted I learn everything there was to know about running a ranch. He'd stay at the teaching until I could do whatever it was he thought I should be able to do, even if it meant staying up all night." A private smile curved his mouth. "However, he wasn't above taking a catnap or two while I worked things out."

"He sounds like a special man."

"He was. He and my mother died a few months back." he said simply, his voice revealing none of the loss he still suffered.

"Oh . . . I'm sorry, Craig." She wished she had known him then and could have shared some of his pain.

He stared into his cup, afraid that if he looked at her he would respond to the offer of comfort he had heard in her voice. *He had to get out of there.* If he stayed, he knew in his soul that something would happen between them, if only because he so desperately wanted it to. "I'd better leave," he said, the words sounding harsh. "It's late, and we both have work to do tomorrow."

Jennifer's first instinct was to protest. She didn't want him to leave. Then reason took over, and she realized it was better for both of them if he left, better if they never saw each other again. "Let me get your coat."

Jennifer followed Craig to the door, desperately wishing there was another way for them to be together, while feeling relieved that her excursion back into the real world, the dangerous world, was nearly over. "When will you be going home?" she asked, blindly searching for parting conversation.

"My plane leaves Monday night."

Four days. Couldn't he tell she wanted him to leave Lexington *now*, not in four days? Why couldn't he have lied to her and said he was leaving in the morning? "Well, if I don't see you before then, have a nice trip." Was that really her? Had she really said something so inane?

Craig stared at her. Everything else in the room disappeared with the intensity of his gaze. "Can I call you tomorrow?" he asked softly, knowing it was wrong.

Her mind insisted she tell him no, but she nodded in acquiescence.

"Jennifer..."

"Yes?"

"I'm going to kiss you, and I don't want you to pull away." He lifted his hands and held the sides of her face. With infinite care and tenderness, he touched his lips to hers. The contact was electric, creating an intoxicating

urge to let the kiss go on until passions became ignited.
But he resisted the temptation and let her go, reaching for
the door, afraid of what he might do if he stayed. Without saying another word, he turned and left.

Jennifer stood frozen, unable even to move to the window to watch him leave. Slowly her hand came up from
her side. She touched her lips. No one had kissed her like
that since David. And she had welcomed and found pleasure in the kiss. A single tear slid unheeded down her
cheek. *Don't call*, she silently pleaded. *Please, Craig,
don't call me tomorrow. I'm not ready to take a chance on
being hurt again.*

CHAPTER FIVE

EXHAUSTION AND FATIGUE helped Craig to fall asleep when he returned to the motel that night, but as soon as he heard a car door slam outside his room early the next morning, he was wide awake and anxious to get started with his day. Despite telling her he would call, he'd decided not to see Jennifer again until he'd made up his mind about contacting his parents. The decision had led him to a course of action he should have taken in the beginning—to let a professional handle the investigation.

After breakfast he called the first of three private detective agencies listed in the phone book. The secretary scheduled him for an eleven-thirty appointment. The rest of the morning he spent walking the streets of Lexington, trying to burn off energy that felt like undischarged lightning.

At eleven o'clock he got into his rented car and drove downtown. The core of the city was being systematically dismantled to make way for what the signs promised would be a spectacular new hotel, office and shopping complex. Craig parked the car and searched for the main entrance to a building that looked as if it too was a candidate for the wreckers' ball. Inside, a meticulously clean lobby was complete with polished floors, potted plants and easy instructions to the tenants' offices.

Jack Chapman's office on the fifth floor was as carefully maintained as the lobby. As soon as Craig entered, the secretary announced him, and he was told to go right in and that Mr. Chapman was expecting him. Thick forest-green carpeting and cherry wood furniture destroyed the last vestige of Craig's stereotype idea of what he would find in a private detective's office.

"Disappointed?" A distinguished looking man in his mid-fifties stood and came around his desk to shake hands with Craig.

"A little," Craig admitted.

Jack Chapman guided Craig to one of two leather chairs facing each other on the opposite side of the room. "Most people are. My wife thinks I should redo the place so it's more in keeping with clients' expectations, but then I would miss the fun of seeing how surprised they are when they come the first time." He smiled broadly. "Now that we have that out of the way, what can I do for you, Mr. Templeton?"

"There are some people I would like you to investigate for me."

"I see. And do these people live in Lexington?"

Craig nodded. "Their names are Frank and Agnes Mitchell."

Jack Chapman let out a soft whistle and sank back in his chair. "What kind of information did you have in mind?"

"Whatever you can get, but primarily I'd like to know what kind of people they are."

"May I ask why you're interested?"

"Is it necessary for you to know?"

"Not really, but there's something you should understand up front. If at any time during the investigation I have reason to believe you are after information about the Mitchells for illegal or unethical reasons, our relationship will be instantly terminated, and only the unused portion of your retainer will be refunded."

"Agreed."

Chapman put his hands together tent fashion and thoughtfully tapped his fingers against his chin while he studied Craig. "What information do you already have?"

"Not much. I know they own Mitchell Farm and that they have three children and that they do their charity work quietly. The oldest son is named Andrew, but I don't know the names of the other two children."

"Are you a relative?"

Craig didn't answer.

"I see . . . By when did you want this information?"

"As soon as possible. I'll pay whatever it takes to—"

"Do you want the information piecemeal, or would you rather have it sent all at once when I'm finished?"

"I'll stop by as soon as you have anything at all."

"All right. I'll probably be seeing you on Monday, then." He stood. "Stop by my secretary's desk on your way out. She will explain the financial arrangements."

Craig shook Chapman's hand again and left. Fifteen minutes later he was back on the sidewalk. He wasn't sure what he'd expected, but it wasn't what he'd found. It seemed almost too easy to have someone investigated. Chapman had simply taken his word that his intentions were honorable. The implications were chilling.

He shoved his hands into his pockets and looked down the street to where he'd parked his car. Now what? He had two and a half days until Monday, and nothing to do with himself. A part of him longed to call Jennifer, if only to hear her voice. Another part demanded he stick to his resolve to handle one problem at a time.

Problem? His expression softened, and anxiety became yearning. Problem was not the word for what was happening between him and Jennifer, but he'd be damned if he knew what was. He started walking, heading in a direction away from his car, not caring where he went as long as it would take time to get there.

JENNIFER REACHED INTO HER DESK DRAWER, looking for aspirins. What had started out as an occasional flash of pain whenever she glanced up from her work too quickly had turned into a full-blown headache. After a sleepless night, coffee for breakfast and a stomach tied in knots, she wasn't surprised her head hurt, just angry that she was still so susceptible to the vagaries of life.

She shook three of the extra-strength tablets into her palm and tipped her cup to see if there was enough coffee left to wash them down. There wasn't. With slow, careful movements she made her way into Lynn's office and over to the water cooler.

Only a few years older than Jennifer, honey-blond Lynn was five months pregnant with her third child. "Headache?" she asked, looking up from her typewriter as Jennifer passed her desk.

"Uh-huh."

"When are you going to refill that prescription Dr. Hunter gave you?"

"I'll get around to it one of these days."

"Before or after those aspirins have eaten a hole in your stomach?"

Jennifer grimaced with pain as she bent over to fill her cup. She knew the number of aspirins she took would catch up with her someday, but she had decided she would rather cope with their effects than with those of the powerful narcotics the doctor had prescribed. "I don't take as many as you think I do," she said. "Besides..." She tried to smile. "How long can this go on? The headaches are bound to get better one of these days, don't you think?"

"Sure they are. Just as soon as you have the surgery you need."

Her pain created an intense wave of nausea, and she reached out to balance herself against the water cooler. "Not today, Lynn," she said, forestalling a familiar argument.

"Then when?" Lynn replied with a sigh. "Face it, Jennifer—you're not getting any better. And you won't until you let the doctors repair those nerves."

"Are you going out to lunch?" Jennifer asked, purposely changing the subject.

Lynn silently stared at her as if trying to decide whether she should let Jennifer get away with the change. Finally she shook her head in resignation. "I'm meeting Bobby at Burger King. You want me to bring you something?"

"No—I brought a sandwich. I was just wondering about the phone. Why don't you turn on the machine before you leave?" It was the coward's way out, but she was afraid that if she heard Craig's voice the resolve she had reached that morning not to see him again would crumble.

"Are you trying to avoid someone?" Lynn asked.

Jennifer's request to have Lynn tell anyone looking for her that she was out of the office for the day was so unusual that she wasn't surprised her friend was suspicious. "Only a salesman who refuses to take no for an answer." She hated lying but didn't have the energy for the truth. No, that wasn't it. Energy had nothing to do with her reluctance to tell Lynn about Craig.

"What's his name? I'll have Andrew take care of him for you."

"I'd rather handle this myself." The last thing she needed was to have more people involved.

"All right, if that's the way you want it. But I've yet to see a salesman discouraged because someone didn't come to the phone. I wouldn't be surprised if he showed up at the front door. Then what are you going to do?"

"One step at a time, Lynn." The phone rang, making Jennifer's heart leap against her chest and a flash of pain shoot through her temples.

Lynn picked up the receiver. "Mitchell Farm." She looked over at Jennifer. "No...I'm sorry, she isn't in today. Is there something I can help you with?" She grabbed a pencil and started writing. "One forty-five, Monday. Got it. Okay, I'll be sure to tell her."

It was all Jennifer could do to keep from signaling to Lynn that she would take the phone. She was sure it was Craig. What made her so afraid of him that she wouldn't accept his call? Without conscious thought her hand came up from her side, and she touched her lips, remembering the burn of his kiss. Not even David had made her feel the way she did when she thought about Craig. He was different from anyone she had ever known—his life rough where hers had been smooth. He was a cougar and she was a house cat. She wanted nothing to do with a man like Craig. He would make demands of her and eventually, if their relationship developed the way she believed it would, he would want to take her away from all that she loved. The familiar would grow dim until it was only a dream. Better to back away now, no matter how desperately she wanted to see him again, no matter how her body cried out in protest.

"It was Gary over at Breeder's Supply," Lynn said. "He wanted you to know they wouldn't be able to make their delivery until Monday afternoon."

Disappointment destroyed anticipation, leaving her feeling hollow. ''Thanks,'' she said softly, mentally berating herself for wanting Craig to phone when she had no intention of taking the call. It was the kind of game she'd always prided herself on not playing. ''Never mind turning on the machine, Lynn. I'll answer the phone while you're gone.''

CRAIG'S DETERMINATION not to call Jennifer weakened as the day progressed. The arguments and reasoning he had used to support his decision not to see her until he had his life squared away diminished in direct proportion to his growing need. Seeking distraction from his thoughts, he stopped to stare in store windows and invariably discovered his mind wandering to the way her face had felt cradled in his hands, the way she had looked when he kissed her, the warmth that had spread through his midsection when her lips yielded to his. He ached to hold her in his arms, to feel the womanly shape and softness of her body against the flat hardness of his own.

Whenever he realized that he'd lost control of his thoughts again, he'd take up his aimless odyssey once more. He stopped for lunch at a sandwich shop long after the noontime crowd had disappeared. He sat by a window and watched the citizens of Lexington passing by. A remarkable number of them were paired off, holding hands, exchanging intimate smiles, radiating happiness. He had never felt so alone. Nor had he ever wanted to be with someone the way he wanted to be with Jennifer. The wanting held him, refusing him any peace.

JENNIFER GAVE THE DOORKNOB a final, unnecessary turn, checking to make sure it was locked. She hesitated before she headed for her car to listen one last time for the sound of a ringing telephone. When she realized what she was doing, she made a disgusted face and stepped onto the walkway. She had been a mental slave to the phone all afternoon, her heart racing whenever it rang, her mind willing it to ring whenever it was silent.

She had started the day praying that Craig wouldn't call, hoping that he, too, understood the futility of their seeing each other again. Now, at the end of the day, more than anything else, she wanted to be in his arms, wanted to feel his lips on hers, wanted to lose herself in the tender compassion she had seen in his dark eyes. It didn't matter if it wasn't forever. When the time would come for him to return to his own life, she would let him go. She was willing to settle for here and now. But even as the thought entered her mind, she knew it wasn't the truth. They were on the edge of being able to stop what they had so innocently started. One step further, seeing each other one more time, would mean no turning back.

With grim determination Jennifer drove past the road to her bungalow and headed for her parents' house. They would be surprised when she just dropped in, but they would welcome her and keep her mind occupied. And maybe, with a little luck, they would come up with a way to keep her busy that weekend.

THE BUILDINGS HAD SPILLED OUT WORKERS on their way home for the weekend an hour earlier, and Craig was finally on his way back to his car when he passed an antique shop and stopped to look at a breech-loading rifle displayed in the window. Bill Mason had taught him to appreciate old guns, and this one was exceptional. During Bill's thirty years as foreman of Templeton Ranch, he had gathered by bartering and trading, one of the finest private collections of antique firearms in Oklahoma.

Craig knew Bill would give a month of his allotted time in heaven to have the rifle in the window.

A slow smile lit Craig's face when he realized that, should he buy the gun for Bill, it wouldn't make a dent in the checkbook he now carried. It seemed money took even more getting used to than he had first thought. He reached for the door just as the owner was coming to close up for the night. When Craig explained what he wanted, the gray-haired man asked him inside, locking the door behind them.

The gun turned out to be everything it had seemed in the window. Craig was taken aback by the price, but knew it was fair, so made the purchase. While he was making arrangements to have it shipped home, a piece of jewelry in the case beside the cash register caught his attention. It was a cameo of a woman so closely resembling Jennifer that she could have posed for the artist.

"May I see that pin?" Craig asked, pointing to the cameo.

The shop owner reached into his pocket for a key to unlock the cabinet. "A fine piece of workmanship," he said, handing the brooch to Craig. "There's a story that goes along with it, but I can't guarantee its authenticity. Supposedly the cameo belonged to the captain of a whaling ship who for some reason couldn't marry the woman he loved. They agreed never to see each other again, but before the captain left, he took a miniature of the lady to remember her by. He had this cameo carved from that painting. It used to be the top to a snuffbox, but as you can see, someone's made it into a pin. Should be easy enough to make into a necklace, though, if that's what you've got in mind."

Craig held the cameo under the light of a nearby lamp. The resemblance to Jennifer was uncanny. "I'll take this, too," he said, not bothering to ask the price.

"Shall I pack it with the gun?"

Craig considered his answer. "No," he said, "I'll take it with me."

JENNIFER MADE IT to almost ten o'clock before she started pacing her parents' living room and realized that if she didn't leave soon they would become suspicious of her behavior. She kissed them good-night and headed home, no better off than when she had arrived, but at least she was hours closer to Craig's departure. Thank goodness he hadn't told her where he was staying. She would probably do something foolish, like trying to find him.

Turning up the long driveway to her home, she tried to avoid looking at the place where Craig had parked his car the two times he had been there. Only blackness filled the spot. She swallowed her disappointment and went inside, not bothering to turn on lights as she walked through the house and headed straight for her bedroom.

She lay across the bed and stared up at the ceiling, her body restless with an ache that haunted her every thought. An image of Craig appeared in her mind. She tried to imagine him working on his ranch, summoning stereotype pictures of cowboys from movies and television programs she had seen. She couldn't make the two merge. What persisted was the Craig she had come to know—a man who seemed to fit into her life and her world as easily as if he had been born to it. And yet she was convinced she was wrong. His words had told her so; his dreams were not hers and never would be.

It wasn't fair. First David and now Craig. What was it about her that seemed hell-bent toward tragedy? She rolled over onto her stomach. With all the men who had passed in and out of her life in the year she'd been keeping the books at the farm, why had she been drawn to Craig? What was it about him that had made him stand out above all the others?

By asking the question, she was seeking answers to negate her feelings, but it didn't work. There was no mystery in her attraction, no black magic controlling her emotions. She admired Craig's strength of will and his eagerness to learn new things. She had seen the way he looked at the farm when he had thought himself unobserved. There was a poignancy to the longing in his eyes that touched her soul. And then he'd told her about being alone, and she had understood because, despite the loving friends and family surrounding her, she, too, was alone.

And she had been so sure he felt the same way about her. But she must have been wrong. If he had, he would have called.

No—she refused to believe she was wrong. Something else had kept him from calling. And then she knew. He not only shared her torment because he was attracted to the wrong person, but he also shared her fear.

CRAIG STEPPED FROM THE SHOWER and grabbed a towel from the wall rack. Preoccupied with all that had gone on the previous week and exhausted from the long day of wandering around the city, he paid little attention to the job of wiping water from his body and left drops glistening on his broad back and clinging to the mat of hair on his chest when he walked back into the bedroom. His gaze immediately fell on the cameo he'd left on the nightstand. Sometime during the evening, between the restaurant he'd gone to for dinner and the bars he'd visited looking for company, he'd accepted that no matter what he did or how it turned out, thoughts of Jennifer were not going to go away. If he left without ever seeing her again, she would haunt him until her memory grew way out of proportion to the time they had spent together. Though he tried to convince himself there was still time to back away, he knew he was lying.

Tenderly, reverently, as though it was her actual skin he touched, Craig ran his finger over the cameo. He doubted that Jennifer had any idea of how beautiful she was, or that she cared. But it wasn't the face the doctors had created that drew him to her. The compassion and humor that flashed in her eyes were all her own. The gentle laugh, the intelligent questions, the tenacity that had brought her through a hell few people had known, had nothing to do with the miracle the surgeons had performed. He lay down on the bed and gently closed his hand around the cameo, pressing the raised image into his skin, creating a tangible feeling of closeness.

For an instant he let himself dream. He imagined Jennifer at the ranch, riding beside him, silhouetted against a brilliant orange sunset, sharing the peace and serenity after a day's work. He pictured her later that night, filling his arms, responding to him with a passion that equalled his own. Threaded through the dream was a well-being created by a far-reaching and loving family; a mother only slightly changed from the yellowed newspaper clipping he had of her and a father who was simply an older version of himself. There were brothers and a sister and nieces and nephews . . . and there were his and Jennifer's children.

His dream filled him with a craving that destroyed safeguards, leaving him defenseless. Could he possibly go back to the way he had been after knowing such promise? So much rested on the detective's report. And what if the finding convinced him to leave well enough alone? He tried to imagine himself leaving Kentucky without ever seeing his mother and father. He couldn't. Even if he didn't tell them who he was, he had to see them. And if he did, would they know? Would they see themselves in him? A part of him wanted to believe they would.

If in the end he decided not to let anyone know who he was, would he tell Jennifer? Would she understand? His hand tightened around the pin. His mind, his body, everything that he was, cried out for the life he pictured with Jennifer by his side.

JENNIFER BRUSHED HER HAIR from her forehead and sat up, leaning against the headboard of her bed. She couldn't see the clock but knew it was late—certainly too late to be sitting on her bed fully clothed. Her mental exhaustion had created a blessed numbness and, as she had so many times before, she automatically began the self-preservation techniques she had developed after David's death, tricks she used to prevent herself spending a night wide-awake. First came a hot bath and then a cup of tea laced with brandy. Next came a book she saved especially for sleepless nights—a seven-hundred-page self-published autobiography written by her great-uncle.

She was in the middle of the twenty-seventh chapter when she heard a car turn onto her driveway. Because Mitchell Farm was several miles from the city and located on a two-lane country road, the quiet of the night was seldom broken by anything harsher sounding than a cricket. Instantly her heart picked up its beat. She took in a breath and had to consciously remind herself to let it out again.

The car stopped; a door slammed. Jennifer reached for her robe and stepped into her slippers. Despite the hour, she wasn't afraid. She knew who was outside as surely as she knew why he had come.

Craig stepped onto the walkway and moved toward the house. His hand was raised to knock when the door opened. Bathed in moonlight, Jennifer seemed an extension of a dream, and for an instant he felt a stab of disappointment. But then he saw her struggle to take a breath, and he knew that what was happening was real. "I tried, but I couldn't stay away," he said softly, hoping she would understand.

"I'm glad," she answered just as softly.

With a hoarse groan he reached for her. He held her close, wrapping his arms around her, absorbing her warmth, radiating his emotion. In that instant he was transported from the loneliness he had known to a place filled with exquisite promise. Long minutes passed, and still he held her, content to feel her response, lost in the miracle of ever finding her at all.

He pressed his face against her fragrant hair; his hands ran across the contour of her back. "I promise I'll never do anything to hurt you," he murmured, holding her as if she were a fragile piece of porcelain. Deliberately, he looked at her. "But I have to tell you that there are things about me you don't know—things I can't talk about yet." His eyes held a poignant plea. "Trust me . . . just for a while longer." The words were all he could offer, but they came from the bottom of his soul. He begged her to understand that he would do anything to spare her more pain, go to any lengths to protect her.

She lifted her face, willing him to kiss her, her actions more eloquent than words.

He took her offering, touching his lips to hers with an aching tenderness. His tongue caressed the corner of her mouth; she turned and met his tiny thrusts with a tentative movement of her own tongue. Craig led her, encouraged her until she eagerly explored what he offered. He held the sides of her face, and his fingers combed through her hair. When he thought he could stand no more, he broke the kiss and gently laid her face against his chest, lightly resting his chin on the top of her head. "I came to ask you to go away with me this weekend."

"Where?" His heartbeat sounded in her ear, telling her how difficult it had been for him to break the kiss.

"It doesn't matter. I just want to be with you, anywhere away from here." He wanted her to escape her shelter, but more selfishly he wanted to leave behind the reminders of the reasons he had sought her out in the beginning.

Jennifer carefully considered her answer, struggling with deeply embedded conflicts. There would be questions when she called her family to tell them she would be gone, but not nearly as many as there would be if she spent the weekend with Craig at home and someone happened to stop by. "When do you want me to be ready?" she asked, giving in to her desire to be with him.

He closed his eyes with a mental sigh of relief. The feeling of victory that swept through him was instantly followed by a stab of doubt. Life was never this easy. Nothing so good had ever just dropped in his lap. "What time can you be ready?"

She looked up at him. "Nine?"

He bent to kiss her again. Her lips parted in invitation, and he tasted the inner softness of her mouth. She filled his senses with a desire that exploded into need. They were transported to a place of lovers, a cocoon that offered refuge from all that divided them, a place where any problem could be worked out.

Jennifer let out a shuddering sigh and leaned her forehead against the base of his throat. "I'll be ready by eight." It was the earliest she could call her family without raising suspicion.

"I'll be here," he answered. He held her close for what he vowed would be the last time that night. He had only come to her tonight because he wanted to see her face when he asked her to go away with him. But as he released her and looked into her eyes, he saw a hunger as raw and compelling as his own. "Jennifer," he said, his voice husky with wanting her, "tell me to leave."

"I can't," she said.

He was lost.

"Everything has happened so fast," she murmured. "I know I should doubt my feelings . . . but I don't, not anymore." She touched the back of his neck and brought him to her. The kiss they shared was a wondrous meeting of lips and tongues, expressing the depth of their loneliness and the consuming need for a night of reprieve from their isolation. Words of protest, rational thoughts were driven from their minds in the explosive release of restraint.

"Where?" he asked, no longer fighting a battle he ached to lose.

She smiled. "Is my bed all right?"

He bent and caught her up in his arms. He was surprised how light she felt, how good. "Thank God you're conventional."

Even though Jennifer had given in to her feelings, a cloak of shyness settled over her as Craig carried her into the bedroom. When he released her to stand beside the bed, she froze. David was the only man she had ever made love to, and it hadn't happened very often. Except for their honeymoon, their lovemaking had been hurried, sometimes even awkward, certainly nothing like Jennifer had imagined it would be when she had been a dreamy young girl. But because she and David had known each other for two years, they had at least had familiarity to guide them. With Craig, she felt unsure, hesitant. She had no idea what to do that would please him or what actions might make him think she was too aggressive.

Craig detected her inner conflict in the sudden tension of her muscles. He held her, waiting for her to tell him she'd changed her mind and wanted him to leave. When she just stood there, he gently lifted her chin and stared into her eyes. "Tell me what's wrong."

She moved her shoulders in an expressive shrug and tried to smile. "I know it sounds strange for someone who's been married, but I'm not sure what I should do."

His heart went out to her. "Would it bother you if I told you I'm not the world's most experienced lover, either?" He'd made love the first time at sixteen—to the woman who'd hired on as cook for the summer. It had been a week after his birthday, and he'd later discovered that she'd been "hired" by one of the summer ranch hands to "make him a man." All the expected and normal things had happened, as they had with every woman he had made love to since, but afterward he had been left with a feeling that something was missing.

Jennifer was surprised and somehow pleased by his statement. She stopped thinking about herself and her confidence grew.

When she didn't answer him, Craig decided that what she was asking for was more time to be sure about what they were doing. "Maybe it would be better if we waited," he suggested quietly.

"Is that what you want?"

"It has nothing to do with what I want." He was filled with a need for her that controlled every thought, every breath. "Jennifer, I don't understand what's happening between us. I only know that in two days you've become such an important part of my life I can hardly think of anyone or anything else. Until tonight I had no idea what it meant to want someone so much it hurt. But it has to be right for you, or it won't be right for me."

Long seconds passed; only the sound of the whispered ticking of the grandfather clock in the living room broke the silence. "I don't want you to go," she told him. Then, realizing he needed more than her words, she reached for the buttons on his shirt. When the shirt was open and free from his jeans, she slowly ran her trembling hands across the taut muscles of his chest. She pressed her lips and then her tongue against his nipples, moving her hands up his sides.

Craig closed his eyes. He felt his world shrinking, growing ever smaller until only he and Jennifer existed. Time and place and doubts disappeared.

Unable to keep from touching her any longer, Craig reached for the sash on her robe. The ecru velvet parted, revealing a thin layer of apricot silk and lace clinging to her body. He lowered his head to the scar at the base of her throat, touching her skin with his tongue, tasting the sweetness. She responded with a heat that matched his own, cradling her hips into his, driving him to distraction. Though he had slept with women, he had never loved any of them. Now he understood what had been missing. Without a deep caring for someone, making love had been mechanical. With it, the experience was beyond his imaginings.

His hands moved across the silk to gently cup her breasts. She sighed and returned the pressure. His thumbs stroked her nipples until they rose to hard peaks. With a fluid movement he brushed the straps from her shoulders and dropped her gown to her waist. He shrugged from his shirt and grasped her arms, slowly pulling her toward him, feeling the touch of her nipples and erotic yielding of her breasts where they made contact with his chest. Then he covered her mouth with his own, his thrusting tongue imitating the act that would soon follow.

Jennifer wrapped her arms around his neck and met his passion with a fire that had destroyed the last of her hesitancy. Craig's hands traveled the length of her bare back, slipping beneath the silk to grasp her buttocks and pull her closer to him.

He reached behind her to hold the blankets open for her to enter the bed, and after he stepped from the rest of his clothes, he joined her. Wherever their skin made contact, the spot became a sensual part of their bodies. "You make me feel as if I could do anything, be anyone," he said.

She pressed her lips to his neck, outlined his jaw with her tongue. Anyone who could give her back the enthusiasm for life that she had thought gone forever could do anything. "You can," she sighed. "You are." Her hand followed the matting of hair on his chest until it disappeared. With sure, deft caresses, she purposely moved lower until she intimately touched him, smiling in pleasure at his sharp intake of breath. Wrapping her fingers around him, she applied gentle coaxing pressure.

Craig reached for her hand and pulled it away. "You're giving me far too much credit for control," he said, his voice low and husky.

"Why would you—"

Her words were lost when he covered her mouth with a thrusting, demanding kiss. She clung to him, seeking release from the sweet torment that burned in her loins, sending an unmistakable message in the rocking of her hips as she moved against him.

Still he waited, fighting his body's demands until he was sure she was ready. Slowly, methodically, he touched her, embedding the memory and feel of her in his mind. He measured her breasts with his hand, the nipple with his mouth. The last thread of control snapped when he caressed the moist folds of flesh between her thighs and heard her whispered demand to be taken.

Their coming together was explosive. Craig's entry was deep, and his thrusts were met by Jennifer with passion-filled abandon. She felt an anticipation building, then a tingling and finally a culminating rush of incredible pleasure followed by wave after wave of release. As soon as reason returned, she recognized what had happened to her, and then she realized she had never experienced a true climax with David. She had a peculiar, unshakable feeling she had just betrayed him.

Coming down from his own climax, Craig didn't immediately notice the transition in Jennifer. When he sensed she had mentally pulled back from him, he caught her chin and made her look at him. "What's wrong?" he asked, once more concern in his voice.

"Nothing."

"I don't believe you."

She blinked away threatening tears. Could he possibly understand what she was feeling? "I was . . . saying goodbye."

He rolled onto this back and brought her with him. When she was nestled into his side, her head on his shoulder, he said, "It must be hard to say goodbye to someone you loved as much as you must have loved David."

"The problem is I thought I already had."

They lay together, each deep in private thoughts, listening to the softly ticking clock. Craig spoke first. ''Jennifer—I don't expect you to pretend David never existed.''

''But it's long past the time I should have got on with my life. There must be something wrong with me.''

''That sounds like something friends might have told you. I know you don't believe it yourself. You couldn't possibly.''

As she listened to him, she absently moved her finger against his chest, making circles, catching the springy hairs and curling them around her fingertip. ''Then why has it taken me so long to reach out to someone again?''

''Because it took me this long to get here.''

She put her arm around his waist and gave him a hug. ''Are you always going to have the right answers?''

''As long as you keep asking the right questions.'' He brushed the hair from her temple and pressed his lips tenderly to the thin scar that paralleled her scalp. They continued to lie together in eloquent silence until Craig felt her breathing slip into the steady rhythm of sleep. Gently, he extracted himself from her arms to get dressed and return to his motel room. Although he made little noise, she woke up.

''Where are you going?'' she asked, fighting to sound wide-awake.

''Back to the hotel.''

''Why?''

''What would the people around here say if they saw a strange car parked in your driveway tomorrow morning?''

She knew he was right, but she didn't want him to go. She started to protest but then reluctantly agreed. She started to get out of bed. He told her he could find his own way out, but she insisted on walking him to the door.

"Tomorrow..." he said, kissing her goodbye.

"Craig?"

"Hmmm?"

"I...uh...thank you." She wanted to tell him how special their lovemaking had been, but couldn't find the words that would express how she felt without sounding clichéd.

He touched his lips to hers in a fleeting kiss. "I know," he said softly.

She slipped her arms around his waist and held him. "I don't know what quirk of fate brought you to Mitchell Farm, but I'm so glad you came."

"I promise we'll talk about that quirk of fate someday soon, Jennifer. Now kiss me good-night and get back in bed."

She raised her face to him and kissed him with a passion that stole his breath. It was all he could do to let her go. He pulled her hands from around his waist and took a step backward. "Now go to bed," he said and turned to leave before he lost his battle and stayed.

CHAPTER SIX

JENNIFER DROPPED HER OVERNIGHT BAG by the front door and ran back into her bedroom for her sweater. It was a glorious autumn day. The air was crisp and clear with a smell of wood burning in fireplaces. The phone call to her parents had gone amazingly well—only a smattering of questions and a command that she enjoy herself on her drive through the country. Of course, she'd left out the one detail of the weekend that could have altered their reaction. She'd neglected to mention Craig. She smiled. It wasn't hard to imagine how different the phone conversation would have been had she been completely straightforward. Now all she and Craig had to do was to get off the farm without anyone seeing them.

She walked back toward the front door and caught her reflection in the mirror. Stunned, she stopped and stared. Was that really her? She studied the person looking back at her. There was animation in the face, the eyes were filled with life, and the mouth was turned up in anticipation. She actually liked the person she saw.

When Craig arrived a few minutes later, Jennifer bounded out the door and threw her arms around him. He caught her to him and swung her around. ''I'm so glad you're here,'' she said breathlessly.

''My God, you look beautiful.'' The rust color of her cashmere sweater accentuated the deep red highlights in her brown hair and heightened her naturally tan complexion. Her cheeks were flushed with color, and her eyes sparkled.

"I really do, don't I?" She laughed. It was a wondrously happy sound. "And it's all because of you."

He looked down at her, dumbfounded by the incredible change in direction his life had taken in the past few days.

Intuitively she understood what he was thinking. "I'm real," she assured him, standing on tiptoe to give him a confirming kiss.

He answered with a deep moan and a meltingly tender taking of her offering. "Let's get out of here," he said.

They loaded her suitcase and left, passing no one as they drove through the farm. When they arrived at the front gate, Craig stopped and told Jennifer to flip a coin to see whether they would turn left or right.

Dozens of coin tosses and several hours later, they were deep into the countryside when Jennifer spotted what appeared to be an inn nestled in a grove of trees. Craig backtracked to a road they had crossed earlier and followed it until they found the building. She had been right: it was an inn. The old two-story building had been lovingly maintained, its shutters freshly painted, the limestone walls and leaded windows scrubbed spotlessly clean.

"Well, what do you think?" Craig asked.

"It's perfect," she answered, already reaching for the door.

She let out a cry of delight when they entered the lobby. A huge fireplace dominated a room that made her feel as if she'd stepped back a half century in time. Potted palms and overstuffed armchairs rested on Oriental carpets; richly polished oak gleamed throughout the room, from the floors to the banisters to the old-fashioned ceiling molding. Behind the desk, a man with a monk's haircut looked up and beamed at them.

"Welcome to Meyer's Country Inn," he said. "Were you folks looking for a place to spend the night?"

"And for someplace to eat," Craig answered. They had stopped for a late breakfast and hadn't had anything since.

"Then today's your lucky day. You've got about forty-five minutes to get settled before we start serving the best food you'll find anywhere around these parts. If you're too hungry to wait for dinner, there are some snacks set out on the buffet next to the dining room."

Craig registered, asking for the best available room. He hesitated for a moment then signed them in as Mr. and Mrs. Templeton from Colby Station, Oklahoma. The signature gave him a keen feeling of pleasure.

The man behind the desk insisted he would show them to their room. When he opened the door, he did so with a blatantly theatrical gesture, obviously proud of the carefully detailed antique interior. He spent a moment showing them the television, hidden in an armoire, and the remote control, tucked in the ornately carved nightstand. He told them to enjoy the room and that the music boxes were for listening, the chocolates on the dresser for eating and the wine on the end table for drinking. His exit was as elegant as his entrance and left Craig and Jennifer smiling.

After the door had closed, Jennifer explored the room on her own. She admired the antiques and commented on the care that had been taken to make guests staying in the suite feel as if they were in their own homes.

Craig dropped the key in a glass dish on the dresser. "Your home maybe, not mine. My mother was a thoroughly modern woman."

Jennifer picked up a corner of the hand-crocheted bedspread on the massive four-poster. "I love antiques. They help me realize there's a continuity to life. The people who made the things in this room are probably dead, and yet their work is still here to be admired and used by us and by the generations that will come after us."

Craig went to her and took her in his arms. He held her without passion, in friendship. "Any regrets about coming today?"

"How could I regret something that feels so right?"

"When we get back—"

She pressed her fingers to his lips. "I don't want us to talk about yesterdays or tomorrows this weekend. Let's forget everything but here and now and how wonderful it feels to be off together by ourselves."

He gave her a wicked lopsided grin, delighted by her suggestion. "Consider it done. As far as I'm concerned, my sole area of responsibility these two days will be to wine and dine you and—" he pressed a kiss to her temple, her forehead, her nose "—to discover where, on this beautiful body of yours, you like to be touched the most."

"Don't you dare start something you can't finish," she warned, exhaling a sensuous sigh.

Craig brought his arm up behind her and glanced at his watch. "We've got twenty-five minutes before dinner. Just enough time for me to undress you."

She moved her head to one side to allow him free access to her neck. "I should be a big hit at the dinner table."

The mental image of Jennifer sitting across from him without clothes created a decidedly different appetite. "Are you really hungry?"

She grinned.

"Of course you are," he groaned, remembering they were miles into the country, and the only readily available food was the dinner served at the inn. He let go of her waist and took her hand. "Let's get out of here while I still can."

They went outside to explore the grounds for the remaining time before dinner. They were watching two squirrels playing tag when Craig put his hand into his pocket and found the tissue-wrapped cameo. He brought it out and handed it to Jennifer.

"What's this?" she asked.

"Something I found yesterday and couldn't resist buying for you. You'll understand as soon as you see it."

An immediate grin covered her face. "It may be crass to admit this, but I love presents." She unwrapped the tissue. When she found the cameo, her expression changed from delight to surprise then to amazement. "That's me," she said, studying the woman's profile. "How . . . where . . . ?"

"The shop owner said it is more than two hundred years old," he said, taking the brooch from her and pinning it on her jacket. "A ship's captain had it made to remember the woman he loved."

She held her lapel out to better see the cameo. "It's beautiful." She glanced up at him. "Or is that something immodest to say since we look so much alike?"

"You have to know by now how beautiful you are without my telling you." He wanted her to keep the radiating confidence she had exhibited that morning, and if necessary, he would prod her into it.

"You don't seem to understand that I've only felt beautiful since I've met you. You'll have to give me some time to get used to the idea."

His answer was cut off by the sound of a bell clanging, calling them to dinner. He took her hand and headed back to the inn, content with the loving smile she had given him, satisfied he had all the time in the world to convince her of her beauty.

Dinner was served family style. A seemingly unending supply of basic but outstandingly good food streamed from the kitchen. There were twelve other guests at the table, none of them under sixty. Conversation centered around the reason most of them were there—the dance held at the inn every Friday and Saturday night—and the big-band style music the small combo played. Everyone good-naturedly insisted Jennifer and Craig join them in the ballroom later that night to see what real music and dancing were all about.

When the diners had retired to the lobby for after-dinner drinks and coffee, Jennifer and Craig tried to come up with a less-than-obvious reason to skip the festivities in favor of going back to the room to be alone. They finally settled on making an appearance at the dance and then slipping out when no one was looking.

Singly and in pairs, more people began arriving at the inn, none of them under fifty years old. They were surprised and pleased to see two "youngsters" among them, and their friendliness was contagious.

When a woman with blue-gray hair announced that the band had arrived, there was an immediate exodus to a large detached building Craig and Jennifer had earlier mistaken for a barn. At the effusive encouragement, they reluctantly followed the crowd.

Once inside, Jennifer openly stared at their surroundings, then tugged Craig's shirt sleeve to get his attention. "Do you get the eerie feeling we've somehow stepped into the *Twilight Zone*?" she whispered, again looking around

the room at the art deco decorations and the overhead re-
volving mirrored ball.

Craig laughed as he put his arm around her waist and
guided her farther into the room. "Come on, this could
be fun." Last week he would never have thought so, but
tonight, with Jennifer, he had every belief in what he had
said.

"Uh-huh. And I suppose next you're going to tell me
you know how to dance to this kind of music?"

He brought her to him and gave her a quick kiss on the
end of her nose. "Since I don't know how to dance to any
kind of music, I can't see that it makes much difference to
what beat I step on your toes."

"You can't dance at all?" she asked incredulously. It
would have been impossible to grow up in her circle of
friends and not know how to dance. So many social
functions revolved around dances that anyone staying
away would have automatically been considered an out-
sider.

"Does it make a difference?"

She thought for a minute. "I'd hate to think of living
the rest of my life without ever dancing again," she said,
her eyes filled with warmth. "But I suppose I could manage."

The innocent implication of her words brought a smile
to Craig's lips. "If you're willing to teach me, I'm willing to learn." When he wanted to give her everything,
what was a simple dance lesson?

She took his hand and led him to an unoccupied corner. "Every song has a rhythm," she said, taking his right
hand and putting it on her waist. "The trick is to move in
time with the rhythm *and* in a fairly predictable way, so I
can follow you."

He took several tentative steps, holding her far enough away so that he could keep an eye on their feet.

"It works much better if you hold me close enough for me to feel your body moving," she said.

Craig brought her closer. When they had almost made it through the song without incident, he looked down at her and grinned. "I think I could get to like this." The sensation of their bodies moving against each other was incredibly intoxicating. He was surprised to discover he was disappointed when the dance ended.

At a break in the music, one of the couples who had eaten dinner with them came over to talk. "Well," the tall thin man said, "what'd ya think?"

"I think I know why this place is so popular," Craig answered.

"I'm surprised the room isn't filled to overflowing," Jennifer added.

"Oh, it would be if the secret ever got out. We kinda keep this place to ourselves. Like it a lot better that way." He shifted his toothpick from one corner of his mouth to the other. "Sure appreciate it if you'd do the same."

"I hope that doesn't mean we won't be welcomed back," Jennifer said, a mischievous twinkle in her eyes.

"Lordy, no," the man's plump companion chimed in. "It's nice to have young folks like you come by once in a while."

The music started, and the older couple excused themselves to return to the dance floor.

Craig took Jennifer into his arms again, feeling fairly confident about what he was doing and positive that he had never been as happy.

No longer afraid they would trip and wind up on the floor if she allowed her attention to wander, Jennifer laid her head on his shoulder and let herself drift with the music. She'd decided it wasn't a *Twilight Zone* they'd stepped into, but a place too good to be true. She had started to wonder if she was in the middle of a particularly vivid dream. In the real world, lives didn't turn around completely in three days, and tall handsome strangers didn't magically appear to sweep women off their feet.

She tilted her head back to look up at Craig. He smiled and brushed his lips warmly against hers. A seed of well-being burst inside her. The impossible was made possible with his touch.

"Ready?" he whispered.

She nodded.

He maneuvered her toward the door. When the song ended and everyone's attention was directed toward applauding the band, he took her hand and slipped outside. Cold, moist air enveloped them; the full moon lit their way as they circled around the back of the inn to avoid running into anyone. When Jennifer shivered, Craig put his arm around her shoulders and drew her close.

"Is your ranch big?" she asked.

"It is as far as ranches go, but that's not to say it's big in the same way Mitchell Farm is. The only paved road is the one leading up to the main house, and if you include a double-wide trailer at the west end, there are only three other houses on the place. There are more miles of fencing on the ranch, but it's not nearly as fancy—barbed wire and steel posts. Along with the trailer, there are a few natural gas wells out on the west end, and except where we grow feed, cattle roam everywhere." His voice became softer, filled with a wistfulness. "It's beautiful country, open and not much changed from the way it has always been." He hesitated before rushing on. "There's plenty of room for Thoroughbreds . . . even a perfect place behind the main house to set up a practice course for jumping horses, if a person was interested in such things."

Jennifer stared down at the pathway. Their relationship was moving so fast she felt a little breathless. "Maybe I could visit you..."

He realized he had scared her with his unbridled enthusiasm. "Jennifer, I'm not trying to push you into anything."

"I know you're not," she said.

"We have lots of time to work things out between us." He brushed a kiss against her hair.

She put her arms around his waist and gave him a hug. "You're very special—not like anyone else I've ever known. From the minute I saw you in Lynn's office, I felt I knew you."

"Then how come I had such a hard time talking you into having dinner with me?"

She smiled. "I didn't want you to think I was a pushover."

"Well, let me tell you, you succeeded."

"Now I have to be careful you don't think me a wanton hussy."

"Oh?"

"When we get back to the room and I..."

"Yes?"

She could feel a blush burning her cheeks. "And I...uh..."

"Go on."

"Discover just where it is on your body you like the most to be touched," she finished, echoing his earlier statement. "And..."

"And?"

"Do all the things I've been thinking about doing since I woke up this morning."

"Which are?"

She stopped and looked up at him. "I think I'd rather show than tell."

He kissed her and felt as if his bones had turned to liquid. "Did anyone ever tell you that you have an incredible way with words?" he murmured.

THE NEXT MORNING Craig slowly rose from the depths of sleep, aware of a pleasant warmth along his left side and a weight pressing against his shoulder. He opened his eyes and smiled. Because he had never shared a bed with anyone, he had been sure he would never be able to fall asleep with Jennifer beside him. And yet here he was, so close to her they could have been attached, feeling more rested than he had in months.

Jennifer's eyelids flickered, and he thought she was about to awaken, but then she settled back into sleep. He stared at her, noting how incredibly long and thick her eyelashes were and how they brushed against her cheek. His gaze lingered on the smooth curve of her naked back where the blanket had slipped and left her uncovered. And on her face, where her hair was pulled back from her temple, he saw a thin straight line from the surgeon's scalpel. He had discovered yet more scars on her body last night when they had bathed together and he had run soapy hands over her lean body. There was a long scar on her thigh where pins had been used to put her leg back together after the accident in Switzerland, and a round one on her elbow where she'd been thrown off a jumping horse as a child and had landed on a fallen crossbar.

Remembering how she had responded to his hands as they had coursed over her body plunged him back into the gut-wrenching arousal he had felt the night before. He closed his eyes and saw her as she had looked stepping from the bathtub, her skin shimmering with drops of water, a tiny smile on her lips. Even the memory took his breath away.

After an initial hesitancy, she had lost all trace of shyness and come to him with an innocent boldness, eager to please and to be pleased. He had wondered at her softness, felt such sweet power at her gasps of delight and such release at his own relinquishing moans. He thought of how her legs had felt when she wrapped them around his waist and what it had been like when she was on top of him. Whatever the intimacy, however performed, it was a bonding, a promise, a commitment beyond words.

Jennifer stirred beside him, and he gently kissed her forehead. She sighed, and a smile formed on her lips. "Good morning," Craig said.

"I don't even have to open my eyes to know it's going to be a beautiful day." She put her arm around his waist and lifted her chin to return his kiss. "How did you sleep?"

"Fantastic. How about you?"

She snuggled closer into his side. "On a scale of one to ten, I'd call it an eight."

"Why only an eight?"

"You wouldn't believe the dreams I had."

"Oh?" When she didn't elaborate, he persisted, "What kind of dreams?"

"I don't think I should tell you."

"Why not?"

"You might get the wrong impression."

"Never."

"Oh, I don't know about that."

Craig rolled over on top of her. "I'm not letting you out of this bed until you tell me."

She gave him a slow, inviting smile. "And they say dreams never come true."

He groaned. "Do you have any idea what you just did to me?"

She lifted her hips to press into him. "Uh-huh," she said, wrapping her arms around his neck and bringing him to her, "just what I wanted to do."

He kissed her, then propped himself up on his elbows and looked down at her, his expression serious. "Thank you," he said.

"For what?"

"For being here with me, for being you." He could have added so much more—how she had given him purpose and made him see a future filled with promise, how she had changed his feelings of trepidation about meeting his family to a confidence that he could handle anything.

She moved against him in unmistakable invitation, wanting him as completely as she had the night before. She caught her breath at his instant impassioned response. When they made love, they did so with a sweet gentleness and poignancy, as if it were the last time they would be together instead of being at the beginning of their relationship.

Time and place disappeared, and they entered a world all their own as Craig touched and held Jennifer, caressing, demanding bringing her to a climax in ways she had never imagined. They made love in the bed, and in the shower while he was standing with her legs wrapped around his waist. They were unable to get enough of each other, unable to let go of the moment. The morning elapsed in tender intimacy without either of them being conscious of the passage of time.

It wasn't until they were lying across the bed in each other's arms and Craig heard Jennifer's stomach growl in hunger that he thought to look over to the nightstand at his watch. "We have ten minutes until we're supposed to be checked out," he said, turning back to nuzzle her neck.

Jennifer let out a squeal and started to get out of bed. "We'll never make it."

Craig laughed as he reached for her, pulling her back into his arms. "Then we'll pay for another day."

"But they'll guess what we've been doing."

"Do you honestly think they have any doubts?"

"Why would they? We registered as Mr. and Mrs.—"

"What possible difference could that make?" He leaned over to take one perfect rose-colored nipple into his mouth. "You've brought out a part of me I didn't know existed," he said softly. "I've never been a moonlight-and-roses kind of person before, but since it's how I want your life to be from now on, I guess I'm going to have to learn."

"I like you just the way you are."

"That's not good enough. I want to give you the moon."

She brushed the hair from his forehead. "What would I do with the moon?"

His expression became serious as he gazed deeply into her eyes. "I'll do anything to make sure you never know pain or disappointment again."

"Craig, you can't promise me that. Life is full of things we have no control over."

"I'll find a way."

She understood what he was trying to tell her. And even though she knew that what he wanted to give her was impossible, she loved him for caring so profoundly.

He tenderly held the sides of her face and stared into her eyes. "It's going to be a great life for us."

And she believed him. With her entire being, she believed him.

CHAPTER SEVEN

IT WAS PAST TEN O'CLOCK when they arrived back at Mitchell Farm. Craig unloaded Jennifer's suitcase and took it inside. She gave him a kiss and invited him to stay for coffee, but he told her he had business downtown early the next morning, and he knew that if he didn't leave then, he wouldn't leave for hours. With another lingering kiss and a promise to call her after lunch, he drove away.

He was up the next morning before the sun. After a shave and shower, he stopped for breakfast to kill time before Jack Chapman's office opened at eight o'clock. He realized with surprise that the main reason for his anxiety to discover what the detective had found out was his longing to finally tell Jennifer why he had come to Lexington. While he still hoped the information would confirm his growing belief that he should make contact with his parents, Jennifer's appearance had filled much of the loneliness that had brought him to Kentucky, so he no longer felt the driving need he had felt before.

Still, the prospect of having a family in addition to Jennifer was a powerful emotional draw. There would be people to call and share news with and visit on holidays. There would be others to care about and people who would care about him. Such ideas represented a completion, a final coming together of his dream. He wasn't ready to let go yet.

He was on his fourth cup of coffee and his second perusal of the morning paper when he decided it was close enough to eight o'clock for him to walk the three blocks to Chapman's office. He arrived a few minutes before the secretary.

She smiled in greeting when she saw him standing outside the door. "Have you been waiting long?"

"Not really." Unless he counted his entire life.

"I know Mr. Chapman has some information for you, but it hasn't been typed yet."

"That's all right."

She laughed. "You wouldn't say that if you'd ever seen his handwriting." She stepped inside and held the door for Craig to enter.

"When does he usually come in to the office?"

"Oh, I'm sure he's been here for hours already. He says it's the only time he can work undisturbed."

"You mean he's here now?"

"Not only here, Mr. Templeton, but anticipating your arrival," a cheerful voice proclaimed.

Craig turned and saw Jack Chapman standing in the doorway of his office. He had discarded his jacket, his tie was askew, and he looked as if he had already put in a full day's work. "Did you find anything?" He was too anxious to spend precious time on formalities.

"I'm sure it's not as much as you'd like, but we do have a beginning. Come into the office, and I'll fill you in while Ms Burnstein types up the report." He handed several papers to his secretary, then ushered Craig into his office.

"I appreciate your spending your weekend working on this," Craig said, taking the chair he had occupied during their previous meeting.

"There's no such thing as a weekend to a detective." He walked over to a sideboard. "Can I get you a cup of coffee?"

Craig shook his head. "I've already had several this morning."

Chapman poured himself a cup, added cream and sugar and came over to sit with Craig. "Now then," he said, leaning back in his chair, "I think I should warn you that this investigation is turning out to be just as difficult as I anticipated. Personal information about the Mitchells is very difficult to come by. Not only have they managed to keep themselves out of the society pages of the local papers—which, for a family of their stature, is no small feat—but they have instilled an unswerving reluctance to gossip in their friends and workers that borders on fanaticism. None of my people managed to gather what I consider any worthwhile information, and they conducted over a dozen interviews."

"Why the conspiracy of silence?" He preferred not to speculate about the possibilities.

"From what I've been able to learn so far, it began twenty-six years ago after their infant son was kidnapped. Up until then, they were among the social leaders of this community. Their pictures or an article mentioning their names was in the paper at least once a week." He blew on his coffee to cool it before taking a sip. "I would imagine losing a child that way was extraordinarily hard to get over, especially since the case was never solved. It's certainly possible and highly logical that the reason they decided to withdraw from public view was to protect the children that followed. As you already know, there were three of them."

"Was a ransom note received?" Even though the newspaper articles had said no note had been received, he had heard there were times when the police kept such information from the press.

Chapman stared at him, his gaze intense, keenly curious. "None that ever got reported. If I were to make a guess at what happened, I'd say the baby probably died before the kidnappers had a chance to send a note. When they realized they were facing a murder charge, they disposed of the body and disappeared."

Craig decided it was best not to show undue curiosity about the kidnapping. Chapman was clever and certainly capable of putting two and two together. "What else have you found out?"

"There's a brief rundown on the two oldest children in the material I gave Ms Burstein. As for the youngest, I should have something on him later today." He readjusted himself in his chair. "The few people we did get to talk to us about the family had nothing but good to say about them. Which means we've been talking to the wrong sources or the Mitchells are an uncommonly well-adjusted group of people." He chuckled. "Andrew seems to be the only one who's stepped on a few people's toes."

"Have you formed an opinion of your own?"

He leaned forward to return his cup to its saucer. "It's too soon. But frankly, I'm always a little suspicious when the reports turn out this one-sided." He stood. "I wish I had more to give you this morning, but as you recall, I told you it wouldn't be easy."

Craig stood also. "When do you think you might have more information?"

"Why don't you give me a call at the end of this week?"

Craig struggled to hide his disappointment. "If you come up with something before then, I'd appreciate it if you left a message at my motel."

"I'll do that. In the meantime, if you happen to come across anything you think might help the investigation, be sure to give us a call." Chapman opened the door for Craig. He looked at his secretary. "Do you have the papers ready for Mr. Templeton?"

"Yes, sir, they're right here." She handed a large manila envelope to Craig.

"Thank you," Craig said, heading for the outer door.

"Mr. Templeton?"

Craig turned to look at the detective.

"Don't be discouraged. We'll find out what it is you want to know. It just may take us a little longer than we first anticipated."

Craig nodded and walked into the hallway. When he was in the elevator, he pulled up the two metal prongs on the envelope and reached for the three typed sheets. On the first was a short biography of his parents. He studied the information and was surprised to discover that his mother was only forty-eight-years old and hadn't been born in Lexington. According to Chapman's researchers, she came from an old and prominent Maryland family that traced its members back to the signing of the Declaration of Independence. Craig suppressed a smile of excitement. These weren't dry facts he was reading. That Maryland family with its holier-than-thou ancestors was his, and he intended to lay claim to every distant relative.

His father was fifty-one, with a birthday in the same month as Craig's. He paused to think about their birthdays. How hard it must have been for his father to see his own birthday arrive the year Craig had disappeared. The report went on to say that Frank Mitchell was the only son of Lawrence and Iris Mitchell, who were both still living and currently residing in Florida. And that there were two sisters, both married, one living in Arizona, the other in California.

An excitement built in Craig as he discovered grandparents, aunts and uncles. The elevator stopped, and he got out, almost bumping into a woman who was as preoccupied as he was. "Excuse me," he said absently, stepping around her. After another near-collision in the crowded hallway, he moved over to a quiet corner to continue reading.

The second sheet began with information about his oldest brother, Andrew.

Andrew James Mitchell—twenty-five-years old, born in Lexington, Kentucky. After grammar and high school in the Lexington area, attended the University of Kentucky, attaining a bachelor's degree in business administration. Engaged to be married to Cybil Winchester. Currently lives in a cottage on Mitchell Farm, but is having a new home built on the farm to use after he is married. At his insistence, the annual charity masked ball—a fifty-year-old tradition in Lexington society—is once again under Mitchell sponsorship. Considered aggressive and at times brash. Opinion about his character among those interviewed has been mixed.

Craig summoned a mental picture of Andrew, recalled his flashing eyes and intent gaze, and wasn't surprised that the reviews would be mixed.

Leaning his shoulder against the cool marble paneling, he settled into a more comfortable position to finish reading the report. His gaze slid down the page to the next indentation, the paragraph that described his sister. When he read the name, the blood drained from his face, and his heart slammed against his chest. As if it were a screaming tabloid headline, the letters stood out, mercilessly mocking him—Jennifer Mitchell Langley.

Jennifer his sister? It couldn't be. There had to be a mistake. His arm dropped to his side. He pressed his back into the wall and closed his eyes, desperately seeking to regain the sane world he had just left. Then, as if drawn by an imaginary beckoning finger, he brought the paper up to continue reading.

Jennifer Mitchell Langley—twenty-three years old, born in Lexington, Kentucky. Attended grammar and high school in the Lexington area. Completed two years of college at the University of Kentucky before marrying David Langley. Three years ago she was critically injured in an accident in Switzerland that killed her husband of one week. She has physically recovered from the accident, but according to sources, there are some lingering psychological problems. Opinion about her character among those interviewed has been overwhelmingly positive

It was a mistake. It had to be. Someone's cruel idea of a joke. How could Jennifer be his sister? They loved each other. *They had made love to each other.*

No, he silently screamed, turning his face to the wall. *God, please don't let this be true.* Let there be some mistake. But even as he tried to deny the facts, they echoed in his mind. Jennifer Mitchell Langley...twenty-three...married to David Langley...automobile accident.

He felt tears sting his eyes. His throat constricted, and there was a weight crushing his chest, making it almost impossible to breathe. He heard an anguished sob and put his hand to his mouth when he realized it had come from him. An urgent demand surfaced, telling him that he had to try to escape or the unbearable agony would tear him apart. He left the building, blindly striking out, not knowing where he was heading, only that he had to get away. He ran and ran until he couldn't run anymore, not hearing the horns that blared in protest as he darted in front of traffic or seeing the panic of those he passed. But the agony would not be left behind. Still he couldn't stop. He ignored the pain in his side and stumbled on. The multistoried buildings of the central city changed to sprawling office complexes and then to housing tracts and shopping centers. But he went on, seeking an escape, needing something, anything, to ease the crushing despair.

As SHE HAD THREE TIMES ALREADY in the previous ten minutes, Jennifer glanced up at the wall clock in her office. It was almost two o'clock, certainly "after lunch" by anyone's standards. She was expecting Craig's call to come in at any time, and the anticipation made it impossible for her to concentrate on the payroll.

Almost without conscious thought, her hand went to the cameo she had pinned to her vest early that morning. Lynn had noticed the piece of jewelry the minute Jennifer walked into the office, and the questions that followed had been immediate and not very subtle. It hadn't taken Lynn long to wheedle the information she sought out of Jennifer and to add things up. But Jennifer didn't mind. It had felt good to share her newfound happiness with a friend who had seen the darker times. After Lynn had wiped sentimental tears from her eyes, she had left her desk to give Jennifer a heartfelt hug.

"Have you told your folks?" Lynn asked.

"Not yet." It was only then that she realized she had told Lynn that she was in love with Craig before she had even told him. It was an error she planned to rectify the minute he called. "Everything's happened so fast... I wanted to be sure first."

"Your dad is going to turn cartwheels."

Jennifer smiled at the image of her conservative, soft-spoken father doing any such thing. But she privately acknowledged Lynn wasn't too far off in her estimation of his enthusiasm. And the really wonderful part was that she was sure he would be as crazy about Craig as she was. In a lot of ways, they were very much alike.

Since she was his only daughter, her father had had a tendency to favor her, and they were, and always had been, close. For the past three years she had seen her own suffering reflected in his eyes. It would be fantastic to see happiness replace the worry.

"And your mother will be right out there turning those cartwheels with him," Lynn added.

Jennifer laughed. "Not to mention Andrew. I think he would like to see me safely married and away from here so he could get Dad's complete attention back to running the farm again." Although it was the truth, Jennifer instantly regretted saying something even slightly derogatory about a member of her family. "Please forget I said that. It seems being happy has made me a little waspish."

"Oh, come on, Jennifer, let's not forget I know Andrew, too. If anything, you were being kind."

"I really hate to think of the possibility of someday leaving Kyle," she said, deftly changing the subject. Her younger brother was much more like her than Andrew. Even at the age of nine, he was intensely in love with Mitchell Farm. If he continued with competitive jumping, she was convinced he would someday win the Olympic medal she had once dreamed would be hers.

"But if you do marry Craig, think of how much fun Kyle will have spending part of his summer on a real ranch."

"I never thought of that."

"I can't understand why," Lynn teased. "You've had . . . what is it, six days since you met this guy?"

"My God, has it really been only six days?" she said, awestruck. How could that be when she felt as if she had always known Craig?

"If the man you're talking about is the same Craig Templeton I've got written in my book, then it's been all of six days since he first set foot on this farm."

Jennifer and Lynn continued to spend the better part of the next hour talking about Craig and how meeting him had changed Jennifer's outlook on life. Then one of the grooms came in to have Lynn check a requisition order for him, and Jennifer went into her office to begin the day's work. She and Lynn ate their sack lunches together but were unable to talk about Craig beyond a few snatches of conversation due to the constant influx of farm people coming in to pick up their payroll checks. Two hours later she grudgingly admitted she had accomplished so little work that day that she might as well have stayed home.

As the afternoon wore on, Jennifer's anticipation turned to anxiousness and then to worry when Craig failed to call. It was four-thirty when she heard a tapping on her door, and Lynn looked in.

"I'm getting ready to leave, but I wanted to see if there's anything you need before I go."

Jennifer forced a smile. "Thanks, but I'm fine. You go ahead, and I'll see you tomorrow."

A bell sounded in the outer office. "Just a minute," Lynn said. "I'll see who that is and be right back."

Jennifer started to call out to her that it wasn't necessary to return, but Lynn was gone before she had a chance to open her mouth. She gathered the paychecks that hadn't been picked up that day and reached for a rubber band. She was on her way to the safe when Lynn came back into the room.

"It was a courier service with a letter for you," she said, with unbridled curiosity in her voice.

Jennifer frowned and held out her hand. She couldn't imagine who would be sending her a letter by courier. She looked at the plain white envelope. There was no return address, and although the handwriting seemed vaguely familiar, it wasn't one she immediately recognized. She slipped her finger under the flap and took the single sheet of paper out of the envelope. Ignoring the text, she searched for the signature and when she saw it was Craig's, a smile of relief and anticipation appeared. Her gaze returned to the beginning.

Dear Jennifer,
I have spent the time we've been apart thinking about us and searching for answers to questions that should never have been asked. I've been unfair to both of us, but mainly to you. You see, I wasn't free to fall in love with you. I have a wife and family in Oklahoma, and they need me. No matter how much I wish it weren't so, I have to return to them.
Please forgive me.

Craig

The paper slipped from Jennifer's fingers and fell to the floor. Lynn picked it up, hesitated a moment, then read the brief message. She put her arms around Jennifer. There were tears in her eyes. "The son of a bitch," she said softly, her voice sounding more sad than angry.

Jennifer held herself stiffly, unable to respond to Lynn's comforting. "I don't want anyone to know about this," she said. "Promise me you will never say anything to anyone. Not even Bob."

"I promise," she said, wiping her eyes with the back of her hand.

Jennifer stood perfectly still until Lynn released her. She then reached for her jacket, put it on and prepared to leave, acting as if nothing had happened. "I think I'm going to go home a little early today," she said in an eerily calm tone.

"Jennifer, talk to me," Lynn pleaded.

She stared at her friend, all traces of the earlier animation gone from her eyes. "There's nothing to talk about," she said quietly and with heartbreaking finality.

CRAIG ARRIVED AT TEMPLETON RANCH in the blackest part of the night. Only the ranch dogs—two nondescript strays—were even aware of his homecoming. He walked woodenly inside the house he had lived in all his life, aware that it no longer seemed like home.

It was a night for crutches, and he felt no hesitancy about using one. The whiskey bottle his mother had kept in the kitchen for colds and sore throats would ease a different ache tonight. He grabbed a glass and poured the golden liquid until it neared the rim. He blindly stared at the counter before lifting the glass and taking a long, throat-burning swallow. Glass in one hand, bottle in the other, he went out on the front porch to wait for the sunrise.

The previous afternoon, after tortured hours of attempted denial, numbed acceptance had finally won out. But the acceptance had not come easily. First there had been a period of desperation when he had tried to convince himself there was another answer. For a while he had even considered ignoring the report, never telling Jennifer they were brother and sister, and taking her away from Lexington as fast and as far as he could. They would live a lie and never be able to have children, but they would have each other. He told himself he could tolerate the compulsive fear that would haunt them the rest of their life that somehow someone would find out about them. In the end, what he couldn't accept was knowing that eventually that kind of life would destroy both of them.

At first he had been too consumed with losing Jennifer to realize just how much more he had lost. And then it had come to him. He would never know his true mother and father. He would live the rest of his life alone, without family and without the woman he loved. The choice about whether or not to contact his parents had been wrested from him.

He had promised Jennifer he would never hurt her. And while he knew the letter he had sent had probably hurt her terribly, in that he had had no choice. Now all that was left to him was to shelter her from the further pain she would feel if she ever found out she had fallen in love and slept with her brother. He was convinced the pain she would suffer at his leaving was nothing compared to what she would feel if he stayed.

And so he had written the kindest letter he could and had sent it to her, severing a love he knew would haunt him the rest of his life, cutting himself off from a family he ached to know, sentencing himself to a solitary existence.

Craig reached for the bottle to refill his glass. Even though he had almost finished the whiskey, the anticipated stupor and emotional deadening he had sought from the alcohol had failed to take place. He might as well have consumed water. He sat the glass on his thigh and absently ran his finger around the rim. When he looked up, he saw the lights go on in Bill and Cloris Mason's house, a sure sign the sky would soon begin to lighten and the ranch would start its almost ritualistic stirrings in preparation for another day. Still, he couldn't bring himself to go inside.

He knew that if he closed his eyes he would see Jennifer. He would hear her laugh and feel her soft sighs and moist lips against his skin. As long as he didn't try to sleep, he would be all right. He leaned back in his chair and propped his feet up on the railing. How long would it take for the hurt to dull to a tolerable ache? How many days did he have to live through before he would be able to think of something else? If he just had an answer. Even if that answer was that it would take years, he could make it through, knowing eventually there would be an end. What he feared and had almost accepted was that the ache that twisted his insides would become a permanent part of him.

He stared at the horizon, watching the false dawn turn the eastern sky a deep purple. More lights went on at the Masons' house, and the breeze brought the smell of frying bacon. Craig put his empty glass beside the now-empty bottle and folded his arms across his chest. He tried to plan his day, but his mind refused to leave Jennifer. How had she reacted when his letter arrived? It tore at him to think of the pain and betrayal he knew she had felt. If only he could go to her one last time.

The thought made his mouth twist in a bitter smile. What would he do if he were to see Jennifer one last time? Tell her he loved her and that he was sorry he had involved her in an incestuous relationship, but that given enough time, they would both recover?

He heard a door open and shut, followed by the measured steps of a man walking across a wooden porch. He silently watched as Bill Mason left the house and made his way over to the barn. When Bill went inside, Craig's gaze wandered back to the house, where he saw Cloris standing at the kitchen sink, washing breakfast dishes. The Masons were the only people left who had been at the ranch longer than he had. More than employees, they had been good and close friends.

Craig felt something stir inside him. He lifted his feet from the railing and stood, not once taking his eyes from Cloris. Purposefully he crossed the distance between the two houses and knocked on the back door. Cloris answered, peering into the darkness while drying her hands on a kitchen towel.

"Craig?" she questioned. And then seeing that it was indeed Craig, she tossed the towel on the counter and reached for him, taking him into her ample arms and holding him close.

While Cloris had always treated him with loving warmth, she had never been a demonstrative person. Her behavior now made Craig realize she knew far more than he had given her credit for. "You knew, didn't you?" he said, his voice resigned.

She let go of him and nervously patted her silver hair. "Yes," she admitted.

"Why didn't you say something?"

"I tried to convince myself your trip to Kentucky was coincidental." She reached behind him and closed the door. "Sit down, and let me fix you a cup of coffee," she said, her practical side surfacing. "You feel like a block of ice and smell like a still."

Craig eased himself into one of the wooden chairs at the kitchen table, his fatigue and the whiskey catching up with him in the warm room. Cloris brought two large steaming mugs to the table and sat down opposite him. His hands slowly wrapped around the cup, and he stared down into the brown liquid.

Cloris broke the silence that had grown between them. "How'd you find out?" she said.

"There was an envelope in the back of the safe that was filled with old clippings about the kidnapping."

"I told your mother to get rid of those."

His head came up. "Why didn't she?"

"She couldn't reconcile herself to your never knowing the truth."

"Then why didn't she tell me herself?" he asked, unmistakable bitterness in his voice and eyes.

"Don't you take that tone around me when you're talking about Wynona. She was a loving, hard-working woman who wanted nothing but the best for you."

"And I suppose that 'best' for me included taking me away from my real parents?"

"She had nothing to do with that," Cloris answered defensively, her voice rising. "Max and Wynona thought they were involved in a private adoption." She let out a deep sigh. "There's just so much you don't know, Craig."

"Then don't you think it's about time I was told?"

Indecision shone from her eyes. She had kept Max and Wynona's secret for so long, it was hard to let go. "Although she tried until it almost killed her," she began, "your mother was never able to carry a baby to term. Once she and Max realized nothing was ever going to change that, they were too old to go through a regular adoption agency. Somehow they got in touch with this outfit that promised them any kind of baby they wanted— for a price. The whole idea bothered your dad, but by then your mom was so het up about holding her own baby in her arms that she would have walked over hot coals if they'd've asked her to. What they did ask for was almost as bad. She was told to tell all her friends and relatives that she was pregnant again and that she'd heard of this new clinic up north where she could get help carrying the baby full term. Then she was to go away—supposedly to this clinic—and stay there until the baby was due. None of us had sense enough at the time to figure out why all the cloak and dagger business, but it was sure plain enough later."

Craig's anger steadily diminished as Cloris talked. It wasn't hard for him to imagine how desperately his mother would want a child and how important it would be to his father that there be someone to pass the ranch on to when he died.

"Naturally they would've agreed to anything. After a while they even started to believe it was a pretty smart idea for everyone to think you were their natural born son. The only problem was there wasn't a baby ready when Wynona was supposedly ready to have hers. She wrote home and told everyone you'd been born sickly, and the two of you had to stay a while. After one excuse and another, it turned into almost a year she was gone before she was given the son they had promised."

Craig thought of the picture of himself he had seen in the clippings. Wynona must have had a hard time passing him off as sickly.

Cloris noticed Craig had finished his coffee and got up to pour him another cup. "To make a long story short," she said sitting back down, "Wynona called to say she was on her way home, and the whole town started preparing for a party to welcome the two of you." She paused. "You never knew your folks the way they used to be before you came along. They were always in on everything that was happening around these parts. A party wasn't a party if they weren't there, and there were always people stopping by the ranch for a visit."

"How did my coming change all that?"

"Wynona was home just long enough to put you down for a nap in that room she'd spent so much time getting ready and to gather the mess of papers Max had left lying around his chair the way he was apt to do on Sunday mornings, and just that quick, things were changed around here forever. You see, while she was cleaning up, she saw a picture of her new son staring back at her, and she learned he wasn't just any baby given up for adoption." Her voice cracked with emotion as she went on. "Your mother agonized over what to do. Even though she'd had you less than a week, she already loved you as much as if you were her own flesh and blood. She was beside herself with knowing they were going to have to give you back and scared to death someone was going to show up at the ranch who might recognize you. Max started phoning people to tell them the welcome-home party was called off, telling everyone you'd taken sick again and that he didn't know when they could come out to see you."

"Why didn't they just call the sheriff and tell the truth?"

"And wind up in prison as accomplices to the kidnapping?" Her voice rose in frustration. "It's against the law to buy babies in this country, and they had used every bit of their savings to get you. There wasn't even any left over for a lawyer to get them out of jail.''

Finally Craig understood. His parents had been victims as much as he had been. ''And so they decided to keep me,'' he said softly.

''Even though your coming changed their lives, they never spent a minute regretting you were here.''

All those years of isolation. Never a day passed that there wasn't a fear his true identity would be discovered—until in the end, the daily pattern had become a way of life. Even the hidden wealth derived from the natural gas wells discovered on the ranch ten years earlier made sense now. Any show of money would have brought attention, and attention was to be avoided at all costs. ''I suppose keeping the clippings where I was sure to find them was her way of—''

''Of saying she was sorry.''

Even his anger had been taken from him. He got up from the table, thanked Cloris for the coffee and headed for the door.

''What will you do now?'' she asked.

Craig stood with his back to her, staring out at the gently rolling grassland. ''I don't know,'' he answered, his voice sounding as hollow as he felt.

CHAPTER EIGHT

SEVEN YEARS LATER

CRAIG GLANCED OUT THE WINDOW of the Templeton Corporation Lear jet as it passed over Las Vegas. On his way home after a month-long business trip to Japan, he began to smile at the familiar sight. Then he looked back down at the sheaf of papers on the table in front of him. If flying over a state he had only seen from the air made him restless, what would it be like when he caught a glimpse of Oklahoma City again?

"Are you ready, Mr. Templeton?"

The crisp, down-to-business tone of Janice Reinhold, Craig's secretary, brought his full attention back to the matter at hand—a memo to the legal department of Templeton Enterprises telling them to update the people who would be leaving for Japan the following month on the current mood of Congress concerning import quotas. With succinct sentences, he finished dictating the memo and moved on to the next problem, one closer to home. Midway through purchase negotiations, the owner of a small winery in California's Napa Valley had upped the price, saying a review of the books and reappraisal of the land had shown the company was far more valuable than first thought. Craig had sent Henry Keily out to California to investigate; the resultant report was sitting on the table in front of him.

He looked across the aisle to where Henry sat, thumbing through the material Craig had brought back with him from Japan. "Janice, why don't you take a break? I want to talk to Henry for a while."

Janice closed her steno pad and stood. "If you need me, I'll be in the back typing the letters you've already dictated."

Craig nodded. Although he had purposely surrounded himself with people who were willing to put in long hours to earn top pay, no one took her job quite as seriously as the never-smiling Janice Reinhold. She had put thirty-five years of her life into the secretarial field, starting when there were few other jobs open to women. Craig was convinced that if she were to start all over again, despite the change in career opportunities that had taken place over the years, she'd pursue precisely the same course with her life. She was the best there was in her profession and was suitably proud of the accomplishment.

Instead of calling Henry over to join him, Craig stood, stretched and crossed the aisle. When he'd returned from Kentucky seven years ago and realized there were too many memories for him to continue living on the ranch, Craig had gone to California to visit his childhood friend for a while. During his stay he had learned the computer company Henry worked for was in financial trouble because of a lack of capital. Henry's enthusiasm for the troubled company intrigued Craig. He had done some investigating on his own and discovered that Henry's confidence was justified. Wells Electronics had been Craig's initial gamble with venture capital. For $200,000, he'd become a full partner in a company that was currently worth over $30 million.

Not only had the investment been financially rewarding, but the time he'd spent learning about the business world had given him an escape from the memories of Jennifer that haunted him wherever he went. The pattern became set. As long as he was completely immersed in work, he was relatively free. When Wells Electronics was on its feet, and the demands on his time had lessened, he'd looked around for other investments. Like the fragile, seemingly inconsequential snowflake that adds its weight to a hillside already heavy with snow and thus creates an avalanche, Wells Electronics snowballed into an ongoing growth of activity that consumed Craig.

He'd moved back to Oklahoma, taking Henry Keily with him. In addition to Henry, Craig had surrounded himself with the best people he could find in the business world, men who were as committed to success and who were nearly as driven by it as he had become. His choice of advisors had paid off beyond his wildest imaginings. But it wasn't until several years had passed that he discovered his feelings about building a fortune had drastically changed. Money had become important only in so far as it signified success. The real pleasure came in the winning. The more brutal the fight, the sweeter the victory.

Henry tossed the papers he was reading into the seat beside him as soon as he saw Craig. With blond hair on its way to light brown, dark green eyes that flashed intelligence and mischief, and a body as athletically trim as it had been when he'd played football for UCLA, Henry was the quintessential free-wheeling bachelor. He was the one person in Craig's daily life who was considered a real friend.

"So how was the trip?" Henry asked.

"Frustrating. I had to keep reminding myself not to try to rush things."

"Was Morita helpful?"

"He was a godsend. I couldn't have got through the endless rounds of prenegotiating meetings without him.

Make sure he stays on the payroll, will you? I want him to work with all the people we send over there.''

Henry laughed. ''Sounds like you had your hands full.''

''I hate to think of the number of times Morita saved my rear end. I'd swear that if there was some way to be insulting, I'd find it.''

Henry eyed him. ''As much as I know you've missed having me around to talk to, I can't believe you had me fly all the way to Los Angeles so you could tell me about Morita saving your backside. What's up?''

Their lifelong friendship had helped Craig and Henry transcend an employer-employee relationship. The rarefied corporate atmosphere that had grown around Craig like an impenetrable aura made his contact with Henry all the more valuable. Craig was absolutely sure that Henry was the only person left who would tell him he was dead wrong about something or, if Craig's demands became too dictatorial, tell him to go straight to hell. ''I'm beginning to sense something's wrong with the stock deal Quist Construction is offering, and I wanted a chance to talk to you about it before we got back to the office.''

''I take it that means you read the material I sent?''

''I also had Janice send all the original correspondence to me so I could go over that again.''

''Okay, why don't you tell me what struck you wrong.''

''That's what's so strange about all this. There isn't anything specific. It's just a feeling I'm getting.''

Henry leaned forward, resting his elbows on his knees and clasping his hands. ''I can't tell you how glad I am to hear you say something's bothering you. I've been having the same kinds of feelings for some time now, but I'll be damned if I can figure out just what it is that's wrong. I've been over and over those reports and—'' He shrugged. ''Nothing.''

"Then let's get out of it while we still can."

"There's still a chance we could be mistaken. If we are, the company stands to lose millions in potential profits."

"I'd rather lose it now than later."

"Do you want me to handle it?"

"Check with legal first to make sure we haven't gone so far that we'll be leaving ourselves open for a lawsuit, then go from there."

"What are you going to do about the winery?"

"I haven't finished your report, but I'm inclined to drop the price and tell them to take it or leave it. They'll fold within a year without our backing, and we'll be able to pick up the pieces for half of what we offered for controlling interest."

"We'd lose goodwill with the other growers in the area if we took over that way."

"How much is their goodwill worth?"

"It's not only the goodwill of the other growers we'll lose, it's the expertise of the present owners. These people have been growing grapes and making wine at that location for three generations. They've built a solid reputation for knowing what they're doing."

"Then why are they facing bankruptcy?"

"Come on, Craig. Since when do wine making and good business policies go hand in hand?" Henry asked, a touch of anger in his voice.

"All right. We'll do it your way this time. Tell them the offer stands as it is for thirty more days; then we drop the price."

The corner of Henry's mouth turned up in a fleeting smile of victory. "Anything else?"

Craig thought for a minute. "Yeah—I want you to gather everything you can get your hands on concerning the Lambert/Ingersol merger so we can go over it this Saturday.''

THE FOLLOWING WEEK PASSED with the usual rapid pace Craig had established as his style. On Saturday he was up at five to shower and shave and go over the Lambert/Ingersol merger material Henry had given him late the previous day. At eight-thirty he gathered the half-finished material and took the elevator down two floors to his office to meet Henry.

They spent the morning undisturbed in the empty offices, trying to decide whether it was in the corporation's best interest to let Lambert Pharmaceutical take over Ingersol Chemical Company, a business one-third owned by Templeton Enterprises. Craig had taken the role of devil's advocate and effectively countered all of Henry's positive statements, which had created hours of nerve-racking exchange for both of them. Finally, after arguing the entire morning and part of the afternoon for a position he didn't believe in, Henry had announced he was leaving and would be back as soon as he'd had time to cool off.

Because it was a familiar termination for their exchanges, Craig had simply nodded and told him he'd be there when Henry got back.

An hour later Craig tossed his reading glasses onto the desk, wearily rubbed his eyes and leaned back in the chair. After a few minutes he got up and went over to the window, where he stared out at the broad expanse of Oklahoma City. From twenty-five stories up, the trees made the city seem an unending carpet of green. When Templeton Tower had still been in the drawing stages, he had chosen this suite of offices for his own because of the view. Radical in design compared to the other high-rise buildings in the city, Templeton Tower had been Craig's way of celebrating the first quadrupling of the money left to him by Max and Wynona. Even before completion, the vacancy rate was projected to be below five percent. It had turned out to be closer to two percent, with a waiting list for the larger suites.

Templeton Tower, along with his recent financial success in a chain of movie theaters and a wholesale import business, had inspired a writer for one of the local papers to call him "the man with the Midas touch." The title had made him smile the first time he'd come across it. His success had taken him seven years and his entire waking energy. Someone's attributing all that work to a "Midas touch" showed a distinct lack of research.

He turned when he heard the door open behind him. Henry was back, carrying two white paper bags.

"You may be able to go all day without eating, but I can't," he said, putting the bags on the glass coffee table on the other side of the room. He sat on the glove-leather couch, peered into one of the bags, looked up and smiled. "That doesn't mean I didn't order something for you, however."

Craig was anxious to finish the work they had started but knew better than to push Henry beyond the extra hours he willingly gave. Henry lacked the drive and killer instinct Craig had developed, but his skill and knowledge were invaluable, and Craig had sense enough to back off when necessary. He went over to join Henry on the couch. "I hope it's not one of those corned beef things you're always ordering."

Henry tossed Craig a sandwich. "I'll bet if you were starving, you'd check to see what was between two slices of bread before you took a bite," he grumbled. "It's ham and cheese on rye."

"Thank God." The rich delicatessen smell assailed Craig, making his mouth water. He had skipped breakfast, planning to call out for something later, but as usual he'd forgotten as soon as he started to work.

"I'm going to knock off around six tonight," Henry said, propping his feet up on the table and taking a bite out of his sandwich.

"Night on the town?"

"As a matter of fact, my sister and her husband are in town for the weekend."

"You should have said something. This could have waited until tomorrow."

Henry shook his head in mock despair. "There's no way in hell I'm coming in tomorrow, Craig. I told you a long time ago you could have my Saturdays, but Sundays are all mine."

"I forgot tomorrow was Sunday."

"If you'd just remember it's one of two days the stock market is closed, you'd be able to keep it straight." He peered inside the second bag and made a face. "I'm not up to another cup of coffee today. You got any beer?"

"There should be some in the refrigerator."

Henry walked over to a built-in wall unit and opened one of the doors. "You want one?"

Craig nodded.

Henry grabbed two bottles and set them on the counter while he looked inside the drawer for an opener.

"They're screw tops," Craig said.

"Of course," Henry replied, closing the drawer. Before he came back he opened another door and switched on the television. "Today's Derby Day, and there's a filly running that's going to make me rich," he offered as an explanation.

Instantly Craig became uncomfortable. For seven years he had purposely avoided everything remotely connected with Thoroughbred horses. "I didn't know you were a gambler," he said, his voice betraying none of his inner turmoil.

"Sandy suckered me into it. She said the odds were too great against a filly ever winning the Derby again, and I said she was crazy. One thing led to another, and I told her to put her money where her mouth was."

Henry had been dating Sandy Maupin for almost two years, the last of which he had spent unsuccessfully trying to convince her to marry him. "So how much are you going to be out when this filly loses?"

He gave Craig a disgusted snort. "You and Sandy."

"How much?"

"Three bucks."

Craig laughed. "That shows real faith, all right."

"You want to make it five?" He took a crunching bite of his pickle. "Put up or shut up, Templeton."

"I don't know anything about the rest of the field."

"What's to know? You want to bet or don't you?"

Craig reached into his pocket for his wallet. "What the hell. If you want to throw your money away, I'll bend over to pick it up."

"We'll just see who's doing the bending when this thing is over," Henry said, leaning back on the couch, a smug smile on his face.

They waited through several advertisements for the coverage to begin. For all his show of nonchalance, Craig was having a difficult time swallowing whenever he took a bite of his sandwich. Finally he gave up the effort altogether and surreptitiously slipped the remainder inside the bag. By the time Howard Snyder, the announcer, appeared on the screen, Craig's heart was pounding heavily against his ribs.

"Good afternoon, ladies and gentlemen. Welcome to what is arguably the greatest horse race on earth, the Kentucky Derby." Snyder's voice seemed more suited to ringside than to the running of the horses. "The smart money here at Churchill Downs today is divided among three horses—a bitter-chocolate-colored filly and two chestnut colts. We're going to tell you something about these magnificent animals in just a minute. But first, let me introduce—"

As if he had returned just yesterday, Craig's trip to Kentucky came back to him. Images, sensations, emotions filled his mind—the serenity and beauty of the countryside deep in autumn, the smell of the crisp air, Jennifer's love-filled, trusting eyes. He sat up straight, struggling to take a lungful of air as the weight of the memories crushed against him.

"Is something wrong?" Henry asked.

"What?" Craig looked at his friend and saw the concern on his face. "No...I'm fine. Just swallowed something wrong."

There was another minute of advertising. When the coverage resumed, it did so with a picture of an almost black horse running freely in a white fenced paddock. "If Mitchell Farm's Nightwind should win the Derby today," Snyder's voice announced, "it will only be the third time since the race's inception in 1875 that a filly has managed to wear the blanket of roses."

Craig felt trapped. There was no way he could ask Henry to turn off the television without giving him an explanation, and there was no logical reason for him to get up and leave his own office to get away. The scene changed, showing various locations on Mitchell Farm, each more poignantly familiar to Craig than the last. The final shot was one of Andrew walking in a breezeway between two paddocks, talking to a man who had been identified as Nightwind's trainer.

Andrew had changed since Craig had seen him last. He no longer looked like a boy recently turned man. He'd put on a good twenty pounds and had added a cocky assuredness to his smile. Seven years was a long time. But then Craig had changed, too. His black hair had developed silver threads at the sides, and his eyes had lost their innocence. At thirty-four he was as thin as he had been at twenty; however, his lankiness resulted more from forgetting to eat than from any concentrated effort on his part. He was as muscular as he'd been before because he had begun exercising at least three times a week when he discovered it was easier to put in a full day at work if he felt physically fit.

The television coverage continued with background information on the two favored colts. Then the remaining seventeen horses in the field were listed along with their jockeys, trainers, and the betting odds.

The segment ended with an interview of the jockey who would be riding Nightwind and his feelings about his mount. Craig went over to get another beer when the advertisement began. He held up the bottle in Henry's direction. "Want another?" Henry gave him a startled look. Craig responded with a noncommittal shrug. Since Craig rarely drank at all, it wasn't surprising that Henry would notice when he took a second.

"Sure," he said, "why not?"

The next segment started with an overview of Churchill Downs, showing the crowded infield, where for twenty dollars, a spectator could join thousands of others who had little chance of actually seeing the race. The camera then swept the grandstand. There, for considerably more money, spectators could purchase box seats on the fourth, fifth and sixth tiers, and possibly rub elbows with the rich and famous who flocked to Louisville each May for the festivities. A succession of beautiful young women filled the screen, each elegantly dressed and wearing a traditional Derby Day hat.

At first Craig dreaded the possibility that Jennifer's picture might flash before him. Then he found that he was actually waiting for it to happen. He ached to see her again.

"It's a big day for the owners," Snyder's voice proclaimed. "Of the 35,000 Thoroughbred foals born three years ago, only twenty have made it to the Derby. And to make the odds even more impressive, only one of them is a filly. Nightwind, owned by Mitchell Farm, may be the sentimental bettor's favorite, but she isn't considered much of a threat by the other owners or by my esteemed colleague, who is working here with me today."

He turned to the ex-jockey standing beside him. "Certainly the Derby has its share of hard-luck stories, Howard," the ex-jockey said, "but perhaps none is more poignant than the one being played out by the Mitchell family today. Of the ten horses entered over the years by Mitchell Farm, the closest any of them has come to wearing the roses is a disappointing third. It certainly doesn't appear the Mitchells have done much to improve their chances by entering a filly that's drawn the number-one starting position.

"Personally I don't like to see fillies running against colts because they don't have the stamina or strength and frankly, I think dangerous situations arise when the horses aren't evenly matched. With Nightwind drawing the number-one starting position, she's going to have to break fast and take the lead. If she isn't held back, she's going to run out of steam before she hits the second turn.''

Craig found himself in a peculiar situation. He wanted a horse to win that he had bet against.

The picture on the screen changed to a shot of the tulip garden and tote board, followed by more shots of women and another interview with a jockey in the paddock. Craig was unable to take his gaze from the television, mesmerized by the possibility of seeing Jennifer. Then, without warning, a picture of Andrew filled the screen. A microphone was shoved at him.

"Was your father able to attend the race today?" the unseen interviewer asked.

Andrew gave the reporter an indulgent smile. "His doctor thought it best for him to watch the proceedings on television. But I'm sure I don't have to tell you that he's here in spirit."

Craig felt the blood drain from his face. His father was so sick he couldn't attend the Derby? A commercial for a luxury car ended the interview. "Dammit," Craig said, only aware that he had said the words aloud when he saw Henry's startled reaction. "It irritates me when they leave something half finished like that," he said.

"Obviously you haven't been reading the sports page."

"What do you mean?"

"For the past week it's been filled with stories about Frank Mitchell."

"What's wrong with him?"

"Kidney failure. I don't understand precisely what the problem is, but he needs a transplant. It seems he has some rare kind of blood or something, and that eliminates most donors. Without any real news, the papers have been having a field day with the human interest thing, saying this is probably Mitchell's last chance to see one of his horses win the Derby.''

"But he has three children. Surely one of them—"

"How did you know that?"

"What? That he has three children?"

"Yeah."

"I must have read it somewhere."

Henry seemed unconvinced but didn't pursue the subject. When the coverage resumed, it was to show the playing of the national anthem. The anthem was followed by scenes from some of the parties that had taken place around Louisville the previous week. Several celebrities were interviewed and asked which horse they favored. The next shot was of the paddock again, only this time the horses had been brought in and were being paraded around in front of their owners.

Still, Craig failed to catch a glimpse of Jennifer.

Next the jockeys mounted their horses and were led out onto the race track. "My Old Kentucky Home" was played, and there were more shots of the crowd. Finally the horses were led into the starting gate and the race began. Nightwind broke fast and took the lead, just as the expert commentator had said she would have to do to keep from being boxed in. At the first turn she was still ahead, but as she entered the backstretch, one of the favored chestnut colts came up beside her and took the lead. Almost immediately the filly seemed to lose heart and drop back in the pack. In seconds she went from first to sixth. Craig sat on the edge of the couch. It was the first race he had watched in which he cared about the winner.

By the time the horses were entering the homestretch, Nightwind was so far back that she wasn't even in the picture. Then, with an incredible lengthening of stride, she appeared on-screen and began closing the distance between herself and the leader. The crowd went crazy as she burst forth, eating up the lengths that separated her from the chestnut colt. The jockey on the lead horse urged him to greater effort as Nightwind neared. The finish line loomed dead ahead. They crossed side by side. Even the commentator refused to make a guess at the outcome, saying it was too close to call.

An unnatural quiet settled over the crowd as they waited for the official results. Long seconds passed. Then pandemonium broke out when the winner was flashed up on the screen. Nightwind had won by a nose.

Henry let out a whoop. "I sure hope Sandy's watching this." He began gathering the remnants of the lunch to throw away. On the television they showed Nightwind being led to the winner's circle. Henry tossed the empty bags and bottles into the trash container and reached up to turn off the television.

"Leave it," Craig said.

Henry gave him a puzzled frown. "I thought you wanted to finish up the Lambert/Ingersol report."

Craig ignored him. A woman in a black-and-white dress with a broad-brimmed hat hiding her face stepped up to Nightwind and stroked the horse's nose when the blanket of five hundred roses was laid across its neck. The jockey, holding a large bouquet of roses, broke one off and handed it to the woman. The camera zeroed in on her as she brought the flower to her face. The commentator identified her as Mrs. Richard Martindale, daughter of Frank and Agnes Mitchell.

Jennifer had married. A sharp stab of disappointment surfaced; he forced it aside. What right did he have to be disappointed that Jennifer had made a new life for herself? Unable to look away, he continued to watch the screen.

She was as he remembered her, only more beautiful. The seven years had matured her face, giving it line, definition, and an aristocratic appearance. "Go home, Henry," he said, his voice an emotionless monotone. "We'll finish the report Monday."

Henry followed Craig's gaze to the television. "Do you know her?"

It was useless to try to deny the profound change that had come over him. "I knew her once...a long time ago."

"Do you want to talk about it?"

"Not now," he said wearily. "If you don't mind, I'd like to be alone."

Henry took his jacket from the back of the chair where he had tossed it earlier. "If you change your mind, give me a call."

Craig nodded absently, not looking away from the television set. When he heard the door close, his shoulders sagged as he abandoned the effort to appear unaffected by all that he had seen that afternoon. His love for Jennifer had't diminished despite denial and time and separation. He would never be free from her.

And time was about to run out for him ever to know his father.

The advertisement ended, and the scene changed to the presentation of the trophy. The platform was filled with people Craig didn't recognize, save two...Andrew and Jennifer. Andrew stood beside a woman who barely reached his shoulder. Craig guessed to be in her fifties; she had black hair turning to gray and dark, flashing eyes. Suddenly, with gut-wrenching certainty, Craig knew he was looking at his mother. She accepted the trophy, looked directly into the camera and in a voice cracking with emotion, said, "We finally did it, Frank."

After Andrew had answered questions about Night-wind's future, the coverage returned to Howard Snyder.

Craig turned off the set and walked over to the window. He was emotionally drained, and for the first time in years, unsure of what to do with himself. He stood at the window for a long time, blindly staring at the horizon, lost in a world of memories.

The sun was almost ready to set when he turned from the window and took the elevator up to his apartment. Desperate for contact with his family, no matter how remote, he opened the wall safe in his bedroom and took out the sealed manila envelope Jack Chapman had sent a month after Craig had returned to Oklahoma. He'd never been able to bring himself to read what was inside the package, but he'd never been able to throw it away, either. So he'd kept the detective's final report all these years, never knowing what made him hang on, yet realizing that he couldn't completely let go.

He opened the envelope as he walked into the living room to pour himself a drink. It wasn't until the whiskey was in the glass that he remembered the last time he'd consumed alcohol alone. A powerful urge to be back on the ranch, sitting on the porch, swept over him, making his mouth twist in an ironic smile. Had he come so far to discover that what he really wanted was to be back where he'd begun?

He sat down on the couch and put his feet up on the coffee table. The envelope stayed on the cushion beside him as he slowly consumed his drink. Finally he reached for the papers and began to read. He skipped the cover letter and went right to the report on his father.

In thorough, methodical steps, his father's life unfolded before him. By the time Craig finished the ten-page report, he felt that a real flesh and blood person had begun to take shape in his mind. For two people who had only spent nine months together, he and his father were amazingly alike. It was as if their personalities were bound by something more powerful than time and space, something so powerful it had survived the long separation. Could he let his father die without ever reestablishing that bond?

Could he go back and take a chance on what his return might do to Jennifer? To return to Kentucky now would be tantamount to admitting the years of sacrifice had been needless.

He turned the last page of the report over and again exposed the cover letter. Because he was the type who read anything in front of him, his gaze swept the typewritten page, picking up bits and pieces, stopping to read a sentence, then drifting on.

Perhaps the most startling discovery, however, concerns the three Mitchell children.

Immediately his attention focused on the paragraph.

Because of the kidnapping of the firstborn son, the Mitchells became almost compulsively protective of the three children who followed. It was, therefore, understandable that only by accident did we discover that all but the deceased child, Eric, were adopted.

Adopted? Craig read the sentence again and then again to be sure he was reading it correctly. Jennifer was adopted? She wasn't really his sister?

With an anguished cry he flung the papers across the room; they scattered like bleached leaves before an autumn wind. Seven years he had lived in hell. And all that time the information that could have freed him had been only steps away.

CHAPTER NINE

AS WAS HIS HABIT when looking for answers to particularly puzzling questions, Craig stood at his living room window and gazed out at the expanse of the city he called home. But that night he was so consumed with the questions that plagued him that his relaxation trick failed to bring the customary results.

How could he possibly return to Kentucky, knowing Jennifer was married? He ran his hand through his hair and then continued on to rub the weary muscles at the back of his neck. Even more unsettling than any of his thoughts about Jennifer was the question of whether or not he could stay away from Lexington when he knew his father was dying. He brought a half-filled glass of whiskey to his mouth, erasing a slow-forming self-deprecating smile. Here he was, agonizing over the decision to go to Lexington or to stay in Oklahoma, as if he had any real choice.

He set the glass on a nearby table and went to the phone to call Mike Stephenson, a sometime business associate who was also his personal physician. Shortly after Craig had set up his center of operations in Oklahoma City, he had been approached by Stephenson for help in rescuing a medical clinic from imminent bankruptcy. The clinic had become Craig's first local business venture and had turned out to be lucrative beyond anything either he or Stephenson had imagined it could be.

A woman answered the phone. "Stephenson residence," she said, her accent a distinct Vermont twang rarely heard in Oklahoma.

"This is Craig Templeton. I'd like to speak to Dr. Stephenson."

"I'm sorry, Dr. Stephenson is busy at the moment. Shall I have him return your call, Mr. Templeton?"

"That won't be necessary," Craig said evenly. "I want to talk to him now."

"I'm very sorry, sir, but Dr. Stephenson is having dinner and—"

"Interrupt him," Craig said, not raising his voice but sending an unmistakable message in the tone.

"I couldn't do—"

He was in no mood to play games. "Get Dr. Stephenson on the phone *now*."

"I'll see if he wants to talk to you," she replied coolly, giving the distinct impression it would do no good.

While he waited, Craig carried the phone over to a chair. Several more seconds passed before a concerned Mike Stephenson came on the line. "What's happened, Craig?" he asked a little breathlessly.

"I want to find out whether I would be a suitable kidney donor for a man who lives in Lexington, Kentucky. And I want it done in strictest confidence."

There was a pause before Stephenson said, "What's this all about?"

"Will you help me or won't you?"

"Are you sure you know what you're doing?"

"Yes."

Again there was a pause. "This wouldn't be about the guy whose horse won the Derby today, would it?"

Mike Stephenson's scope of knowledge and information never ceased to amaze Craig. "Can you do it?"

"What do you mean by strictest confidence?"

"Until we find out whether I'd be a suitable donor, only you, me and Frank Mitchell's physician will know anything about it."

"Is there some reason other than to procure medical records that you wanted Mitchell's physician informed?"

"I just assumed that was the only way we could get donor information about him."

"In other words, if I can get the information without anyone else knowing, you'd prefer it was done that way?"

"What are you getting at, Mike?"

"There's a kidney procurement network for patients who are in need of transplants. Hospitals that are involved in the program are periodically provided with updated serum samples from these patients so they can act quickly to establish matches whenever a kidney becomes available. I have access to these samples."

"Will you do it?"

"What if the match turns out positive? You can't seriously be planning to donate one of your kidneys to someone you heard about on a television program. That's carrying charity a little far, don't you think?"

"Will you do it or not?"

Mike Stephenson let out a sigh. "Of course I will. Come into my office Monday and—"

"This can't wait until Monday. I want to get the tests over with as soon as I can. Tonight if possible. Tomorrow at the latest."

"What's the rush?"

Of the number of answers he could have given, Craig chose the simplest. "It's the way I want it done."

"All right. I'll see what I can arrange and call you right back."

"Thanks." Craig replaced the receiver and walked back over to the window. The ethereal beauty of the city's blanket of lights brought him no peace. Again, as it had the day he had found the clippings, his life had taken an irreversible turn. With a shrug of acceptance he turned and walked away.

BECAUSE THE NEXT DAY was Sunday, and the usual places Mike Stephenson would use for lab work were closed, Craig went to the hospital to have the tests run that would tell him if he was a good candidate to donate a kidney to his father.

Stephenson called him at the office late Monday afternoon with the results. "I just got off the phone with the lab at the hospital."

"And?" Craig took off his reading glasses and tossed them on the desk before leaning back in his chair.

Stephenson hesitated for a long time before answering. "You're a remarkably good match," he finally, reluctantly admitted.

Craig let out a sigh. He closed his eyes and leaned his head against the chair. "Thanks, Mike. I owe you one."

"I'd settle for an explanation."

There were only two other people who knew the relationship between himself and Frank Mitchell—Bill and Cloris Mason. But if he went through with his plan, the information was bound to come out, anyway. "Frank Mitchell is my father."

A stunned silence filled the line. "Are you absolutely sure about this?"

Craig's mirthless laugh punctuated Mike's question. "Think about it, Mike. What better proof could you want than the lab results?"

"Listen, I've gone along with this thing up until now because I didn't believe there was a snowball's chance in hell you'd be a match. Now that it's turned out I was wrong, I've got to step in and say my piece. Frank Mitchell—your father—is a very sick man. I don't know if you're aware of this, but kidney failure doesn't even show up until a patient's function drops below five percent. It's even possible he could be too sick to make it through transplant surgery. This isn't a guaranteed thing, Craig. No one can promise you the kidney will take."

"When the match is good, and the donor is either a sibling or a party in the parent child relationship, the success rate is almost ninety percent," Craig replied.

"I see you've been doing your homework. Then you must have also found out that there are some very real dangers involved for the donor. This isn't a simple matter of generosity. You will be subjected to at least five hours of major surgery. In the end you'll be left with one functioning kidney, which could be destroyed in a relatively minor automobile accident or by a stubborn infection. Did your research also tell you that there are some physicians in this country who refuse to use a live donor because of the risks involved to them?"

"What's my alternative, Mike? Do you honestly think I could live the rest of my life knowing my father died because I was concerned that some day something might happen to me?"

"You're thirty-four years old, Craig. You have a long life ahead of you. Too long to be relying on just that one kidney."

"And it's a life I'd just as soon live with a clear conscience."

"Promise me you'll think about it for a couple of days before you commit yourself."

"Mike, believe me, I appreciate your concern, but I've already done all the thinking I need to do."

"There's nothing I can say to get you to change your mind?"

"Nothing."

"I suppose you want me to make the arrangements," he said with a sigh of resignation.

"I'll take care of telling my father, but I'd appreciate your contacting his transplant team."

"They'll want more tests than the ones you took at the hospital Sunday."

"That's all right."

"When do you want to leave?"

"I'll get back to you on that sometime tomorrow."

"In case I forget, be sure to stop by the office and pick up a copy of your medical records to take with you. It will save time when you get there."

"I appreciate all you've done, Mike."

"Don't take it to mean tacit approval," he grumbled.

Craig thanked him again, hung up and reached for the list of private phone numbers he kept in his desk. He turned to the M's for the number of Lewis McDade. Lewis was the attorney Craig used whenever he needed advice about anything personal and didn't want to involve the company's legal advisors. The number he called bypassed McDade's secretary and was picked up by Lewis himself.

"Craig...it's been ages since I've heard from you," Lewis's booming voice announced. "I thought maybe you'd decided to take up residence in Japan."

"I have a job for you," Craig said, skipping the small talk they usually engaged in before getting down to business. He could almost picture the large man's posture changing as he responded to Craig's intensity.

"What is it?" the attorney asked, his earlier good cheer replaced by a cool professionalism.

"I think it would be better if I explained in person."

"Give me a second to check my calendar." He was back almost immediately. "Can you come over now?"

"I'll be there in fifteen minutes."

An hour later Craig was sitting across from a thoughtful Lewis McDade, trying to ignore the cloud of pipe smoke that filled the room and burned his eyes. McDade claimed his well-used pipe was an integral part of his thought process whenever he was working. Therefore, despite repeated warnings from his doctors about the danger of smoking and complaints from his wife about the smell, he refused to give it up.

"Let me get this straight," McDade said, tapping his pencil against the tablet he had used to take notes while Craig talked. "You want me to contact the Mitchells through their attorney to let them know you will be visiting them?"

It was the least traumatic and most convincing way Craig had been able to devise to inform two people that the son whom they thought long dead was still alive. "Do you think the things I've told you will be enough to convince them I'm not some con artist?"

"Not alone they wouldn't be. However, when combined with the medical evidence, I don't think there will be much room for doubt." He hesitated before going on, clearly uncomfortable with what he would say next. "Has it occurred to you that there is a possibility not everyone will be as delighted as your parents will undoubtedly be to see you reappear?"

Craig shifted position in the overstuffed leather chair. "I assume you mean Andrew?"

"Not only Andrew. The other two children, as well."
He looked down at the paper in front of him. "I believe
you said their names were Jennifer and Kyle?"

"Yes."

"And then there are the respective spouses of these
people. How will they feel about the sudden reappearance of the long-lost son, who they naturally will think is
returning to claim his rightful place in the family? Along,
I might add, with his rightful inheritance."

"Quite honestly, I've been too wrapped up with the
medical problem to give much thought to anything else."
But not so wrapped up that there hadn't been unguarded
moments when thoughts of Jennifer intruded to the ex-
clusion of everything else. "Perhaps it would be best for
everyone concerned if we kept the initial meeting small.
Just Frank and Agnes and myself." It would certainly be
easier on him if Jennifer weren't present. "Could you
make those arrangements?"

McDade clasped his pipe between his teeth as he added
another line to his notes. "You can consider it done."

TWO DAYS LATER Craig arrived at the Lexington airport.
He'd taken a commercial plane instead of the company jet
because he'd wanted as few people as possible to know
where he was and to speculate about his reasons for being
there. The running of Templeton Enterprises had been left
in the capable hands of Henry Keily, the only person besides Stephenson and McDade who was aware of what
was going on.

Henry had been stunned when Craig filled him in on his
true background. After taking a while to absorb the information, he became an unanticipated ally in Craig's
decision to be a donor for his father.

A friend first and business associate second, Henry had shown up unannounced at Craig's front door the previous night. He had been carrying a large bag filled with Chinese food and a six-pack of imported beer. "I knew you wouldn't be able to sleep, so I thought I'd keep you entertained," he'd said. They hadn't parted company until dawn.

As soon as Craig picked up his rental car and headed toward town, he realized that the seven years he had been away from Lexington had done nothing to dull the memories. Except where new construction had changed the scenery, the streets seemed as familiar as those he traveled every day. Although he could have bypassed the downtown area and arrived at the farm earlier, he chose not to, unconsciously delaying the moment he would come face-to-face with his parents by telling himself he was simply curious to see if things had remained the same in the center of the city, too.

They hadn't. The downtown was still in transition. Everywhere the old was being replaced with the new. The wrecker's ball had even taken the building that had housed Jack Chapman's office. Craig considered stopping to get out and walk around and then thought about what he was doing and why he was doing it. He was taken aback to realize that he was postponing what was supposedly the fulfillment of a dream because he was afraid. Where was the person whose reputation among his employees was one of unfailing composure? Although he was sure he was the only one able to detect the change, the events of the past week had left him shaken.

Acknowledgement of the delaying tactics for precisely what they were was all it took for Craig to get back on the road to Mitchell Farm. He arrived at the front entrance less than half an hour later.

He felt a tightness in his chest when he saw the brass plates embedded in the limestone fence that proclaimed the area beyond to be Mitchell Farm. When he reached the first division in the road he turned left instead of right, the direction he had always gone before. Lewis McDade had told him to watch for a Georgian style brick house with a large circular driveway in front.

When he found the house, he hesitated before turning onto the driveway. The two-story home was impressively large. With its regal columns and portico, it had an aura of age and history about it. Even though Craig had no sense of recognition, he somehow felt a part of what he saw.

He took a deep breath and drove toward the house. The front door opened before the car came to a stop. A woman whom Craig recognized from the television coverage of the Derby—his mother—stepped out onto the porch. She was followed by a man whom Craig so closely resembled that he was sure it could be no one other than his father. Craig got out of the car and slowly walked toward them. His throat felt dry; his stomach was in knots.

It wasn't until he reached the bottom step that he saw there were tears in his mother's eyes. But more than the tears, he saw recognition. None of the information he had sent through Lewis McDade had been needed. He could see that she recognized in him the seed of her union with his father. He was her son.

His mother's hands trembled as he came to her, and she reached up to touch his face. "I knew you weren't dead," she said softly, her belief vindicated at last. She tried to smile. "You've become a fine young man...so handsome. Just like your father."

Craig could hold back no longer. He enfolded her in an embrace, holding her close, feeling her shoulders shake as she released tears held in check for a lifetime. He looked over to his father. Tears formed narrow trails of moisture down his sunken cheeks.

Agnes released Craig and stepped back. For a moment he was unsure of what to do. Then, tentatively, his father raised his arms. It was all the encouragement Craig needed. He hugged the desperately ill man, praying the surgery would be successful and that this first embrace would not be the last.

"Welcome home, son." Frank's voice cracked with emotion.

"Come inside," Agnes said. "There are others who are anxious to meet you."

Craig held back. He felt drained, vulnerable. He couldn't chance seeing Jennifer the way he was now. There was no telling what he might do, what he might say. "I thought this was supposed to be a private meeting."

"Oh, it is," Agnes said, taking his arm. "Just the immediate family, as you requested."

"Everyone's here, except your sister," Frank said. "She's out of town at a jumping competition and couldn't be reached, so we left her a note telling her to come over when she gets back."

Relieved at the temporary reprieve, Craig followed them inside. They walked through a large entrance hall with a black-and-white marble floor, cherry wood antique furniture and hand-painted paper on the walls. Craig studied his father as they moved through the room. Despite the excitement of the moment, which should have brought color to his cheeks, he looked ashen. Every movement seemed an effort for him. Why wasn't he in a hospital?

The room Agnes entered became funeral-service quiet as Frank and then Craig entered behind her. Four people rose to their feet when they saw him: a woman, two men, and a boy Craig guessed to be in his midteens. Only the boy smiled.

Agnes clasped her hands in front of her, effectively hiding their trembling. She gave Craig a lingering, possessive look. "Eric . . ." she began, and then flushed in confusion. "I'm sorry," she said. "You'll have to be patient with me. It's going to take me a while to remember your name is Craig now." She began again. "Craig, I'd like you to meet Andrew, your oldest brother, and his wife, Cybil."

Andrew's face held a puzzled frown as he reached out to take his brother's hand. "I have this crazy feeling we've met somewhere before."

Agnes's quick reply kept Craig from having to answer. "It's probably because he looks so much like your father." Her voice was filled with happiness and more than a little pride.

Craig met Andrew's intent gaze and knew it was only a matter of time before he would remember their previous meeting. When he moved to take Cybil's hand, he looked into her eyes and was surprised to see undisguised appraisal. Apparently satisfied with what she saw, the appraisal changed to an unmistakable, if fleeting, invitation. Craig was immediately on guard. Since moving up in the business world, he had come to recognize women like Cybil. They were like pieces of merchandise, available to the highest bidder. And to Cybil, he imagined he was like the new kid on the block who was about to win all the marbles.

"And this is Richard Martindale, your sister's husband," Agnes said, steering him to a rather tall man who greeted him with a limp handshake.

"Richard . . ." Craig nodded. So this was the man Jennifer had married. Craig fought to control an almost overwhelming surge of jealousy. It was an unfamiliar feeling and soon passed, leaving in its wake a sharp curiosity. The man Jennifer had chosen to live her life with was as different from the man Craig had been as the horses he had owned at the ranch were from the ones raised on Mitchell Farm. Richard looked like an ad for *Gentleman's Quarterly*. Everything about him, from his Corinthian leather Loafers to his Rolex watch, proclaimed him to be a man of wealth and leisure.

"And finally—this is your youngest brother, Kyle."

Craig held out his hand. Shyly Kyle started to reach for it, changed his mind and threw his arms around Craig. Stunned at first, Craig didn't immediately respond. When he did, he held his youngest brother in a heartfelt hug, easily reciprocating Kyle's enthusiasm.

"Wow," Kyle said, stepping back and looking slightly embarrassed at his outburst. "I must be living right or something. Most kids have to put up with a screaming baby and messy diapers when they get a new brother."

Craig laughed, as did everyone else in the room. He liked his youngest brother, who seemed to be all arms and legs attached to a body that looked as if it couldn't possibly catch up. Kyle's engaging grin and ingenuous eyes reminded him of Jennifer. It wasn't hard to understand why her voice had taken on a special quality when she'd talked about him.

"Have a seat . . . Craig," Andrew said. "We're anxious to hear all about you."

Craig hid the flickering smile of understanding that curved his lips. Andrew still wasn't convinced he really had a new brother. He chose a chair situated with its back to the door so that he could see everyone.

"Can I get you something to drink?" Agnes asked. When Craig showed surprise that she intended to serve them herself, she explained that, on occasions reserved strictly for close family, she preferred to dispense with the domestic help she employed on a part-time basis.

Spotting the coffee service on the sideboard, Craig said, "Coffee would be fine."

Frank started to speak when Andrew interrupted him. "Your attorney didn't mention what it is you do in Oklahoma City, Craig."

Craig had given Andrew more credit for subtlety. "I work with investments."

"Oh, a stockbroker," Cybil chimed in.

"No...I work for a company that specializes in investment capital." Craig wasn't sure what made him reluctant to divulge his true position at that company. But he balked at being quizzed. He refused to let his success or his financial status color their impressions of him. Looking up to take the coffee from Agnes, he caught Richard staring at him, a look of unguarded hostility in his eyes. Although Richard's expression changed immediately, Craig was sure he hadn't mistaken the message.

"Have you always lived in Oklahoma?" Frank asked, his voice little more than a dry whisper. He looked even more tired than he had only moments before.

Craig nodded. "I grew up on a cattle ranch in a fairly unpopulated section of the state."

"Were...uh, were—" Agnes struggled with the words. "Were the people who...were they good to you?" she asked, and an unspoken plea that he tell her yes was written on her face.

Craig's heart went out to her. She wore the pain she had suffered stoically and with incredible dignity. "Their names were Max and Wynona," he said gently. "And yes, they were good to me." Someday he would tell his parents all he had experienced since leaving them. Someday when it was just the three of them.

"Were you a cowboy?" Kyle asked.

"I think 'rancher' might be a better term."

"What made you decide to give up ranching and go into the world of business?" Andrew asked.

Craig took a sip of the aromatic coffee, using the action to delay his answer. "It just seemed like the right thing to do at the time," he finally said.

"Do your parents...uh...do Max and Wynona still live on the ranch?" Cybil broke in, her voice a sultry caress. She crossed her legs, revealing a tempting length of thigh. With purposeful movements she pulled her skirt down.

"They were killed in an automobile accident several years ago." There was a quick exchange of meaningful glances between Cybil and Andrew. Craig pretended he hadn't seen the exchange that told him they were undoubtedly wondering who there was to confirm his story about the kidnapping if Max and Wynona were dead.

Richard spoke. "I'm sorry my wife wasn't here to meet you, Craig. But I'm sure she will be as delighted as we all are to have you back in the fold." He chuckled. "So to speak."

"Thank you." Despite the words and outward demeanor, Craig could feel hostility radiating from Richard. "I appreciate the warm welcome I've received from everyone."

"What's it like in Oklahoma?" Kyle asked, oblivious to the undercurrent of tension permeating the room.

Before Craig had a chance to answer, Frank interrupted. "Let's not wear Craig out with questions on his first day home, Kyle. I'm sure you'll have plenty of opportunity later."

"Your father's right," Agnes said, looking over to her husband. A flash of concern passed through her eyes. "Craig would probably like to rest a bit after his long trip. Why don't we call it an afternoon, and then we can all get together again for dinner this evening?"

It was obvious Frank was the one his mother was worried about, but Craig welcomed the chance for privacy. There were thoughts and emotions he needed time to sort out.

Everyone had started to get up when the sound of the front door opening drew their attention. "Mom...Dad?" an achingly familiar voice called out. "Where are you?"

Agnes signaled from the living room door. "We're in here, dear."

"What's this about Eric being found?" Jennifer asked, her heels striking the marble floor as she crossed the foyer, her voice filled with excitement.

"Come in and see for yourself," Agnes answered.

Craig sat frozen in his chair. It was so unfair to let Jennifer walk in cold and see him. But there was no way he could warn her. He heard her come up behind him. Slowly he rose from the chair and turned.

Jennifer brushed a kiss on her mother's cheek as she came into the room. She had hurried over as soon as she'd returned home and found Richard's note telling her he was at her parents' house. There had been a cryptic sentence saying Eric had reappeared, but that was all. She hadn't even bothered to change clothes in her rush to get there. "So tell me what—" Her glance swept past Agnes and landed on Craig. The blood drained from her face; a pain sliced through her chest, stealing her breath.

"I want you to meet your brother," Agnes said.

CHAPTER TEN

CRAIG HELD OUT HIS HAND, as much to steady Jennifer as to perform the expected ritual. Automatically she put her hand in his, and the contact swept away the years they had spent apart. He ached to forget everyone and everything still separating them and to take her into his arms.

Like a blind man suddenly sighted, he stared at her, absorbing every change seven years had brought. She no longer wore her hair in loose curls. It now hung smooth and sleek, curved under at the ends to lightly brush her chin and neck when she moved her head. Bangs touched her forehead and were swept back at the sides. Her eyes still held pain, but they were more wary now. Her mouth was set in a grim line of determination. She had matured, and the maturity had etched her face into a breathtaking beauty.

She was wearing snug-fitting riding pants and a tailored jacket. There was a scarf at her neck…held in place by the cameo he had given her their last day together. For the first time Craig felt a ray of hope. She had not forgotten him any more than he had forgotten her.

Jennifer saw his gaze land on the cameo, and her hand went to her throat. What was Craig doing here? It was all wrong. Somehow her dreams had gone haywire. But it wasn't the middle of the night, and she wasn't dreaming. Her mother had said he was her brother. How could that be? He couldn't be her brother. They had... Oh, my God, she silently gasped, understanding at last.

In the space of a caught breath, in an anguished heart-beat, seven years disappeared. Why, after staying away so long, had he come back now? "So..." she finally managed to say, "you're my long-lost brother."

Craig had placed himself so that he and Agnes were the only ones who saw the transformation that took place on Jennifer's face. Nothing in his entire life had been as difficult as his seeing her again and knowing he could not have her. "I realize it's a surprise to find out I'm still alive after all this time—"

"Surprise is hardly the word," she told him, desperately fighting to control her runaway emotions, trying to deny that, despite the circumstances that had thrust her into marriage with Richard, her feelings for Craig had not changed. How could that be? She hated him for leaving her the way he had. For seven years that hatred had been her key to survival. She had clung to it like a lifeline. Only at night, in her dreams, had the lifeline failed.

"I wish I could have found an easier way to break it to... everyone."

"I doubt there is an easy way to do something like this." A touch of anger seeped into her voice. "How long have you known? How did you find out?"

Agnes broke in. "Why don't you save those questions for tonight, Jennifer? We've all decided to let Craig rest this afternoon and to get together again for dinner."

A look of panic filled Jennifer's eyes. She couldn't come back. She couldn't be around Craig. There were too many memories, and they were too fresh. "I can't," she said. "Come to dinner, that is. I have something else planned."

Richard moved past Craig and put his arm possessively across Jennifer's shoulders. "I'm sure whatever it is, you can get out of it, sweetheart. After all, it isn't every day you add a new member to your family."

"And be sure to bring Nicole," Agnes said. "She'll want to meet her new uncle."

"No!" Jennifer replied, far more loudly than she had intended.

"Of course we'll bring Nicole," Richard corrected her, giving his wife's shoulders a squeeze.

"She's been up late every night this week," Jennifer said.

"And one more night isn't going to hurt her," Richard reasoned. "After all, it isn't every day she gets a new uncle."

"Thank God," Andrew said, coming up beside them.

Agnes flinched at Andrew's seeming rudeness.

"Where would we put them all?" Andrew quickly added, trying to lighten his remark with humor.

Richard responded to Andrew's comment with a nervous laugh. "Well, I guess we'll be taking off, then. I'm sure Jennifer would like to get home to take a bath and change out of her smelly clothes."

Craig tried to keep from looking at Jennifer, knowing his ability to hide his feelings had been stripped from him, leaving him exposed. Because it was expected, he walked to the front door to bid the two couples goodbye. It was there that his and Jennifer's gazes met again for a brief instant, and his soul was laid bare for her to see.

Jennifer closed her eyes against the intimacy, turned and refused to look back as she walked to her car. She needed time alone to regain her composure, to find the strength to see Craig again that evening.

"I'LL DRIVE," Richard said, coming up beside her and reaching for the keys in her hand.

"Don't you have your own car?"

"Andrew brought me."

"Oh." She reluctantly relinquished the keys and went around the Mercedes to get in the passenger side. Even though it was still early afternoon, she had caught the unmistakable smell of alcohol on Richard's breath.

They were halfway down the driveway when Richard spoke again. "Well, what did you think of this supposed brother of yours?"

Jennifer clasped her hands around her knee and stared out the window. "What do you mean?"

"Do you think he's who he says he is?"

The first time she had seen Craig came to mind. She remembered how he'd looked standing in Lynn's office, and she recalled the peculiar feeling that she had seen him before. It had never occurred to her she'd felt that way because he looked so much like Frank. "You must admit there's an uncanny family resemblance," she said. Pieces of the puzzle were beginning to fall into place. They traveled the remaining mile to their home at Martindale Farm in silence.

CRAIG WAITED IN THE LIVING ROOM for Agnes to return after seeing that Frank went to bed. Unable to sit still any longer, he got up and started to pace the room. The news that Jennifer had a child had left him numb. Not until Nicole's name had been mentioned had he realized he had subconsciously hoped there would be a way for him and Jennifer to get together again.

The child changed everything. The claim Richard held on Jennifer—the link forged between them by the birth of Nicole—represented a far stronger bond than any Craig might have. He stopped in front of the window and looked out at the rolling acres of fenced pasture. He was filled with such longing that it was tearing him apart. He had to get the surgery over with and leave Kentucky as soon as possible.

"You used to love to look out windows when you were a baby," Agnes said, coming up behind him.

Craig turned to her. "I guess in that respect I haven't changed much."

She sat down in the chair beside him. After several minutes of silence had passed, she looked down at her hands, which lay folded in her lap. "Why did you come back after all this time?" she asked.

Her question startled Craig. "I don't understand."

"I have this feeling you've known who you are for a long time. Why did you decide to come home now?"

He couldn't bring himself to lie to her. "I heard about Frank's kidney problem."

She dipped her head in a slight nod. "That's what I thought."

"How did you know?"

She looked up at him and gave him a sad smile. "I've always known you were still alive. When you were a baby, there was something special between us. You never cried because somehow I could anticipate your needs as clearly as if you had told them to me. I've never stopped feeling this connection. If something had happened to you, I would have known. The feeling would have stopped."

He knelt down in front of her and took her hands. "Those years must have been terrible for you."

"In the beginning I could hardly function. Then we adopted Andrew, and because he was a sickly baby and demanded so much of my attention, my life got easier. By the time Jennifer and Kyle came along, I had learned to cope."

"Why did you adopt instead of having more children yourself?" It was a question that had burned for an answer since he had read Chapman's report.

"You were a difficult birth. After you were born, I couldn't have any more children of my own," she explained simply.

He looked down at their hands. Hers were nearly lost in his. He thought about Wynona and the children she had tried to have and how she, too, had finally turned to adoption out of desperation. "You know why I've come, don't you?"

"I think so, but I'd rather hear you say."

He took a deep breath. "I've had the test, and I'm as good a match to become a donor for Frank as he's likely to get."

She looked deeply into his eyes. "Your father will never agree to letting you give him one of your kidneys," she said calmly.

Craig frowned. "Why not?"

"Now that you have been returned to him, he'll never permit you to risk your life, no matter how noble or pressing the cause."

That possibility had never occurred to Craig. "Then it will be up to us to convince him."

She smiled. "I'm pleased to see you got your stubbornness from my side of the family." Her eyes filled with tears. "But are you really sure you know what you're doing?"

"You're going to have to trust me on this. The decision was easy for me to make, but it wasn't one that I took lightly. I've talked to my own doctor and done as much reading as there was material I could find on the subject—I know what I'm doing."

She touched the side of his face, and her palm pressed into his cheek as he turned to meet her touch. "When I'd go to bed at night, I'd pray that whoever had you would raise you with love. I believe my prayers were answered."

He brushed the tear from her cheek with the back of his finger. "Someday, when this is all over, I'll tell you about Max and Wynona."

She nodded in agreement. After the moment had passed, she sat up straighter in the chair. The vulnerability disappeared from her face and with its absence, her entire demeanor changed. "I can wait to hear about them, but I think you'd better tell me what's going on between you and Jennifer before she returns this evening."

JENNIFER STEPPED INTO HER SHOES, grabbed her purse and headed for the door, where Richard was waiting. He gave her a quick once-over. "Beautiful, as always," he proclaimed. "But where's the cameo?"

"I decided not to wear it tonight."

"My, my, a first." He held her coat for her.

"You say that as if I never go anywhere without it."

"Do I? I'm sorry—I'm really quite aware you've never pinned it to your nightgown."

"Why are you making such a big thing about this?"

"Perhaps it's just because I want this new brother of yours to realize what a gorgeous sister he has, and on you, jewelry is like the bow on a delectable package."

"I'm sure he doesn't care one way or another how I look. Why should he?"

"Ah, my dear, you wouldn't say that if you had seen how he looked at you when we were leaving."

"You're imagining things." She finished buttoning her coat, looking down to hide the flush she felt warming her cheeks. "Are you ready?"

"Aren't we waiting for Nicole?"

"She isn't coming."

"Why not?"

"She isn't feeling well."

"How strange. She was perfectly all right this afternoon when we came home."

"Well, she isn't perfectly all right tonight. Besides, I've already made arrangements for Barbara to stay."

"Did you call the doctor?"

"Richard, she isn't sick—just tired."

"I must say I find your behavior about all this rather odd."

She hated it when he resorted to puffing himself up like a pompous country squire. "All right, I'll tell you why I don't want Nicole going with us tonight. I saw the look in Andrew's eyes, and I listened to you talk about Craig all the way home, and I don't think Nicole has any business witnessing the two of you taking potshots at her new uncle." She looked at him to see whether or not he believed her. His return gaze bored into her.

"How easily his name rolls off your tongue," he said softly.

She let out a disgusted groan. "That's exactly what I'm talking about. You're behaving like—"

"A jealous husband?" He took her into his arms and tried to kiss her, but she turned her head before their lips met. "Don't you think I have cause, my dear? In all the years we've been married, not once have you looked at me the way you looked at this supposed brother of yours."

She tried to twist out of his arms, but he held her tight. "I refuse to listen to this nonsense."

"Nonsense?" He pulled her closer, insisting she look at him. "Do you love me?"

"Of course I do."

"Are you telling me the truth?"

"What is it you want me to say?"

"I don't want you to say anything. If you truly love me, show me that you do by making love to me right now." He nuzzled the side of her neck as his voice dropped to a husky whisper. "Do you have any idea how long it's been, Jennifer? Can't you see that I need you?"

It was everything she could do to contain the panic that gripped her. She knew she was being unfair, but she couldn't bring herself to sleep with him. Not anymore. In the beginning she had tried so hard to love him, and when that had failed, she had told herself it didn't matter. She could still be a good wife. She owed him so much. He had been so kind to her after Craig left. He had been a good father to Nicole. "They're waiting for us, Richard," she pleaded.

He released her, flashing a disarming smile. "Just teasing, my dear. We wouldn't want to get something started just to be interrupted by someone wondering what was keeping us, now would we?"

She knew he had been serious but was grateful he chose not to pursue the tryst. She touched his arm. "Richard . . . you have no reason to doubt me."

He put his hand over hers and smiled. "That's all I needed to hear, my darling. Now, shall we get going?"

THAT AFTERNOON Craig had been saved from answering Agnes's question about Jennifer when Frank came into the room, saying he was unable to sleep. Deciding nothing would be gained by waiting, Craig had told his father why he was there. Afterward, the discussion had become heated as he and Agnes joined forces in their effort to talk Frank into allowing Craig to give him a kidney. Finally, when they were all emotionally drained and reaching the breaking point, Frank had given in. Agnes immediately left the room to call the transplant team, afraid to wait until morning and give Frank a chance to change his mind. The chief surgeon made arrangements for Craig and Frank to go into the hospital the next day for a final series of tests. If all went well, the actual surgery would take place the day following.

That evening Andrew and Cybil arrived for dinner first. Richard and Jennifer came in fifteen minutes later. When they were all gathered around the table, Frank rapped his knife against his crystal water glass. "I have an announcement to make," he said, his voice filled with emotion. "Day after tomorrow, if everything goes according to plan, it will no longer be necessary for me to spend half my life hooked up to that damned dialysis machine." He looked at the ceiling to blink away the tears that had formed in his eyes. "It seems sometimes wonderful gifts come in great big packages. Craig has returned home to give me the greatest gift of all—life."

There was a moment of stunned silence, broken only by a tiny gasp of surprise from Jennifer as everyone turned to look at Craig.

Craig had asked Frank and Agnes not to tell anyone about the transplant. They had refused to keep the news from the rest of the family but had agreed to do everything possible to keep the story out of the papers. Craig had been forced to capitulate when he had been unable to come up with a good enough reason not to tell his siblings. He kept his gaze on his father, as the rest of them raised their glasses to honor him in the toast. It wasn't until the first course was served that he dared to look across the table at Jennifer. It was a mistake. Just having her near tore at his insides; looking at her created an open wound for all to see.

Somehow they got through the meal. Afterward they went into the living room, where Jennifer nervously paced the carpet for several minutes before announcing that she was going outside for a short walk to settle her meal.

"Why don't you take Craig with you," Frank said. "You could show him Changeover's new colt."

Jennifer looked at Craig, her eyes holding a silent plea for him to stay behind. "I don't think he would—"

"Nonsense," Frank interrupted. "It's about time he discovered what the Mitchell family is all about."

"Maybe tomorrow would be better," Craig said. "After all, I couldn't see much in the dark, anyway."

Frank chortled. "We've got all the modern conveniences around here, even in the barns. Electric lights are just one of them."

"Go on," Agnes said. "It will give you a chance to get to know each other."

Craig glanced back to Jennifer. To argue further would focus too much attention on them. "It looks like you're stuck with me." He tried to make the statement sound as innocent as it should have been.

She tried to smile. "Or that you're stuck with me."

"Maybe I'll go, too," Richard said, standing and stretching as if the thought had just occurred to him.

"Why don't you stick around here?" Frank suggested. "I'd like to talk to you about that stallion your dad bought last week."

Richard tossed Jennifer a meaningful look before sitting back down. "Don't be gone long, dear. Remember, we've got an early day tomorrow."

"I won't," Jennifer answered, struggling to hide her unreasoning anger at Richard's cloying possessiveness.

Before they left the house, they stopped by the closet to pick up Jennifer's coat. Craig handed it to her, standing back while she put it on, afraid to chance even an accidental touch by helping her.

They were almost a hundred yards from the house before Craig broke the unnatural silence that hung between them. "I'm sorry," he said.

She crossed her arms over her chest. "What for?"

"For coming here without finding some way to warn you . . . for leaving the way I did seven years ago."

"What had happened before is history. Something both of us would be better off forgetting."

They left the driveway and started down the road to the barns. It was unseasonably cold for May, but neither of them seemed to notice. The sky was clear, and the lack of nearby city lights made the stars stand out in sharp relief. A quarter moon provided just enough light to guide them on their way.

"How have you been?" Craig asked.

"Fine . . . wonderful. My life is filled with activity; I'm having a grand time." She sounded brittle instead of casual, as she had intended.

"I understand you're jumping competitively?"

"Among other things." Again she sounded cutting.

He reached for her arm and brought her to a stop beside him. "Can we at least be friends?" he asked gently.

Her eyes had adjusted to the dark enough to let her see the poignant plea written on his face. "I don't know if that's possible," she admitted. "I've spent too much time hating you. There's no way I can make those feelings disappear overnight." When she saw the flash of pain her words had provoked, she was surprised it brought her no satisfaction.

He let out a deep breath. "I noticed you still wear the cameo I gave you."

She lifted her head to look deeply into his eyes. "I use it to remind me how foolish I once was."

"Jennifer...you have to realize by now that I had no choice."

"You used me."

"I loved you." And he still loved her, but he had lost the right to tell her so.

She extricated her arm from his grasp. "As I said before, that's history now." She turned and walked away from him.

Craig caught up to her and again reached for her arm to stop her. "We're going to have to find some way to get along with each other while I'm here or be prepared to pay the consequences."

"What is that supposed to mean?"

"Agnes is already suspicious that there's something between us. And if I'm not mistaken, Richard is having similar thoughts."

"Well, they're both wrong. There's nothing between us." She looked down at the pavement to hide her eyes, knowing he would be able to see the truth if she didn't. How could it be that despite the years, despite the pain, nothing had changed? She felt as if she loved him as completely, as desperately as she had the day he had left. Obviously the hatred she had convinced herself she harbored was nothing but a sham, a feeble attempt at self-defense.

"Jennifer, I'm so sorry," he whispered. "I know I hurt you by leaving the way I did but—"

"But what? You had no choice? There's always a choice, Craig. There's always another way to do something."

He let go of her arm and shoved his hands into his pockets. "You're right," he said, "But at the time, I sincerely believed the choice I made was the one that would be the least painful."

"For whom?"

He stared at her, not answering, knowing she was lashing out at him to exorcise the hurt.

"How could you possibly convince yourself that a letter telling me you were already married was kind?" she demanded.

"Because of the alternative."

"Which was?"

"Telling you that you had fallen in love with your own brother."

"How could you know what was happening between us and still let it go on?"

"I had no idea you were a Mitchell until that last day. How could I? Your name was Langley. Whenever you talked about Agnes and Frank, you never once referred to them as your mother and father. I've thought about that a thousand times and never understood why."

Jennifer looked away as she caught her breath in a silent sob. "Because it would have been unprofessional of me. If you remember, I was working in the office, and I thought you were here on business." Moisture pooled in her eyes. She took another anguished breath. "If only you had trusted me enough to tell me the truth." Her voice cracked with unshed tears.

Craig jammed his hands deeper into his pockets to keep from reaching for her. "I tried to spare you."

She moved over to the fence, leaned her arms on the post and stared at the empty pasture. "Why did you come here?"

"Then or now?" He moved over to stand beside her.

"I know why you're here now, but I can only guess why you were here then."

Craig leaned his back against the fence so that he was facing in the opposite direction and not looking at her as he told her about his first trip to Lexington.

By the time he had finished, her heart was breaking anew for the two naive young people they had been. "If you had just told me then," she said softly. "I would have told you that we were brother and sister in name only. We would have held each other...and laughed..." How different their lives would be today. At least before he'd told her why he'd left, she'd had her anger to help her get through the days. Now she had nothing. She would live forever knowing what might have been...if only.

"That's a mistake I'll carry with me the rest of my life."

She turned to look at him. "Then you weren't really married?"

"No," he said softly. "Not then, not now, not ever."

"You've lived alone all this time—because of me?"

Before he could answer, headlights cut through the darkness, pinning them against the fence like insect specimens on a board. Craig shielded his eyes with his hand but couldn't tell what kind of car was heading toward them.

"It's Richard," Jennifer said in a spiritless monotone.

He searched her face. She looked drained. Her eyes were those of a battle-weary soldier. "Are you all right?"

She stared at the approaching car. "Yes," she answered. But it was a lie. She would never be all right again. She felt like a caged bird that had been allowed to see the outdoors. Her life in that cage would go on, but it would never be the same. The car pulled to a stop beside them.

"You've been gone so long that I was getting worried something might have happened," Richard said, leaning out the window.

"We lost track of time," Jennifer replied.

"How nice. That must mean the two of you are hitting it off. Now why don't you both hop in, and I'll drop Craig by the house on our way home."

Craig walked around the car with Jennifer and opened her door. Once she was inside, he leaned down and said, "I'll get back on my own. The night air feels too good to pass up."

"Well, good night then," Richard said.

"Good night," Jennifer added, reaching for her seat belt, not trusting herself to look at Craig even for the second it would take her to tell him goodbye.

Craig closed the door and stood aside while Richard made a U turn and headed back the way he had come. He remained where he was long after the taillights had disappeared over the hill.

Why had Jennifer married Richard? Had she been so lonely, so hurt by what he had done that she had chosen a man like Richard to spend her entire life with? Was it possible she didn't see him for what he was?

If only the child weren't involved. If there were no child to suffer the consequences, he would go after Jennifer with every honest and dishonest method he had picked up the past seven years, even if it meant buying her freedom from Richard. And he was convinced he was a good enough judge of character to recognize how easily that could be done. But he knew too well the effects of taking a child away from its natural parents. How could he ever justify doing to Nicole what had been done to him?

CHAPTER ELEVEN

LONG AFTER he and Jennifer arrived home, Richard donned his bathrobe and wandered through the dark house, too consumed with anxiety to continue to lie in bed. Unlike Jennifer, who had gone to sleep almost as soon as she had crawled under the covers, he had tossed and turned for hours before he'd finally given up the attempt and left the bedroom.

He had been like this since he'd first heard about the return of the Mitchells' prodigal son. In the space of a day, his future had taken a nosedive. Now, instead of being second in line to inherit the Mitchell millions, Jennifer was a weak third, with two male heirs in front of her. Worse yet, it looked as if the old man would live, after all. With Frank still alive, Richard would have to scrap his plans to buy the property coming up for sale next to Martindale Farms.

Dammit! It was so unfair. He had put seven years of back-breaking effort into making Jennifer happy, just waiting for the day she would come into her share of the Mitchell money and free him from the stigma of being involved with a second class breeding farm. He wanted that money. He deserved it. Without Jennifer's inheritance, he would never be able to crawl out of the hole he was in. His dream of buying top-quality breeding stock and matching the mares with equally good stallions had turned to dust. Worst of all, he would never be able to pay off his gambling debts without that money, and Coscarelli was getting tired of waiting.

Living his entire life next to the Mitchell Farm had made him acutely aware of just how second class his own family's operation was. A hunger had grown for what the Mitchells had, until it became his driving force. From his first memory of such things, he had been filled with a consuming rage to know that when the Mitchells had a promising mare—and they had hundreds—they had their pick of stallions. At Martindale Farms it was a matter of having to choose the best of the rejects to service their mediocre stock. On his twelfth birthday he had made himself a secret promise. Somehow, someday, he would have what the Mitchells had. And he didn't care how he got it.

All through high school he had cultivated Jennifer, slowly setting her up, carefully planning for the day when he would ask her to marry him. And then, out of the blue, she had started going with David Langley. Richard had considered it an incredible stroke of luck when David was killed. But no matter how charming he made himself, Jennifer refused to go out with him. He took some solace in knowing it wasn't just him; she refused to go out with anyone. He could wait. The stakes were worth it. He had bided his time until finally she had been the one to call him for a date. The biggest surprise had been her immediate acceptance of the casual marriage proposal he had made two weeks later. Then there had been her insistence they secretly elope that next weekend. It wasn't until much later that Jennifer's behavior had made sense to him.

He glanced over at the picture hanging above the mantel. It was a portrait of Jennifer, painted four years earlier and given to him as a Christmas present by the Mitchells. Somehow the artist had managed to capture the haunted look that came into her eyes whenever she thought she was alone. It was a look he had come to despise, one that represented his failure with her. Despite every effort on his part, all he had ever managed to make her give him was her body. She had never given him her soul. And in the past year, he'd had neither. It couldn't go on that way. He'd played the gentleman for too long. It was time to start claiming his rights as a husband.

JENNIFER STARED at the bedroom ceiling, listening to Richard's measured footsteps as he moved around the house. She knew he thought she was asleep. He was still unaware that she had learned to mimic the regular breathing and relaxed posture of sleep a long time ago.

She rolled to her side, hugging her pillow. She carried such guilt for what she had done to Richard, for what she still did. He had married her in good faith, thinking she loved him. He had been so good to her, so kind and loving. And she had never been able to reciprocate those feelings. When she had reached the point that she could no longer pretend passion for him, he'd told her he didn't care if they stopped sleeping together, just as long as they were together in every other way. How could she even think of leaving him? She owed him so much.

They had reached an understanding that they both seemed able to live with, and their lives had settled into a reassuring routine in which, while there were no peaks of joy, there were at least no valleys of despair. Everything had been neat and orderly—until Craig's return.

Now her body burned with need, where before she had felt frozen with dispassion. She ached for the touch of a hand holding hers, dances in the moonlight, a secret smile. With a desire more powerful than any she had ever known, she wanted to live the promise Craig had given her so very long ago.

She brought the pillow up and buried her face in the soft down to muffle the sob that racked her. What crime had she and Craig committed? What sin? What terrible thing had they unconsciously done that was so bad they had been sentenced to live their lives in such unhappiness?

CRAIG AND FRANK WENT INTO THE HOSPITAL the next day. After checking in, Craig was taken to radiology, where fluorescent dye was injected into his kidneys. They were then X-rayed to see if they were normal. After the X ray he went to the lab, where more blood was taken. He was on his way back to his room when Arnold Vitrale, the head of the transplant team, met him in the hallway.

"You're scheduled to meet with me in my office later this afternoon to discuss the surgery, but since I have some time free, why don't we go there now?" he said, holding his arm out in the direction he wanted Craig to go.

"That isn't necessary," Craig replied. "My own doctor thoroughly explained the procedure to me."

"I'm not asking you to indulge me in my frequent need to talk shop or to spend an hour or two in idle conversation, Mr. Templeton. I happen to take the 'informed consent' rule very seriously. I want you to be aware of everything that will happen to you tomorrow, from the hair that will be shaved from your body to the chances your father has for a full recovery."

Realizing it was useless to protest any further, Craig followed him down the hall.

The surgeon's office was much like the doctor himself, sparse and antiseptic looking. Nothing personal intruded on the professional. The only thing out of sync with the sterility was a tidy mustache on the doctor, precisely trimmed so that it fit in perfectly with the geometric angles of the middle-aged man's narrow face.

Once Craig was seated, Vitrale went around the desk and sat opposite from him. He spent a minute studying a file that lay open before him. When he looked up, he said, "I'm sure you're aware by now that you are your father's best chance to live out his normal life expectancy. While his sisters would be preferable matches, they are too old, and their health isn't what it should be for them to be donating something to someone else. That leaves a natural child with suitable cross matches as a close second best."

He laid the file down once more and leaned back in his chair. "Personally, I much prefer using cadavers as donors, but there are so many younger people ahead of your father that I'm afraid if we wait, it will be too late. He's already exhibiting renal failure damage to other parts of his body."

"I thought he was on dialysis," Craig said.

"Ah, yes, what people have come to think of as the 'wonder machine.' For all that's been written about hemodialysis, very few articles have bothered to tell the public the procedure is not perfect. Personally, I consider it little more than a holding measure to be used to keep the patient alive until he can receive a transplant. With dialysis, the blood is only partially cleaned. The complications of kidney disease—hypertension, cardiac failure, anemia and abnormal blood coagulation, to name a few— still appear even with the wonder machine. Tragically, most people assume that the thousands of patients waiting for transplants are doing so simply because it is inconvenient for them go through dialysis."

"Does my father have any of those symptoms?"

"Some hypertension and anemia. But, everything considered, he's basically a healthy individual. Otherwise, I'd never consider the surgery. Your father will be on immunosuppressant drugs for the rest of his life, so it's critical that he goes into this thing as healthy as possible."

"It sounds as if you believe his chances are pretty good," Craig said.

"They're a hell of a lot better than they would be without the transplant." He pressed his hands against the desk and pushed his chair away to give him room to stand. Walking across the room, he indicated a diagram of the torso of the human male that hung on the wall. "Let's talk about the actual surgery itself. On you, we'll be making the incision here." He pointed to an area on the flank that was near the ribs. "Now on your father, it will be here...." He circled an area beside the right hip.

Craig twisted around in the chair to see better. "Why the difference?"

"Since your father has no antibodies against his own kidneys, there's no reason to put him through the ordeal of removing them. By placing your donated kidney in your father's pelvic region, it also makes it easier for me to get back inside, should it ever be necessary."

"How long before you'll know if the transplant has taken?"

Vitrale leaned against the wall. "We'll know within twenty-four hours if wastes are being removed properly. However, it only takes a minute after the restoration of blood flow during surgery for us to see the normal color and tissue resiliency return to the kidney. Within half a year the single kidney in both of you will increase in size and output to match the workings of two."

Craig had heard the basic facts of the operation from Mike Stephenson, and he had read statistics in the articles he'd found, but Vitrale had brought a drama and intensity to the procedure that had been missing before. "I assume we'll be operated on at the same time?" Everything he had learned before said so, but he was curious to see if Vitrale conducted surgery in the standard way.

"You'll be in adjoining rooms in order to avoid any delay after your kidney has been removed. The kidney itself will be transported from room to room submerged in an ice cold isotonic bath. Normal sterile procedure will be heightened for your father because of the additional suppression of his immune system. The last thing we want is to have an infection set in when he can't fight it off."

"How long before I'll be able to go home?"

"I'd say someone in your overall condition should be out of here in about a week."

"And my father?"

"He'll be here at least two weeks. He should be able to return to full activity in about six."

"Then it would be reasonable for me to make reservations for next Wednesday?"

Vitrale's eyes narrowed suspiciously. "What kind of reservations?"

"To fly back to Oklahoma City."

"Absolutely not. You'll need a week or more of convalescent care and a clean bill of health from me before I'll release you."

"I have a doctor at home who—"

A quick condescending smile preceded his reply. "I don't care if your personal physician is Christiaan Barnard. I'm not turning you loose until I'm satisfied you're all right."

For the sake of avoiding argument, Craig agreed to the terms. Once the surgery was over, and he was out of the hospital, he'd do whatever he pleased. Until then, it saved time and energy just to go along. He asked to sign the consent for surgery and left to return to his room.

He took a few minutes to unpack the personal things he had brought with him before heading down the hall to Frank's room. He found his father alone, sitting up in bed reading a magazine that had a chestnut Thoroughbred on the cover.

"Come in," he said, noticing Craig standing in the doorway. "I sent your mother home for a few hours, but she'll be back later tonight. Meanwhile, it's just you and me."

"You were the one I was looking for, anyway," Craig said, pulling a chair up to the bed. "How are you feeling?"

Frank thought for a moment. "A little scared . . . a little excited. How about you?"

"I guess I don't have enough sense to be scared. This is the first time I've been a patient in a hospital."

Frank closed the magazine and laid it on his lap. He absently began thumbing the edge of the pages as he talked. "I'm glad we got this chance to be alone for a while." He paused, looking flustered. "I've been giving it some thought, but I'll be damned if I can figure out a proper way to thank you for what you're doing."

"I'm not doing this for thanks."

He eyed Craig closely, as if he were seeking the answer to his next question from the way Craig responded rather than from any words he would use. "Then just why are you doing it?"

"If I were to take the time to stop and count, there would probably be a hundred reasons—most of them selfish."

"I'd like to hear some of them, if you don't mind."

Craig leaned back in the chair, stuck his legs out in front of him and crossed them at the ankles. He rarely talked about his feelings to anyone. He scratched his chin and ran his hand through his hair. It was difficult for him to give Frank the naked honesty he wanted, but realizing his father's need, Craig tried. "It's not very often a man is given the opportunity to do something special with his life. I didn't want to let that opportunity pass."

"Seems to me, even if you were anxious to make your mark, the possible consequences should have made you stop and think twice about what you were doing."

"The only thing that gnawed on me was how I'd feel if I didn't try."

The room grew quiet, its only sound the magazine pages being rifled by Frank's thumb. "We've got a lot of years to make up when this is behind us."

Craig didn't have the heart to tell him that he didn't plan to be around long enough after the surgery for them to get to know each other, so he simply agreed and moved on to another subject. "Have you decided whether or not to enter Nightwind in the Preakness?"

Frank chuckled. "Is that just an idle question, or is the racing and breeding business starting to show up in your blood now that you're back in Kentucky?"

"What I know about it you could put on a saddle and still have room for a fat jockey."

"The decision is Andrew's. I figured I had enough to keep me busy without worrying about what to do with Nightwind, so I turned the job over to him."

"I'm sure she's in capable hands, then."

"Should be. Andrew's been around the business all his life."

"Still, I would think that like anything else, some people would be better suited to the job than others."

"I suppose so. But I've always thought the ability to do well in this business was something in the blood. Kind of like a special talent that's passed on from one generation to the next."

The words could have been Max's. He'd heard them often enough while he was growing up on the ranch to know them by heart. How strange that he would wind up being raised by someone who so closely resembled his own father. Craig looked at the man who had been partially responsible for giving him life. The disease that ravaged his body had taken its toll on his physical appearance, but it had done nothing to the penetrating sharpness of his eyes. "What is it you're trying to tell me, Frank?"

"I just want you to know there's a place for you at Mitchell Farm. I expect it might take a while, but now that we've gotten to know each other a little better, I'm confident that in the end you'll feel the calling."

"I appreciate the offer," Craig said. "But how would Andrew feel about my coming into the picture so late?" He knew exactly how Andrew would feel, but he was curious to hear what Frank had to say about it.

"Oh, I expect it might take a while for him to get used to the idea, but he'll come around."

"And what about Richard?"

This time Frank's eyes flashed suspicion. "What makes you think Richard would care one way or another? He has his own place to run."

"Does that mean Jennifer doesn't figure in what eventually happens to Mithcell Farm?"

"Jennifer will be taken care of when the time comes. She and Kyle both know that to keep the farm from being broken up there's a standing family tradition that it just automatically goes to the eldest son."

"Only now it seems there are two of us who fit the description," Craig said softly. "Which seems to defeat the purpose."

"I don't want you to get the wrong impression, Craig. I have no intention of shoving Andrew out of the way just because you've returned. I don't operate that way."

Craig smiled. "That's all I wanted to hear."

Frank stared at him, studying Craig as if unsure of something. Slowly a smile formed that turned into a chuckle. The chuckle became a laugh, the laugh a roar. The raucous sound brought a nurse to investigate. After Craig assured her Frank was all right, she shook her head and left, muttering to herself.

"You were testing me," Frank said as soon as they were alone again. "You wanted to see how far I would go to get you back here. What would you have done if I had said I would disinherit Andrew?"

"I think you already know the answer to that," Craig said dryly.

They stared at each other for a long time, each taking measure of the other.

"You could have shown up with curly red hair and bright blue eyes," Frank said at last, "and after today, no one could have convinced me you weren't my own true son."

"What's going on in here?"

Craig turned to see Agnes standing in the doorway. She was dressed in tan slacks and a red silk blouse and was wearing an expression of such serenity and happiness that she looked years younger than she had just the day before.

She came across the room and gave Frank a kiss. "The nurse said you two were being obnoxiously loud and if you didn't settle down, she was going to move you to the children's ward.''

''Actually. . .'' Frank gave Craig a conspiratorial smile as he took his wife's hand in his. ''We were trying to decide the best way to divide things among the heirs when you and I are gone.''

Agnes looked from father to son. ''Well, you were wasting your time,'' she said with an indifferent sigh, ''because I have no intention of leaving.''

A bittersweet feeling came over Craig as he listened to the repartee between the two people whom he had begun to find it easier and easier to think of as his parents. How different would he be now if he had been reared by them? What kind of a man would he be? But then, dwelling on the past had never been his style. Other than being desperately in love with a woman he could not have, he considered the person he had become under the guidance of Max and Wynona was precisely the man he wanted to be.

SURGERY WAS SCHEDULED for seven the next morning, which meant that Jennifer had to start her day far earlier than usual in order to make arrangements to get Nicole to school and arrive at the hospital on time. She had tried to talk Richard out of accompanying her, but he had insisted on being there just in case she should need him. They had arrived at 6:00 A.M., so that Jennifer could spend a minute with her father before he was taken to the operating room. She visited awhile, gave him a kiss and then left him and her mother alone.

''Shall we drop in on Craig?'' Richard said as they walked down the hall to the elevators.

''I don't think that's necessary,'' Jennifer answered too quickly.

''I just thought it would be a nice gesture on our part.''

"He probably wouldn't even know we were there. The pre-op medicine they give people before surgery makes them so drowsy that sleep is far more important than visitors." It was everything she could do not to snap at him for putting pressure on her.

"And if anyone should know about such things, it would be you, as many times as you've gone through this yourself."

"I'm sorry," she said, responding to the wounded tone in his voice. "I don't know why I'm acting so bitchy this morning."

He put his arm around her. "It's perfectly understandable. You're worried about your father." He pressed a quick kiss to her temple. "But I'd rather be with you when you're in a bad mood than with any other woman I know who was in a good mood."

They reached the elevators just as one of the doors slid open to unload its passengers. Richard looked at the overhead arrows to make sure it was going up before he held his hand against the door to allow Jennifer to enter first. When they were inside and all alone, he took her into his arms before pressing the button that would take them to the fifth floor. "I've missed you," he whispered huskily against her hair. "I hope that whatever's wrong between us can be worked out before I go crazy with wanting you. If only you'd talk to me—tell me what I've done wrong."

Jennifer held her hands against his chest. "I've told you over and over, Richard, it isn't you. It's me."

"That's impossible. You're the most perfect woman I've ever known. Whatever's wrong between us has to be my fault. If I were more attentive...or perhaps a better lover," he said softly, encouragingly. He didn't believe either, but he hoped the protestations would put her on the defensive and create enough guilt that she would eventually come around.

"Please don't say that. You're a wonderful lover, Richard." It wasn't the truth, but she couldn't bring herself to bruise his ego any more than she already had. How could she tell him his lovemaking was mechanical and passionless when he'd been following, word for word, the best-selling sex manual she'd found hidden in his drawer. How many husbands would go to such lengths to please their wives? "And I can't think of a way you could be more attentive. I know it's unfair of me to ask, but could you be patient with me for just a while longer?"

"If only you'd let me help you with whatever it is that's bothering you. I feel so left out of your life, sweetheart." It stuck in his throat to beg her when what he really wanted to do was teach her what it was like to be made love to by a real man.

If she weren't so valuable, he wouldn't hesitate to damage the goods a little in the teaching process, either. Patience, he told himself. The day would come when he would have the upper hand. As soon as he gained control of her share of the Mitchell fortune, she would learn what it really meant to be a wife.

Jennifer leaned her forehead on his shoulder. Again she was overwhelmed with guilt for having used him the way she had. "Just give me a little longer," she whispered.

"Jennifer, I would give you my life if you asked." He cupped his hand beneath her chin and made her look at him. A surge of satisfaction swept through him when he saw tears gleaming in her eyes. He had been stupid to worry. She was putty in his hands.

JENNIFER FOLDED HER ARMS across her chest and leaned against the doorframe as she looked down the hall for what must have been the hundredth time, watching for Dr. Vitrale. He'd promised he would come to the surgery waiting room as soon as the operation was over. Four and a half hours had passed, and still there was no word. It took everything she could do to keep from pacing the floor to work off her nervousness.

Agnes put aside the book she was reading and looked over at her daughter. "I could use a cup of coffee, Jennifer. Would you mind getting it for me?"

She gave her mother a grateful smile. It never ceased to amaze her how intuitively Agnes handled her three children. No, she reminded herself, it was four children now. "Does anyone else want anything?" she asked, glancing around the room. Andrew and Cybil declined, Richard asked for tea, and Kyle wanted a Coke.

She was halfway down the hall when Kyle joined her. "Richard was coming to help you, but I told him I would," he said.

"Thanks." She put her arm through his and matched her pace to his leggy stride. "Another inch or two, and you'll be as tall as I am," she teased, looking up at him. He had spent his early teen years in agony, convinced he would never get taller. Now, at six feet two inches and still growing, he was torn between basketball and resuming the horse jumping competition he had temporarily abandoned the previous year.

"Saying it doesn't make it so, Jen. You've become the runt of the family, whether you like it or not. Especially now that Craig's here. He makes you look like a midget."

They waited a few seconds at the elevator before deciding to take the stairs. "What do you think of him?" Jennifer asked.

"Who? Craig?" He held the door for her to enter the stairwell first.

Jennifer gave him an "uh-huh" as she passed him.

"I like him—a lot." He took the steps two at a time, exhibiting a lanky gracefulness.

"Why?" Jennifer asked as she reached the first landing.

"He treats me like an adult."

"What do you mean?"

"In case you haven't noticed, strange things happen to people when they get near thirty. They become so stuck on what it's like to be in the 'real' world that they don't even see anyone who can't vote and doesn't pay taxes. Craig's not like that." He stepped in front of her to open the door that led to the third floor. "Why'd you ask me about him, anyway?"

"I was just curious."

"Oh, yeah—like bears don't do it in the woods."

Jennifer groaned. "Is that the best you can do?"

"It is in mixed company." He bounded down the hall, shooting imaginary baskets. "Come on, Jen—what's up? How come you want to know how I feel about Craig?"

"I trust your judgment. I've been worried about Mom and Dad."

He gave her a who-do-you-think-you're-kidding look as he stopped in front of a row of vending machines. "Mom and Dad have never been happier. I heard them talking last night when I came to visit Dad. They're planning to ask Craig to move back here and take over running part of the farm."

"They can't do that," Jennifer gasped.

Kyle hesitated before dropping his money into the Coke machine. He stared at her. "I don't know why not. Seems to me it's the only fair thing to do. He is the oldest, you know."

"But what about Andrew?"

A scowl twisted Kyle's face. "Craig showing up is probably the best thing that could have happened. If Andrew ever gets control of the farm, he'll destroy it."

Jennifer's mouth dropped open. As much as by the words, she was stunned by the anger and frustration in Kyle's voice. "Why did you say that?"

"The only thing Andrew cares about is money. Quality can go to hell. He'd stab his best friend in the back if it made him a dollar."

"Don't you think you're being a little unfair? Andrew has had a lot of responsibility thrust on him since Dad got sick. He's probably just—"

"Andrew has loved every minute of it. He holds his position over everyone's head like he's been made some sort of god, and we're all supposed to bow down to him. John's even getting fed up with him."

Jennifer sorted through the Johns she knew, and only one made sense, the farm's head groom. "John Wilkins?"

Kyle nodded. "He wouldn't talk to me about Andrew until I said something first. But then he really let go. Did you know he's thinking about retiring?"

"Because of Andrew?"

"Why else?"

John had been the head groom at Mitchell Farm for as long as Jennifer could remember, and it had been a standing joke that the only way he would leave was in a hearse. His knowledge was one of the farm's most precious intangible assets. "And Dad doesn't know any of this?"

"We didn't want to say anything to him because he's been so sick."

Jennifer leaned heavily against the wall. She felt as if Kyle had knocked the wind out of her. "What are we going to do?"

Kyle took a drink of his Coke, then wiped his mouth with his sleeve. A slow, menacing grin appeared. "*We're* not going to have to do anything now," he said, his maturing voice dropping, as it occasionally did, in timbre. "I figure once they're on their feet again Dad and Craig will be able to handle Andrew without any help from us."

Jennifer leaned her head against the wall and closed her eyes. Where had she been all this time—in a vacuum? Why hadn't she been able to see what was going on? She spent just as much time each week on the Mitchell Farm, where her jumping horses were stabled, as she did at the Martindale Farm. So how could she have missed what was happening? Kyle and John shouldn't have had to go through what they had with only each other for support. If she had shown any strength of character, they would have come to her. But they hadn't. What kind of person had she become these past years?

"I'm sorry, Jen," Kyle said, coming up to stand beside her. "I never should have dumped this on you. You've got enough to worry about already."

Her eyes snapped open. "What do you mean by that?"

"Richard."

"What about Richard?"

"You know."

"No, I don't know. Stop beating around the bush and tell me what you're talking about," she demanded.

He shrugged and backed away. "I didn't mean anything by what I said. I just thought... Aw, hell, you know. I just thought things could be better between you two."

She stared at him, looking for some small clue that he was only guessing about her and Richard. She was disappointed. "How did you know?" But before he could answer, she threw another question at him. "Does anyone else know?"

He set his Coke down and jammed his hands into his pockets. "I don't think so." He shrugged. "Hell, half the time, I don't even think Richard knows himself."

"Then what makes you so smart?"

"Everyone's been so busy this past year with Dad and all that I've been pretty much left on my own. It's given me a lot of time to watch and listen to what's been going on."

"You know you're too darn smart for your own good, don't you?"

He grinned. "Not to mention devastatingly handsome."

Serious again, she said, "Kyle . . . please don't say anything to anyone about—"

"I haven't up till now. I can't see any reason to start."

If it wouldn't have embarrassed him, she would have given him a hug. "If I'd been allowed to do the picking, I couldn't have chosen a better brother than you."

"Finally someone sees me for what I am—Mr. Wonderful."

Jennifer groaned. "Let's get going before I change my mind."

They arrived back at the surgery waiting room just as Dr. Vitrale, still wearing his surgical greens, came down the hall. "Everything went according to plan," he said as he entered the room, a rare smile on his face. "But as I said earlier, I'm going to keep Frank's visitors down to just one until further notice. However, Mr. Templeton is free of any visitor restrictions. They've already seen each other in the recovery room and swapped a few stories, so you needn't be concerned about the two of them worrying about each other.''

"Is Frank awake now?" Agnes asked.

"Yes, and he'll probably stay awake. As you know, we didn't have to put him under as deeply as we did your son. I expect Craig will sleep off and on until some time tomorrow." He looked around the room. "Are there any more questions?" He waited for several seconds. Then, when no one spoke, he said, "Well, if you should happen to think of any, don't hesitate to call." He accepted their collective thanks and handshakes and left. For several seconds the only sound in the waiting room was a soft swishing as they listened to the doctor's green paper slippers slide along the tile floor out in the hallway.

"I guess Cybil and I will go on home since we won't be able to see Dad today," Andrew said.

"As will Jennifer and myself," Richard added.

Agnes looked at Richard. "I'd like Jennifer to stay with me today, if you don't mind." It wasn't the request she had made it sound; it was a command. She turned to Andrew. "I want you to drop Kyle off at school on your way home."

"Aw, Mom, that's not fair," Kyle protested.

"No...it's a C plus in civics that isn't *fair* when your grade could be an A with just a little effort on your part."

After a few minutes of leave-taking, only Agnes and Jennifer remained in the waiting room. "I hope you don't mind my asking you to stay," Agnes said. "This isn't Barbara's day off, is it?"

Barbara was the housekeeper who had been with Jennifer since Nicole's birth. "Actually, it is. But she agreed to stay until we came back from the hospital so someone would be there when Nicole gets home from school."

"And you don't mind leaving Nicole with Richard tonight while you stay here with me?"

"What's this leading up to?" Jennifer asked, suddenly suspicious.

Agnes brushed an imaginary piece of lint from her skirt before she looked up to meet Jennifer's demanding gaze. "Since I can't be two places at once, and no one in this family had the decency to volunteer to stay with Craig, I want you to do so."

"I can't," Jennifer breathed. She had reached the conclusion that her only chance to make it through the time Craig would be in Lexington was to stay as far away from him as she could.

"Why can't you?" Agnes demanded.

"Mother, please don't ask me to do this."

Responding to the panic in her daughter's voice, Agnes softened her tone. "We can't let him lie in that hospital room thinking no one cares about him. Not after what he's done for your father."

"But why me?" The words were little more than a choked whisper.

"Because I think you care, even if you'd have me believe you don't."

Stalling for time, Jennifer reached for her coffee. She stared down into the black liquid. If she had any sense at all, she would leave the hospital now and not return until Craig was gone. She couldn't stay with him. She wasn't strong enough to be around him and pretend she didn't love him. But then, was she strong enough to let him think no one cared?

CHAPTER TWELVE

JENNIFER PACED THE HALLWAY outside Craig's room. The orderlies had brought him from the recovery room only minutes before, and they were still inside with the nurse who had accompanied them. Jennifer's back was to the door when it opened. She turned and saw a young man dressed in white come out. He smiled at her and said, "The nurse will be finished in a minute, and then you can go in."

"Thank you." She mouthed the words but made no sound. She resumed her mindless pacing. Her mouth felt dry, and her palms were wet. She ran her tongue across her lips and wiped her hands on her skirt. Time had never passed as slowly.

"Excuse me."

Jennifer jumped at the sound. She had been lost in her own world and hadn't seen the nurse come out of Craig's room. "Were you talking to me?"

"I said you could go in now. Your husband is—"

"He's not my husband. He's my . . . brother."

"Your *brother* is ready to receive visitors." The nurse's smile was automatic and hurried as she moved past Jennifer. She was halfway down the hall when she turned and called out, "He's sleeping now, but if he should wake up and need one of the floor nurses, there's a buzzer attached to the pillow that you can use to call them."

Jennifer looked at the door to Craig's room. Panic that had been growing in her like cultured yeast in a warm oven finally bubbled over, so that every breath she took seemed to be an effort. Despite the nurse's assurance that it was all right to go inside, she held back. To enter Craig's room was to face herself. No longer would she be able to hide behind the mask of complaisant acceptance she had worn the past seven years.

In the end, it was knowing that Craig was all alone that prodded her into moving. She took a deep breath and slowly opened the door. The heavy orange-and-green striped curtains were drawn against the brilliant midday sun; the small reading light over the bed provided the main source of illumination. After scanning the room, she forced herself to look at the unnaturally still form lying on the bed. She let out an involuntary cry as she saw how deathly pale and lifeless he looked. She had never imagined him this way, stripped of his vitality...utterly vulnerable. Her fears for herself disappeared, and she was drawn to him. Slowly she moved across the room.

The sides of the bed were drawn up, and the covers were neatly folded across his chest. His arms had been laid on top of the blanket with toy soldier stiffness. One hand had needles taped to its back with tubes running from the needles to bottles of clear liquid suspended on a metal stand beside the bed. His breath was shallow and regular with sleep. Dark circles ringed his eyes.

For long minutes she could do no more than stand beside the bed and stare at him. Memories touched and swirled around her like the autumn breezes of long ago until she grew dizzy with their force. As if it were yesterday, she remembered how Craig had pursued her and won her heart...and how he had broken it. She felt the hurt all over again. But this time it wasn't for herself alone that she ached; it was for both of them. She knew now that she hadn't been wrong. Craig had loved her as much as she had loved him. And he had suffered as much as she had at the loss of their love. But the knowing brought her little comfort.

It did, however, bring her peace. It freed her from the bitterness she had used to shelter her wounded pride. Yet, without the hatred and the bitterness, there was no refuge for the pain.

She was caught between a man whom she loved and one to whom she owed her sanity. Without Richard she doubted she could have survived Craig's leaving. He had been kind and loving when she had desperately needed someone to provide a sheltered place for her to heal her wounds. He had never stopped loving and caring for her. And he adored Nicole. If he were ever to find out how she hungered for another man, it would destroy him. She had walked the streets of that particular hell. She could not condemn Richard to go there because of her.

She blinked away the tears that blurred her vision as she looked at the face of the man she was convinced she would love the rest of her life. She touched his hand, curling her fingers into his palm. The contact was like the release of a long-held sigh. She had come home, if only for these precious few hours they would have alone together. She would capture the time she had been given with him and selfishly store it against the lonely years ahead. If only for this one afternoon, she would stop pretending and allow her feelings free reign.

"I love you, Craig," she whispered, her trembling fingers brushing the hair from his forehead. "I will always love you." She breathed a kiss against his dry lips. "Know this and carry it with you until the day comes when you find someone who is free to love you as you deserve to be loved, openly and without reservation.'' She caught her breath in a stifled sob, turned and covered her face with her hands. God, how desperately she ached to be that woman.

RICHARD ARRIVED HOME from his meeting with Oscar Coscarelli, teetering on the edge of panic. Coscarelli had arranged their private get-together to accept the already previously postponed second payment on Richard's gambling debt. The normally soft-spoken loan shark had been visibly upset with the news that there would be another delay and had shown a violent side to his personality he'd previously kept well hidden.

Richard leaned against the wall and pressed the palm of his hand against his stomach, trying to ease the burning that was turning into a constant companion. He'd known at the time he was a fool to get involved with a man like Coscarelli, but the bet had seemed to be such a sure thing. The favorite horse was supposed to have been drugged. Which should have meant that even if the horse had won, the tests would have disqualified it later. But something had gone wrong. *Dammit, it was supposed to have been a sure thing.*

But the sure thing had turned out to be drug-free, leaving him with a debt he couldn't begin to pay off and a lender who maintained his reputation for collecting what was owed him with broken bones.

Three weeks he'd been given. How in the hell was he supposed to come up with that much money in three weeks? He'd already tapped his father for all the old man could raise. And another bank loan was out of the question. He went into the family room and poured himself a brandy, purposely moving as quietly as possible to avoid alerting Jennifer that he'd returned home. The alcohol hit his stomach with a wrenching jolt.

Like it or not, he was backed into a corner, and there was only one escape route. Even though it was a dicey proposition and an avenue he hated to pursue, he had to find a way to talk Jennifer into breaking the trust fund her grandparents had left her. He rolled the thought around in his mind, looking at it from every possible angle. He didn't doubt for a minute he could get the money from her. What concerned him was that he should manage to handle the transaction in such a way that he would come out looking like a hero to his dear sweet wife.

The brandy had begun to work its familiar magic, helping him to ignore the increasing pain in his stomach. An idea began licking the edges of his mind. The easiest way to manipulate Jennifer into thinking well of him was to tell her he needed the money to help someone else. Slowly a smile formed on his face. The answer was so obvious that he was disappointed it had taken so long for it to occur to him. He'd tell Jennifer his father was in trouble and that it was his old man who had run up gambling debts. In order to save his pride, it would be absolutely imperative they keep everything quiet.

His grin of satisfaction turned into a chuckle as he poured himself another drink and headed for the bedroom. Now that he had a solid course of action, he was anxious to get started. But after a thorough search, he discovered Jennifer wasn't anywhere around the house. It took a few minutes to remember he'd left her at the hospital with Agnes. Then he found a note from Barbara saying she had taken Nicole to the sitter's. He tossed the brandy that remained in his glass to the back of his throat and poured himself another before heading out the door.

Several hours later, he was at the hospital. As soon as he entered, he checked at the nurses' station for Frank's room and was told no visitors were allowed.

"I'm aware of that, but I'm looking for my wife," he told the gray-haired nurse in a voice he normally saved for the hired help. "She's either in with Mr. Mitchell or somewhere with her mother."

"Would that be Mrs. Martindale you're looking for?"

"That's right."

She peered at a chart on her desk. "I believe she's still in room 538 with Mr. Templeton." The iciness in her voice was more than a match for Richard's. "If you'd like, you can check for yourself." She returned to her work, dismissing him as easily as she would the janitor.

What in the hell was Jennifer doing spending her time with that interloper Templeton, when she should be with her parents? "Thank you," he told the nurse, his tone turning conciliatory, his normal engaging smile back in place.

He left the station and turned down a corridor, glancing at the room numbers to make sure he was headed in the right direction. As he approached Craig's room, it occurred to him that it was strange all of the doors were open except the one for room 538, but he gave it no more than a passing thought. Before going inside, he stood in the hallway, taking a minute to compose himself. His hand was flat against the smooth ash surface, ready to give the door a push, when something made him look through the small glass window first.

He saw Jennifer sitting beside a hospital bed, her hand stuck through the side bars, clutching her newly discovered brother's hand as if he were her long-lost friend. She had a look on her face she had never shown him—a loving tenderness that up until then she'd reserved exclusively for Nicole. Mesmerized by what he saw, he could neither enter nor move away. He continued to watch as the silent drama unfolded, perversely fascinated as he saw Jennifer tend to Craig's every need. She dipped and wrung out a washcloth in the steel basin sitting on a stand next to her and then gently placed the cloth on his forehead. When she had finished, her fingers trailed caressingly down the side of his face. If he moved, she readjusted his covers. She got up to check the IV bottles, sat back down and took his hand in hers again. Richard was about to look away in disgust when he saw his prudishly conventional wife raise her brother's hand and press her lips against the palm. Instantly the disgust turned to fury.

What in the hell was going on in there?

His first almost overwhelming impulse was to burst into the room and demand she give him an explanation. But Richard made a point of rarely acting on his first impulse. He purposely took several deep breaths while he allowed time to pass. Although it galled him, the hesitation made him realize that, for the moment, doing nothing was the wisest course of action. He backed away from the door and started down the hall, his rage scarcely in check, a balloon in search of a pin. It was everything he could do to contain his fury as he worked his way out of the hospital to the parking lot.

The bitch! All those years of catering to her every whim, and the minute he was distracted by his own problems, she went chasing after another man. And her own brother, for God's sake. The idea was sick. Perverted. It didn't matter that there was no blood between them. He was still her brother.

He stepped onto the sidewalk when a sobering thought struck. Could he have misjudged her all these years? Was it possible Jennifer was smarter than he'd given her credit for being? Could she be going after Craig because now he was the heir apparent to the Mitchell millions? Everything he thought he knew about Jennifer told him he had to be wrong. But it was the only sane explanation for her behavior. He couldn't dismiss the possibility. After all, if the situation had been reversed, he would have used it to his advantage. But naive little Jennifer? Never. There had to be another explanation.

"Richard?"

He swung around to see Agnes coming toward him. Dammit—of all people to run into. "Agnes... what are you doing out here?"

"I was about to ask you the same thing."

He affected a smile. "I thought I'd forgotten to lock the car. But what about you? I expected to find you at Frank's bedside. Or did you leave Jennifer in charge?"

"Frank's taking a nap, so I decided to come outside for a little exercise. I feel as if I've done nothing but sit for two days." She took a step forward. "Why don't I walk you out to your car, and then we can go up to see Jennifer together. I assume that's who you've come to see."

He needed more time before he saw Jennifer again. If he went back in there too soon, she would suspect there was something wrong and would rag him to find out what it was. "I just remembered I promised the sitter I'd pick Nicole up an hour ago. I think I'd better get her first and then come back."

Agnes studied him in the dim light. "Are you all right?"

"Of course I'm all right. What could possibly be wrong?"

"You seem upset."

"Just in a hurry."

"When shall I tell Jennifer you'll be back to pick her up?"

"You'd better make it at least an hour—no, make it two. If Nicole's hungry, we'll have to stop by somewhere to get her something to eat. I haven't had much time to spend with her lately. It will give us a chance to catch up on things."

"That's very thoughtful of you," Agnes said.

Richard smiled. "Yeah, I'm a real peach of a guy." He was careful to put enough teasing into the sentence to keep her from detecting the sarcasm.

"Sometimes I think you're almost too good to be true," Agnes said before she returned his smile. She fluttered her hand in a tiny wave as she headed for the hospital's side door.

Richard watched her leave, wondering, as he had a dozen times since marrying Jennifer, if Agnes could possibly know more about him than she let on. He'd never been quite sure he'd succeeded with the mother as well as he had with the daughter. Or, he reminded himself, the way he'd *thought* he'd succeeded with Jennifer. He clamped his jaw against the gnawing ache in his stomach. If Jennifer thought she was going to dump him for Craig, she had another think coming. There was no way in hell he was going to be left standing out in the cold after all he'd done to earn his position by the fire.

JENNIFER SENSED CRAIG'S SLOW ASCENT from the depths of his drugged sleep long before any physical clues became evident. Methodically she cleared all traces of her long vigil, emptying and returning the metal bowl she'd been using to the cupboard and pushing the chair she had sat in all day back against the wall. She was careful not to come too close to the bed while she waited for him to awaken, for fear she might unconsciously do something that would give her away. She stood in the shadows and watched his restless movements, listened to his soft moans when he turned the wrong way, and pretended she had every right to be there.

Craig's eyes fluttered open, closed and then opened again. A puzzled frown appeared and deepened and then was erased with a look of recognition. His gaze swept the lighted portion of the room before his eyes narrowed and zeroed in on the corner where Jennifer stood. "How long have you been here?" he asked. The words sounded slurred as he moved his tongue around to try to restore moisture to his dry mouth.

"Not long. I just dropped in a few minutes ago to see how you were doing before I left for home."

"Stand in the light so I can see you."

Reluctantly she complied, stopping several feet from the side of his bed.

"Closer."

She took another step forward.

"You look exhausted," he said.

"It's been a long day—for all of us."

"Is your head bothering you?"

"I don't understand what you mean."

"I thought maybe you looked so wrung out because you've had one of your headaches."

"I don't get headaches anymore."

"Oh? What made them stop?"

"I had the operation I needed." But only after she'd almost dropped Nicole one day after a particularly sudden and debilitating attack.

They had been together such a short time seven years ago, and yet Craig felt as if they'd always known each other. Moments like these made him realize he had a lot to learn about her. "How's your dad?"

"Don't you mean how's *our* dad?"

"Did the kidney take?"

"As far as I know. I haven't heard anything since… It's been a few hours since the last report."

"What time is it now?"

She glanced at her watch. "Almost nine." She'd had no idea it was so late. Richard would be wondering where she was. The last thing she needed after the day she had already put in was to have him chasing after her, asking questions she couldn't answer. She had to get to a phone.

"You've been in here with me all day." It was a statement, not a query.

"Mom and I have been taking turns between you and Dad." It wasn't exactly a lie. Agnes had been in twice to check up on Craig and to see if she needed anything.

"I see."

"How do you feel?"

One side of his mouth came up in a lopsided grin. "I've felt better."

"It's almost time for your pain medication. Do you want me to get the nurse?"

"No—I don't want you to leave."

"But she's just right down the hall."

"I'm all right."

"I have to leave, anyway. It's late. Nicole will be wondering where I am. And Richard—"

"Will you come back tomorrow?" The surgery or the medicine—something—had left him incapable of subtlety. The more he saw her, the more he wanted her. No, it wasn't want anymore. Long ago the want had turned into need. Without her his life was a desert; she represented rain. He lived in darkness; she offered light. When he was with Jennifer, he was incapable of maintaining the noble, unselfish path he had decided to take for Nicole's sake. The promise she held was too great.

"I . . . can't," she breathed, struggling to sound normal. She was so tired, exhausted from the battle to hide her feelings and from the effort to convince herself that what she was doing was right. Her eyes burned. Her throat grew tight with the effort to hold back tears. "Nicole has riding lessons tomorrow, and she likes me to go with her."

"In the evening, then?"

Please don't do this to me, she silently begged him. "Richard and I are having friends for dinner."

"Then perhaps the next day."

"Yes . . . perhaps." She had to get away from him before she broke down. She should have followed her instincts and left before he woke up. It would have saved them the additional pain of yet another parting.

"Maybe it would be best if you left now," he said, silently acknowledging that if she stayed any longer he would tell her things she had made evident she didn't want to hear.

She bent to retrieve her purse from beside the bed. "Would you like me to come back after I check on Dad to let you know how he's doing?"

"Why don't you just ask Agnes to stop by on her way home instead?"

Realizing he didn't want to see her again, even for the few minutes it would take to give him the report on Frank, made Jennifer feel as if prison doors had irrevocably closed between them. She knew he was right, but her heart cried out against the injustice. "I'll do that," she said softly. She looked at him one last time before turning and walking to the door. Then she left the room without a backward glance, afraid to trust herself even for the few seconds it would take to stop and say goodbye.

THE REST OF CRAIG'S WEEK passed with the precision and lack of spontaneity of an assembly line. At Vitrale's prescribed day and hour, Craig left his hospital bed and started the exercise program he'd been told was necessary to get his terribly insulted body back on the road to full recovery. Because he'd never known illness, he became an impatient patient. It irritated him to have to yield to weaknesses where before there had only been strength.

The first time he experienced an attack of dizziness, he analyzed and studied it as if it were a phenomenon somehow not associated with him and therefore unnecessary for him to take into consideration as he moved across the room. The result was classic and predictable. He wound up flat on the floor with a cut on his forehead and three torn stitches in his side. A stern lecture that included the possible ramifications of another such fall followed his unauthorized trip to the bathroom. The lecture had been unnecessary. The accident had convinced him he was not as invincible as he had first thought. For the remainder of the week he followed every instruction to the letter. The long hours of inactivity, when his thoughts invariably turned to Jennifer, also made him realize he had to get out of the hospital and on his way home as soon as possible.

There were clever and amusing cards and two flower arrangements from Jennifer but no more visits. Kyle, however, came by every day. In the beginning he stayed only a few minutes, but as they came to know each other better, the visits grew longer. Agnes conscientiously divided her time between father and son, and toward the end of the week, received permission to take Craig to visit Frank in a wheelchair.

The day before Craig had been told he could expect to go home, Dr. Vitrale came to his room and pronounced him fit enough to check out of the hospital that afternoon. After Vitrale left, Craig reached for the phone to change the plane reservation he had made to fly to Oklahoma city. Because of the difficulty he'd had getting reservations in the first place, he knew it would be next to impossible to exchange tickets so late. But he had to try. After checking several carriers and learning that the fastest way he could get home was by way of Chicago, he decided to spend one last night at the farm. By the time he was ready to leave the hospital, he discovered he had started to think of his final night in Lexington as a symbolic farewell.

When Agnes arrived for her regular twelve o'clock visit, she was surprised to see that Craig had packed and was sitting in a chair waiting for an orderly. "And just where do you think you're going?" she asked, her tone demanding as she stood in the doorway, hands on her hips.

"I've been sprung a day early."

"And why wasn't I informed of this wonderful news?"

Craig laughed. "Have you always been this suspicious, or is it something I bring out in you?"

"You've only seen the tip of the iceberg. Since I was three years old and caught my father filling the Christmas stockings, I've never taken things at their face value again."

Craig eyed her. "For some reason I get the feeling you're trying to tell me something."

She smiled benignly. "I can't imagine why." She systematically began checking drawers and closets. "Now," she said, snapping the lock on his suitcase closed after dropping in an overlooked razor, "you wait here while I tell your father where we're going. I won't be ten minutes."

"You don't have to leave the hospital to take me to the farm. I can call a cab."

"Over my dead body."

He didn't attempt to argue. In all the years he had been in business, he'd met few people as formidable as the utterly feminine and deceptively unimposing looking woman who stood across from him. "I'll wait," he said. He would have liked to go with her to see Frank for the last time before he left, but he was convinced Agnes would detect his reason, so he refrained from asking.

True to her word, Agnes was back in precisely ten minutes. She had a nurse and an orderly who was pushing a wheelchair in tow with her. "Hop on," she said to Craig, pointing to the wheelchair. "You're going home."

THE DRIVE FROM THE HOSPITAL to the farm was like a dose of medicine for Craig's soul. It was a glorious Kentucky day, and he immediately opened the window to fill his lungs with the pure sweet air, to purge himself of the antiseptic hospital smells.

The countryside was lush with the fulfilled promise of spring. Frisky foals ran beside their mothers on thick carpets of grass. The trees that lined the narrow roadways appeared overburdened with shimmering leaves; the sun felt warm and wonderful against his skin.

"It must be especially good to get outside after being cooped up for so long," Agnes said, glancing over to him.

"Words can't express the feeling."

"You do know you're going to have to be careful not to overdo things for a while, don't you? You're not as well as you think you are."

"Been talking to Vitrale, have you?" He saw the color rise in her cheeks and smiled.

"It's good advice no matter where it's coming from."

"Well, you don't have to worry." He reached up to touch the lump on his forehead. "I may be hardheaded, but one of these is enough to last me for quite some time."

"I'm glad to hear it. That means I can trust you to behave yourself when I go back to the hospital this afternoon." She turned off the main road to enter the farm property.

A profound sadness came over Craig as they drove by the lengths of white fence and rows of paddocks on their way to the house. In the short time he had been at Mitchell Farm, he had come to feel a sense of belonging. He would miss it when he was gone.

No one was at the house when they arrived. "Kyle won't be home until later this evening," Agnes said, removing Craig's suitcase from the trunk. "Which means you have the afternoon all to yourself. After you've taken a nap, why don't you wander around the house a bit? Poke into anything you like. It'll help you get to know the place and make it easier for you to think of it as home. There's a whole shelf of family albums and some history books on the farm in the library. And there's plenty of food in the kitchen if you get hungry." She waved off his attempt to take his suitcase as they walked into the house.

"But don't fill up too much. I'm only going to stay at the hospital a couple of hours, so I'll be home in plenty of time to fix supper for you. Before I go, I'll write down Jennifer's and Andrew's telephone numbers and leave them beside the hall phone in case you should need to get in touch with someone in a hurry. They're both within ten minutes of here." She stopped and looked at him, as if taken aback by what she had just said. "What's the matter with me? I shouldn't even be thinking of going back to the hospital until I've made arrangements for someone to come and stay here with you.''

Craig met her steady gaze with one that was meant to intimidate. ''There's a point where I put my foot down, and you've just reached it.''

She yielded without further argument. ''Are you sure you'll be all right?''

He put his large hands on her small shoulders. ''Not only will I be all right, but the quiet will be good for me. It will help me recharge my batteries. When someone has lived his life pretty much a solitary creature, having a family around takes some getting used to.''

She gave him a quick kiss. ''Call me if you need me?''

''I promise.'' He walked her to the door. As soon as she turned onto the main road, he went back inside.

The massive entrance hall seemed cold and cavernous as he stood there alone. Deciding he would never be able to sleep that night if he took a nap, he chose to explore the house. He wanted the rooms and how they looked to be set in his memory for the years to come. That way, when he thought of his parents, he would be able to picture them in their house as they went about their daily lives. He started with the room to his left, the one Agnes had called the library.

The large sliding doors silently disappeared into their sleeves, revealing a large rectangular area where three of the walls were covered with floor-to-ceiling bookshelves. The fourth wall held a massive fireplace that was flanked by two bay windows. Above the fireplace was a painting of a man. The painting drew his attention, and he crossed the room to have a closer look. At first he thought his father must have posed for the picture as a young man but then realized the clothing was from a much earlier time.

The resemblance to Frank was uncanny. Both men possessed the same square jaw and deep-set dark eyes. Their hair was thick and black, their bodies tall and lanky. There was even an aura of self-assuredness that tied them together.

A sense of recognition struck like a well-aimed baseball. He spotted a small gold plate attached to the bottom of the picture frame and stepped up to the hearth to read the engraving. There were just two words and a date written on the plate. Lawrence Mitchell—1935.

Again Craig looked up at the man in the painting. Lawrence Mitchell, unless he was wildly mistaken, was his grandfather. Staring at the painting produced an eerie feeling, much like looking in a mirror and seeing a slightly altered version of himself. He shook his head in wonder. The original Mitchell genes must have been powerful. How else could they have mixed with others for so many generations and remain so remarkably undiluted to pass such striking characteristics from father to son?

He turned from the painting and glanced at the bookshelves, wondering where to begin looking for the photograph albums and history books Agnes had told him about. His gaze skimmed the rows of books, seeking something out of the ordinary. He found what he was looking for on the bottom shelf of the back wall. After giving a cursory examination to yellowed photographs of unknown relatives, he took the most recent albums over to a loose-cushioned chair in front of the fireplace, propped his feet up and began going through childhood pictures of Andrew, Jennifer and Kyle.

An hour and a half later, a car door slammed and woke Craig from a dozing sleep. He jumped and made a grab for the album he had been leafing through when it started to fall from his lap. The resulting pain in his side stole his breath. He slowly left the chair and went over to the window to push the curtain aside. Agnes's Jaguar was parked out front.

He turned when he heard the front door open, prepared to see his mother and surprised when it was Kyle who came into the room. "I thought you were staying after school today," Craig said.

"Practice let out early, so I took a bus over to the hospital." He sat down sideways in one of the twin damask-covered chairs, hanging one leg over the arm, sticking the other straight out in front of him. "Mom said you were here all by yourself, so I decided to come home and keep you company."

Craig gingerly stretched, trying to loosen a kink he'd acquired in his neck while sleeping in the chair. "I'm glad you're here. You can save me the trouble of looking through all those books to pick up a little history about this place."

"You don't like to read either, huh?"

Actually, Craig did like to read, but he wanted to hear what Kyle had to say. "Not when I've got someone like you around," he said.

Kyle's suspended leg started to swing; his heel tapped lightly against the chair. "How far back do you want me to go?"

Craig glanced at the painting. "For now, why don't we start with Lawrence Mitchell?"

Kyle looked from Craig to the painting and then back again. "It's hard for me to remember you've never met Grandpa. You'd like him . . . and Grandma, too."

"I take it that means they're still alive?"

Kyle laughed. "Everyone should be so alive. We hardly see them anymore. If they aren't off cruising or mountain climbing somewhere, they're in California or Florida staying at one of their condos and playing golf.''

Craig smiled at the sound of envy in Kyle's voice. "How did the farm do when Lawrence had it?''

"All right. As far as I know, the farm's always been in good hands. I guess when you're raised knowing something like this is going to be yours someday, you take the responsibility seriously.'' He grew quiet, thoughtful. "Maybe sometimes you take it too seriously.''

"How could you take that kind of responsibility too seriously?'' Craig asked gently, aware of the change in Kyle. Though wary of pushing him too hard, Craig was curious to hear his answer.

He shrugged. "I don't know.'' He waited for Craig to fill the silence with another question. When he didn't, Kyle reluctantly expanded his answer. "I think sometimes Andrew gets so wrapped up in what he's doing he forgets he's just the caretaker for the farm until the next generation is ready to take over.'' He gave Craig an intense look, as if trying to decide how far he should go and whether or not his new brother would understand what he was trying to say.

"You see,'' Kyle continued, "the farm isn't like other kinds of businesses. It's something that's meant to go on living even after the people who take care of it die. That way, a little bit of those people can go on, too.'' He stopped talking and stared at the carpet as if it had suddenly developed a compelling fascination. When he looked up again, his face was flushed a spotted crimson.

"Don't ever feel embarrassed because you feel strongly about something,'' Craig said quietly. "The most boring people I've ever met are the passionless ones.''

"You'll see what I'm talking about after you've been here awhile.''

Craig knew that Jennifer would understand why he had to leave and that Frank and Agnes would never understand his going, but that they would forgive him. Kyle would do neither. "I already know what you mean, Kyle. I once felt the same way about the ranch where I grew up. Max and Wynona—my other parents—felt about their place the way you feel about Mitchell Farm."

"Is that why they took you? Because they needed someone to pass their ranch to?"

"Max and Wynona had nothing to do with the kidnapping. But I think you're right about the reason they kept me after they found out who I really was."

"Why don't you live on the ranch anymore? What happened that made you leave?"

"Nothing was the same after I found out who I was."

Kyle frowned in puzzlement. "I don't understand. I thought you just found out who you were a couple of weeks ago."

Craig was going to have to be more careful. Kyle was too sharp for him to let his guard down the way he just had. "I've known about the kidnapping for several years, but I could never see much sense in turning everybody's lives upside down just to get reacquainted. When I heard about Frank being sick, all that changed."

"If I ever found out I was kidnapped, nothing could keep me away from my real parents. Weren't you ever curious about them? Didn't you want to know if you had any brothers or sisters?"

Craig leaned forward, resting his elbows on his knees, staring down at his hands. "I had some things I had to work out first."

"What kind of things?"

Kyle wasn't going to let go. He had the brash curiosity of youth and wasn't hesitant to use it to his advantage.

"Why don't we talk about my reasons another time and go into the kitchen to get something to eat? I'm starved."

"Just tell me one thing," he insisted. "How long have you known?"

Craig studied Kyle. Although he couldn't understand why, the answer was obviously important to him. "I'd just as soon not everyone knew that."

"You can trust me. I won't tell anybody."

There was no doubt in Craig's mind that Kyle meant what he said. But from the time they had spent together in the hospital, he also knew that, given enough information, Kyle would be able to put pieces of his and Jennifer's puzzle together that were better left apart. Because Kyle was the only sixteen-year-old Craig knew, he wasn't sure whether his younger brother was extraordinarily intuitive or simply a typical teenager. His gut instinct told him it was the former.

"Well?" Kyle prodded.

"It's been about six or seven years," he finally answered. Instead of the rash of questions Craig had assumed would follow, Kyle grew silent, thoughtful. Craig was on the verge of questioning him about the silence when the sound of a car coming up the driveway stopped him.

Kyle untangled his legs and arms from around the chair to go over to the window to look outside. "It's Jennifer and Nicole," he said, a peculiar mixture of relief and anticipation in his voice.

CHAPTER THIRTEEN

"GRANDMA...GRANDMA," a child's voice echoed in the hallway.

"We're in here," Kyle answered.

A young girl wearing jodhpurs and a riding jacket came bounding into the library. She was halfway into the room when she noticed Craig and stopped. The smile disappeared and was replaced by a puzzled frown. She looked from Kyle to Craig and back again.

"Come in and meet your new uncle, Nicole," Kyle said.

Instead of going over to Craig, she moved toward Kyle, never taking her eyes from the stranger as she sidestepped across the room. When she reached his familiar form, she leaned her shoulder into his thigh and peered up at him. "How come he looks so much like Grandpa?" she asked in a hushed tone.

Craig stared at Nicole hard. He realized he was frightening her by how intently he was looking at her, but he was unable to stop. She was tall for her six years, with long black hair that almost reached her waist. Her eyes were large and so dark they could have been black. Although her features were immature, it was evident they would someday be pronounced and angular—just as her great-grandfather's and her grandfather's were. *Just as his were.*

Even as the implications became clear, he managed to remain outwardly calm. The desire to cross the room and take his daughter in his arms was modified by how unfathomable and upsetting his actions would seem to her.

There was the sound of a sharp intake of breath behind him, and he looked up to see Jennifer standing in the doorway. The color left her face as her gaze swung from Craig to Nicole and then back to Craig again.

"What's wrong, Mommy?"

"Nothing," Jennifer said. But the reassuring smile she tried to give her daughter never made it to her lips. What she had feared the most had come to pass. She could see the uselessness of trying to deny who Nicole was written on Craig's face. Unable to bear the anger and hurt she also saw there, she looked at Kyle. "Have you introduced Nicole to Craig?"

"I was about to when you came in."

"Well, why don't you finish and take her down to the barns to see John? If you don't mind, I'd like to talk to Craig alone for a little while." There was nowhere to run anymore. It was time to face him and try to make him understand what she had done.

Kyle put his hand on Nicole's shoulder and guided her across the room. "Nicole, this is your Uncle Craig. Craig, this is Nicole."

As she had been taught to do, Nicole held out her hand. "I'm pleased to meet you," Craig said, his heartbeat sounding deafening in his ears. A band of emotion wrapped itself painfully around his chest. Aside from all of himself that he could see in Nicole, he could see Jennifer, too. The innocent love that had created the child in front of him returned with breathtaking force, filling him with a longing that destroyed his old boundaries of loneliness.

"I'm pleased to meet you, too," she said softly, staring at him with open curiosity.

"Come on, Nicole. Let's go see what John is doing." Kyle affectionately ruffled her hair as he led her out of the room.

When Craig heard the front door close, he got up and went over to the window. He saw Kyle reach down and pick Nicole up, lifting her high into the air and around to his back. She swung her legs over his shoulders with a graceful ease, indicative of the number of times she had ridden that way before. As soon as she was settled, they started down the driveway. They hadn't gone far when Nicole turned and saw Craig watching her. She gave him a tentative smile and brought her hand up in a tiny wave. His heart skipped a beat.

He watched them until they were out of sight before he turned to Jennifer. "Why didn't you tell me?" he demanded softly. "You had to have known what it would mean to me to find out Nicole was mine."

"She isn't yours," she said, her tone defeated. She felt as if she had been stripped of everything, even her ability to give her protection to those she loved. In the beginning she had thought to shield Nicole and Richard from Craig. But once she had come to know Craig again, she realized he was the one who needed sheltering. She had sensed that his never being able to claim Nicole as his own would haunt him for the rest of his life. The torment and frustration she saw on his face told her she had been right. "She's mine . . . and Richard's. He was with me when she was born and has been with both of us ever since. He's the only father Nicole has ever known."

"None of that matters now."

"You're wrong. It's all that matters." How long would she have to fight a battle she desperately wanted to lose? "Don't you see?" Her voice held a wrenching plea for him to understand. "We don't count anymore. Nicole and

Richard are the only ones who count now. We have no right to destroy two completely innocent people." She had thought the pain couldn't be any worse. How little she'd known. Seeing her own heartbreak reflected on Craig's face was tearing her apart.

"What makes you so sure that if Nicole knew I was her real father it would destroy her?"

"She loves Richard."

"I wouldn't ask her to stop loving him."

"Yes you would. You'd never be satisfied with a long-distance relationship. Eventually you'd want to take her away from him and have her live with you."

"She's not the only one I would take from Richard if I could," he said, his voice stripped of all pretense, naked with longing.

She recoiled at the intimacy. "You're too late." She had committed herself to Richard, and he had done nothing to deserve the breaking of that commitment.

"I refuse to believe that."

"You have no choice." She met his determination with a monotone that conveyed finality.

The man he had been seven years ago would have responded to the plea in Jennifer's voice to leave her and Richard and Nicole alone, but the man he had become wouldn't. Before he had known Nicole was his, he had been willing to sacrifice what he wanted for her sake. Now nothing could make him leave. "Do you have any idea what it means to me to know I have a daughter?"

"Yes...." she answered, her throat tight with unshed tears.

God, how he loved her. Every part of him cried out with the need to touch her. He held his hand out to her, mutely begging her to understand and to respond to his need.

Through the haze of tears she saw the movement, felt the yearning, and blindly turned to get away before she caved in. She was almost to the doorway when he caught her. "No," she cried, struggling against him. "Please don't do this . . . we can't . . . it's wrong . . ."

Craig let go of her arms and reached up to cradle the sides of her face between his hands. His fingers reached into her hair. He stared deeply into her eyes, communicating his love with an unspoken poignancy. Slowly he lowered his head to kiss the tears from her cheeks. His lips brushed her skin in fleeting caresses, each lasting a fraction of a second longer than the last, as if he, too, were fighting a battle for control he had no hope of winning. When the tears were gone, he reverently kissed her temples and her forehead.

She held herself rigidly, afraid to move even to escape. She tried telling herself she was in a dream, no more real than those that came to her each night. But she forgot to tell herself she was not allowed to respond to this dream. With a tiny cry of longing, she moved to accept his kiss.

Their lips melded and then parted. With aching tenderness his tongue explored remembered crevices, tasting the sweetness of the velvet lining of her mouth. The world they occupied ceased to exist, and they were transported to a place of innocence and fantasy, a place where those who loved long and faithfully were rewarded with a life of happiness.

Jennifer wrapped her arms around his neck and felt the taut muscles of his shoulders as he moved to draw her closer. She took a deep breath and brought the clean smell of him into her lungs. She ran her tongue across his lips and marked the taste. An ache filled her loins and scorched her breasts.

"My life has been empty since I left you," he said, his mouth brushing her temple. "I tried everything to forget but nothing worked."

"I know," she said softly. "Not a day passed that I didn't remember how it was between us those few days we were together."

"You should have hated me."

"I tried...." Over and over again she had tried. Whenever she lowered her guard and his image appeared, she had ruthlessly shoved it aside, telling herself he didn't deserve her love. But it had never worked. She would see him in Nicole's smile or feel his presence in an autumn breeze and know that what they had shared had been real. She had loved and been loved with a passion and completeness the ensuing pain couldn't destroy.

Craig covered her mouth with his, trying to absorb her pain and take it into himself. Love was supposed to bring happiness, but it had nearly destroyed them both. And now there was no way they could seek that promise of happiness without bringing devastation to others. "Do you want me to go with you when you talk to Richard?"

The simple, thoughtful question caused her world to come crashing back down around her. How could she do what Craig suggested? It was so unfair to Richard. None of the pain she had suffered was his fault. She couldn't repay his years of kindness with such terrible cruelty.

Her confusion about what was happening created a panic in her to get away, and she accidentally hit Craig's side as she twisted out of his arms. He doubled over as pain sliced through him, its violence causing waves of darkness that temporarily blinded him. He held his side with one hand and groped for something to hang on to with the other.

Jennifer swung back around at his gasp of pain. "Oh, Craig. I'm so sorry." She caught his arm and put it around her shoulders to lead him to a chair.

"I'm all right," he told her with an effort that belied the words.

She knelt on the floor in front of him, holding his hand while she watched for signs that the pain was lessening. When she was finally convinced he was going to be all right, she laid her head against his thigh and with a sad sigh said, "What happened between us today can never happen again."

Craig leaned his head back in the chair and closed his eyes. "Is your marriage to Richard so wonderful you would trade it for what we could have together?"

Her heart broke anew at the loneliness in his voice. "I owe him," she said softly.

"By now you must have paid him back tenfold."

"The kind of debt I owe can never be repaid."

"What is this magnificent thing he's done that makes you feel that you're chained to him forever?"

"He asked me to marry him."

"That's it?"

"I never told him," she whispered. "I knew I was pregnant with your child, and I never told him. He thinks Nicole is his."

Long minutes passed. Finally Craig answered her. "It doesn't matter."

A flash of anger brought her to her feet. "How can you say that? It matters to me. It sure as hell matters to Richard. And it matters a great deal to Nicole. Richard is the only father she has ever known. She loves him."

"But she doesn't belong to him."

"According to the state of Kentucky, she does." She folded her arms across her chest and walked over to the window. "In case it hasn't occurred to you by now, Richard's name is on Nicole's birth certificate."

"If necessary a blood test could change all that."

"You wouldn't," she gasped, seeing the determination in his eyes. "What's happened to you, Craig? You're not the same man I once knew. He could never have contemplated something so cruel."

He slowly rose from the chair and went over to stand beside her. "The man you knew seven years ago had died. Since then, I've learned to function in a different world. One in which it's the fittest who survive."

"I don't think I like the man you've become. I'm beginning to wonder if I still love him."

He caught her chin and made her face him. "You're lying, and we both know it."

She turned away. "I have to go. Richard is waiting for me."

He grabbed her arm before she could move out of his reach. For long seconds he stared at her, penetrating the shield she had tried to put up between them. "I love you, Jennifer," he said softly. "I'll never love anyone else."

The words, the look, the message were filled with such tenderness that they stole her anger. Her body lost its unmalleable stance and she stopped fighting him. "God help us . . . I love you too," she admitted.

Slowly he brought her to him. The kiss he gave her was filled with an aching poignancy. Without words he told her how lonely his life was, how empty he felt.

For an unguarded instant she gave him all that he wanted, and they knew how sweet life could have been for them. But it was only a moment before the control she had used to get through the years without him forced her to abandon the fantasy. She broke the kiss and pressed her hands against his chest. "I have to go," she said.

"He isn't what you think he is, Jennifer," he told her as he released her.

She responded more to the sadness in his voice than to the words. "What do you mean?"

"We'll talk about it another time."

The words telling him that there wouldn't be another time formed in her mind, but she knew he would refuse to believe her. Only her actions would prove how sincere she was in her determination to keep Richard from being hurt because of her. "I'm sorry about Nicole," she whispered, catching her trembling lower lip between her teeth.

"I know."

She ached to tell him how often just looking at their daughter filled her with loving memories that made her day to day existence bearable. But she knew the words would only cause more suffering. "If you had just come to me then," she whispered, hardly aware she'd spoken aloud.

"I tried to save you."

Tears burned her eyes. She had to leave before she broke down again. "When you go back to Oklahoma, I'll write and tell you about Nicole—and I'll send you pictures."

"And you think that will be enough to satisfy me?" he asked gently. "Surely you don't think I can be bought off that easily."

"Then what would it take?"

"To make me leave?"

"Yes."

"You and Nicole on the plane with me."

"That can never happen."

"Don't be so sure."

"Why can't I make you understand?" Her eyes held a desperate plea. His answer was a cold look of determination. "Damn you," she said, angry that he would do nothing to ease her burden. She turned and left, wanting to get away before she broke down completely.

As soon as she was gone, Craig went to the phone and canceled his plane reservation to Oklahoma City. He then put in a call to Henry Keily.

"Craig! I've been going crazy waiting for you to call. I was going to give you one more day before I—"

"I'm sorry if I worried you. I know I promised to get in touch before now, but . . . well, things haven't gone exactly as I'd planned. I'll tell you about it later. Right now I want to hear how everything's going there."

"You were right about the winery people. They've agreed to our price, and I'm just about to close the deal. Any last minute instructions?"

"Go with your instincts."

"Also, we've heard from Korato Morita and—"

"You're going to have to handle that one, too. I'm going to be here longer than I'd originally planned, so whatever comes up in the next few weeks is all yours."

"Were there problems with the surgery?" Henry asked hesitantly.

"No . . . it went off textbook perfect. I'm staying because of some personal problems I have to work out."

"Is there anything I can do?"

It was like Henry to volunteer to help without asking any questions first. "As a matter of fact there is. I want you to check into the background and any present business dealings of a Richard Martindale of Lexington, Kentucky. Use the Wulff Agency and stress discretion."

"And I suppose you want it done yesterday?"

Craig smiled. "I'm willing to wait however long it takes."

"Is that all?"

"For right now."

"Will you be calling for the report, or do you want it sent to you there?"

"I'll get back to you about that." The next half hour was spent discussing upcoming business deals and the best people in the company to assign to each of them. After hanging up, Craig stood with his hand on the receiver for a long time as he thought about the unexpected turn his life had taken that afternoon.

He was a father.

The idea both dumbfounded and pleased him beyond measure. He and Jennifer had a child—a stunningly beautiful child. There was no way he wouldn't fight for her with every means at his disposal. Despite all that had gone before, Nicole was his, not Richard's. Nothing, no one, could change his mind about that.

Craig headed for his bedroom to unpack, feeling more hopeful about his life than he had since he'd left Lexington seven years before. He knew he was in for a battle— he had no illusions that Richard would give Jennifer up easily. He was about to enter the most important fight of his life, and it was one he was willing to do anything to keep from losing.

RICHARD STOOD ON THE FRONT PORCH, sipping a snifter of brandy while he waited for Jennifer and Nicole to get out of the car. It had been almost a week since he'd witnessed the little farce at the hospital between Jennifer and Craig, yet it seemed as fresh as if it had taken place that morning. He could hardly stand to be around her anymore. If it weren't for the money that would someday come his way, he would have taught her a lesson she would have carried with her the rest of her life and then thrown her out on her ear.

As usual, Nicole was bubbling over with excitement. Jennifer, he noted with pleasure, looked terrible, wan and lifeless, as if she hadn't slept in a week. He bent down to accept Nicole's kiss.

"Hi, pumpkin," he said. "What's gotten you so stirred up?"

"Uncle Kyle took me to see John, and John let me help him feed the horses."

"Do you think that's work a proper young lady should be doing?" he said, the disapproval strong in his voice.

"John made me be careful not to get dirty. See?" She turned around for his inspection.

"Well, you seem to have done a good job of staying clean. But next time, I'd prefer you just watched. That kind of work is best left to the people who are hired to do such things."

"Oh, Daddy. That's no fun."

"Nicole!"

"All right," she said, hanging her head in dejection, expressing a world of disappointment in two words.

"And how was your day?" he asked Jennifer as she came up to the porch.

"Long."

"Why don't you let me fix you a drink? You look as if you could use one."

She leaned over Nicole, who stood between them, to accept his kiss on the cheek. She didn't want a drink but knew that refusing his offer to join him while he continued to drink would only put him in a bad mood.

They entered the house and then went into the family room, where Richard poured Nicole some orange juice before putting ice in a glass and splashing a healthy shot of bourbon over the top. He handed the glass to Jennifer. When she turned to walk from the room, he stopped her by saying, "Don't leave yet. I'd like to talk to you."

The last thing she wanted was to talk to anyone, especially Richard. But her feelings of guilt for what had happened earlier with Craig made her smile and act pleased to be with him. She sat down on one of the leather chairs facing the window, kicked off her shoes and propped her feet up on the matching footstool. "I'm all yours," she said, giving a tiny shudder at the aptness of the unintentional double entendre.

"Nicole...why don't you go to your room and get changed for dinner?" Richard said.

"But I wanted to tell you about Uncle Craig first."

Richard brought his drink up to his lips to hide the immediate angry snarl that twisted his mouth.

"Why don't you tell Daddy after dinner, Nicole?" Jennifer rushed to suggest, detecting Richard's peculiar reaction to the casual mention of Craig. A warning bell sounded. Could he know about her and Craig? Impossible. But then why was he so angry?

Reluctant to leave, Nicole glanced from Richard to Jennifer.

"Go on now," Richard said, draining his glass. "Mommy is right. I'd prefer not to hear about your new uncle on an empty stomach."

Jennifer's sense of foreboding grew. Richard never used sarcasm with Nicole. She waited until Nicole was gone before she said something. "What's wrong? Why did you talk to her that way?"

"Nothing. At least nothing that involves Nicole." He assumed a properly worried and solicitous attitude and came over to sit in the chair opposite hers. "However, there is something that requires our immediate and wholehearted attention."

She put her feet on the floor and leaned forward, giving him, at least in appearance, what he wanted. "What is it?"

Long dramatic seconds passed before he spoke. "It's my father. I'm afraid he's in a bit of trouble."

"What kind of trouble?"

"If he can't come up with a quarter of a million dollars by next Friday, he's going to lose the farm. And I'm sure I don't need to tell you what that means for us."

Jennifer caught her breath. Richard hadn't been exaggerating. While she had no fear for herself, she understood his concern. The Martindale Farm operated the same way Mitchell Farm did; Richard, as the oldest son, was therefore the heir. If the farm went, he would lose everything he had spent his entire life working for. "Why? How?"

"None of that matters right now."

She struggled to make some sense out of his news. "I assume he's tried all the usual sources to borrow the money?"

"He has. No one will lend him a dime."

"I don't understand. Your father's credit has always been good before now."

Richard got up to pour himself another drink, making a show of his reluctance to tell her more. "Banks frown on lending money to pay off gambling debts."

"Your father owes $250,000 in gambling debts? How could he—"

"He told me the bet he made was supposed to be a sure thing and that he couldn't pass up a chance to improve the breeding stock on the farm. You know how frustrating and embarrassing it has been for him to have you as a daughter-in-law. Your presence has constantly reminded him what a second-rate operation he has, when his lifelong dream has been to turn his place into one as good as Mitchell Farm.''

The difference between Richard's background and hers had been an unspoken barrier between them from the very beginning. Richard chaffed at the disparity between their families' wealth. She had tried in every way she knew to convince him that it made no difference to her and had never succeeded. But not once had she detected the slightest hint that it also bothered his father. ''I never knew...''

''It's not important now. What is, is that he's learned his lesson and has promised me that he'll never get involved in anything as foolish again. But if we don't find some way to help him this time, it won't make any difference. There won't be a Martindale Farm to worry about.''

She put her drink on the table beside her. ''How are we ever going to come up with that kind of money?''

Richard allowed the pause that followed to grow until it reached an almost unbearable length. ''I really hate to ask this of you, but what about using the trust fund your grandparents gave you?''

She was too surprised to answer immediately. ''I thought you knew. I passed the trust fund on to Nicole right after she was born.''

His hand closed tightly around the fragile brandy sifter. ''How could I know?'' he said softly. ''You never bothered to tell me.''

''Perhaps not...I don't remember.''

''If you haven't been using the interest from the trust fund,'' he said, careful not to sound accusatory, ''where have you been getting the money you've been spending since we were married?''

''From you.'' Their conversation was assuming a bizarre quality.

"Surely you don't mean to tell me you've been living all these years on the measly allowance I give you every month."

"It isn't measly—it's very generous. It so happens I don't need any more."

He leaned forward and put his glass on the table beside hers. "I guess that's it, then. I'll have to tell Father he's out of luck. And, I'm sure I don't have to add that we're out of a home." It was a last-ditch effort, and he carried it off with consummate skill.

Her heart went out to him. "Don't talk to him yet, Richard. I'm sure that between the two of us we can come up with something."

"If you're thinking of asking your father to advance part of your inheritance..." He let the thought dangle, giving her room to insist.

"I could never do that."

The muscles convulsively tightened at his jaw, making it difficult for him to reply. "Then I can't conceive how you intend to raise that kind of money."

"I have jewelry I can sell. Have you considered selling your interest in Nightwind?" As a special thirtieth birthday present, her parents had given Richard partial interest in Nightwind when she was only a colt. While her earnings had been phenomenal, Richard's portion was nowhere near enough to settle his father's debt—but the sale of his shares might be. He would be giving up a large amount of future earnings because Nightwind's real value wouldn't show up until she began producing colts of her own. But there seemed to be little other choice. "And my horses will bring in some. We can—"

"For God's sake, Jennifer, don't be grubby. Besides—except for Nightwind, which I wouldn't even consider selling because he was a gift from your parents—you're talking peanuts. It's too little and, by the time we ran around trying to sell all of your things, it would be too late.''

"I realize the resale value of most jewelry is negligible, but I have some—"

"What do I have to do to make you understand? We don't have time to hit every pawnbroker in the state to get the best price on your grandmother's pearls. I need a quarter of a million dollars, and I need it now.'' Uncharacteristically, he ran his hand through his carefully combed hair, disturbing the classic lines. When he looked at her again, his face held a compelling plea. "Can't you borrow the money from the trust fund even if it is in Nicole's name?''

"I wish I could, but it isn't set up that way. The money can only be used for her benefit.''

"And I suppose keeping a roof over her head isn't beneficial enough?''

"I don't know what to say, Richard.''

"Then don't say anything.'' His hands curled into fists as he got up. He had to get away from her. He was afraid that if he stayed he would lose the minimal control he had left and tell his dear wife precisely what she could do with the offer of her paltry pieces of jewelry and her pathetic show horses.

With a lithe grace, he knelt down in front of her. "I'm going to leave for a while to see if I can't work some of this frustration off before I wind up taking everything out on you and Nicole.'' He kissed her. "Forgive me, darling?''

"There's nothing to forgive, Richard. I just wish you'd let me help you.''

He took her hand in his and brought it to his lips. "I'll never deserve you,'' he said, nearly choking on the conciliatory words. "Don't worry if I'm a little late.''

She nodded and watched him leave. When he was gone, she reached for her drink. She was too stunned by all that had happened to move from her chair. The prospect of losing the farm had shown her a side to Richard she had never seen before and made her realize how desperate he had become.

How like him it was to keep the problem from her until there was nowhere else for him to go. He had undoubtedly hoped to spare her entirely. It didn't surprise her that he thought her incapable of raising the money. The only jewelry he had ever seen her wear was the cameo Craig had given her. He had never seen the collection of diamonds and other precious stones that had been passed from mother to daughter for generations of Mitchells, and she had never spoken to him about it. Most of them were in antique settings inappropriate for current styles, and the rest just seemed too much trouble to bother about. They were kept in a safe deposit box and someday would be passed on to Nicole. If one or two of the pieces were needed to help Richard, then they would be used for a good purpose. The jewelry had been given to her with no strings attached. Only tradition bound her to keep them intact.

She picked up her and Richard's glasses and walked over to the bar to wash and put them away. Tomorrow she would go downtown and start the necessary proceedings for the sale of her great-grandmother's engagement ring—a blue-white, nearly flawless five-carat diamond. She was sure it would bring more than enough money to get Richard's father out of trouble. And she would sell the emerald necklace to improve the breeding stock. It was the least she could do.

CHAPTER FOURTEEN

LYING ACROSS THE BED, his hands behind his head, Craig watched the orange glow of sunset reflect off the white walls of the bedroom he had been given to use while he stayed at the farm. The window's sheer curtains moved softly in the light breeze and created fleeting images of color on the clear canvas formed by the ceiling.

Agnes had been right—again. She'd taken one look at him when she arrived home from the hospital and demanded he take a nap. He wasn't sure how long he'd been asleep, but the smells of cooking drifting up from the kitchen told him it had been long enough.

As he had been told to do until he was fully recovered from the surgery, Craig sat up slowly and waited several seconds before attempting to stand. In addition to the rumbling in his stomach, a desire to spend some time with Agnes led him to the top of the stairs. He was about to descend when he heard a male voice raised in anger coming from the direction of the kitchen.

"I have a right to know where I stand."

The reply came from a woman, her voice too hushed for Craig to make out the words.

"I won't be put off about this anymore. Do you or do you not intend to let him come here and stick his nose into the running of the farm?"

As the female voice grew louder, Craig placed it as Agnes's soft Kentucky drawl. Occasional words began to come through.

"...can't...home...rights..."

"He doesn't know a damn thing about horses, and you're going to let him move right in, aren't you? Clever man, this newfound brother of mine. He 'donated' what was probably the most costly kidney in history."

"Keep...voice...hear you."

"I don't care if he does hear me. You can't really believe Craig has returned after all this time because of uncontrollable altruism. What do you know about him? What do any of us know about him? You haven't done as much checking into his background as you would someone you'd hired to paint the fences."

"...all I need to know."

Craig heard a noise behind him and turned to see Kyle coming down the hall.

"Loud, aren't they?" he said, obviously embarrassed that Craig had overheard Andrew.

"I was trying to decide whether or not to go down and interrupt them."

"If I were you, I'd let Mom handle him. She's about the only one who can."

"I take it he isn't too pleased about my return."

"You have to understand about Andrew. He thinks Mitchell Farm already belongs to him."

The disembodied voices below traveled in waves, thundering up the stairs and then quietly receding. "Isn't he forgetting Frank?" Craig said.

"Dad's been sick so much the past few years that the running of this place has fallen to Andrew. It's going to be hard for him to give any of it up now that Dad's coming back."

"I can't see that he's got much choice."

Kyle looked down at his feet. "It's not Dad he's really worried about, anyway. It's you."

"What makes him think I'm a threat to him?" Craig asked quietly, interested in Kyle's version of the answer.

Kyle gave him an incredulous, slightly suspicious look. "You're the oldest now."

"Andrew can't think Frank and Agnes would throw him out and turn the farm over to me just because—"

"Andrew really believes in this oldest son thing the Mitchell clan is hung up on. I overheard him tell Richard that's why he and Cybil haven't had any kids yet. He said he didn't want a son snapping at his heels until he was good and ready to have him take over."

When Craig hesitated a minute to consider what Kyle had told him, Andrew's angry voice filled the silence.

"There's no way in hell I'm going to let him have any part of this farm. I've put too many years into this place to share it with some damned cowboy just because he's lucky enough to have the right blood type."

"Kind of melodramatic, huh?" Kyle said.

"Actually, he sounds pretty determined."

"Yeah, but he doesn't have a leg to stand on. You're the oldest, and if Mom and Dad wanted to turn the whole thing over to you tomorrow, they could."

Craig eyed Kyle, wondering about the hopeful note in his youngest brother's voice. "I don't know about that. The courts might have a different opinion if Andrew cared to push it that far." Craig had no interest in taking over Mitchell Farm, but he was intrigued by Kyle's apparent desire for him to do so.

"How could they? It's a family tradition."

"But Andrew's right. He's put his entire life into Mitchell Farm."

"And he'll destroy it if he gets control," Kyle said, his anger mixing with frustration.

Craig was taken aback by the impassioned outburst.

"That's one of the reasons Mom and Dad are so glad you've come back," Kyle went on, almost pleading now. "They know the farm will never be the same once Andrew takes over, and it scares them."

"They've told you this?"

"No...not exactly."

"Then how can you be so sure about how they feel?"

"I hear things...and I pay attention. Before he got so sick, Dad and Andrew used to fight all the time about how to run things around here. Dad was always telling him the farm wasn't in business to see how much money it could make, it was here to produce the best horses money could buy." Kyle's eyes sparkled with emotion. "There's a difference, you know," he said hopefully.

"Yes, I know, Kyle. It was the same where I came from."

Below them they heard a door slam, followed by the sounds of a car leaving. Kyle started down the stairs, and Craig reached out to stop him. "Would you mind letting me talk to Agnes alone for a while?"

Kyle shoved his hands into the pockets of his jeans. "All right. But don't be too long—I'm starved." Craig was almost out of earshot when Kyle added, "When are you going to start calling her Mom?"

Craig looked up at Kyle. Everything was so black and white at sixteen. The grays didn't come until later. "Some things take time," he said, wishing he had a better answer.

Kyle hesitated, as if waiting for Craig to go on. When there was only silence, he shrugged and turned toward his bedroom. Craig felt the weight of his brother's disappointment. He was beginning to realize there was far more than companionship involved in having the siblings he had craved while growing up.

He found Agnes washing lettuce at the kitchen sink. She glanced up at him as he entered. "You heard, didn't you?"

Craig nodded.

"I'm sorry you had to find out how Andrew feels about your return this way, but it was bound to come out sooner or later." She put the lettuce into a colander to drain and dried her hands.

"I can't say I wouldn't feel the same if our situations were reversed."

She gave him a weary smile. "Well, as far as I know, you're the last of the missing Mitchell children, so there's not much chance we'll ever find out how you'd react." She pulled open a drawer and took out a knife. The tomatoes on the cutting board separated into evenly cut wedges at her quick strokes.

"Do you think it would help if I told him I have no interest in taking over Mitchell Farm?"

"How can you say you have no interest in running the farm when you've just returned? You haven't even had a chance to look around."

He was too stunned to answer immediately. Of all people, he'd expected Agnes to be the one to fight for Andrew's rights. Could he have misjudged so completely her seemingly fierce loyalty to her children? Or was it that she, too, was so afraid of Andrew's plans for the farm that she was willing to put her trust in a virtual stranger? "I have a life in Oklahoma," he said with gentle insistence. "Eventually I'll have to return to it."

"But you have a *heritage* here." She began tearing the lettuce into bite-size pieces and tossing them in a crystal bowl.

"So does Andrew." Because she had turned her back to him, he couldn't see her face. The only clue that something was wrong was the abrupt stillness of her hands. He went to her and stood beside her, giving of himself the only way he could. He knew she needed the comfort of reassuring words, and arms wrapped protectively around her, but that type of easy familiarity was not a natural part of him.

"There's no reason why the two of you—"

"There's every reason in the world. Andrew would never accept me."

"If he were told that he had no choice, he would have to learn to accept you."

"Why does everyone seem so intent on cramming me down Andrew's throat when it's something neither of us wants?"

"I don't understand how you can say you don't want to be a part of the farm when you've only been here a little over a week. That's not enough time to make such an important decision."

"You're evading my question." She glanced up from the cutting board and Craig saw tears in her eyes. He had heard in her words none of the agony that he saw on her face. The pitting of one son against the other was tearing her apart.

"The farm must survive," she said, a lone tear escaping her eye.

How often had he heard the same from Max and Wynona about the ranch? It was never the people who counted; it was the land. Without his consent, his entire life had been dedicated to that premise and almost destroyed because of it. He refused to be a part of its perpetuation. But his resolution was tempered by the gentle pleading he saw in his mother's eyes, and he decided to wait for another time to make his point. He bent and placed a kiss on the top of her head. ''Why don't we talk about this later? I promised Kyle I wouldn't hold up dinner.''

She smiled and reached up to lovingly touch the side of his face. ''You're so much like your father.''

He didn't have the heart to tell her the number of times he'd already been told how much like Max Templeton he was. Craig returned her smile and determinedly overcame his hesitancy to take her in his arms.

THE NEXT MORNING Jennifer rang the buzzer to call the safe deposit teller to the front of the bank. While she waited, she dug her key from her purse. Several minutes later she was alone inside a small room next to the vault. In front of her, on a low counter, was a metal box filled with an assortment of personal papers, silver dollars given her by her grandfather, and the Mitchell jewels. She loosened the drawstring of a small felt bag and emptied its contents onto her hand. In amongst several lesser quality rings was the five-carat blue-white diamond. She slipped the marquise-cut stone into her pocket and returned the others to the felt bag.

The emerald necklace was in its original box. It had been a long time since Jennifer had seen the necklace, and she wasn't prepared for its stunning symmetrical beauty. The large center stone was flanked by two matching stones of lesser size. All three were surrounded by brilliant-cut diamonds. The necklace seemed as if it had been designed with Nicole in mind. Her dark hair and creamy skin would someday provide the perfect showcase for the breathtakingly beautiful jewels.

Jennifer had thought the decision to sell the jewelry settled. But that had been before she held the ring and necklace in her hands and thought about the women who had worn them over the years. She realized they were not hers to dispose of so easily. She could not sell them without at least consulting her mother about the decision. And someday she would have to find a way to tell Nicole what she had done with this part of her inheritance and why.

Jennifer returned the ring and necklace to the safe deposit box and left the vault. She stopped in the lobby to call her mother and make arrangements to meet her for lunch. A half hour later she was at the restaurant, sitting at a table in the back where they were unlikely to be disturbed by friends stopping by to ask about her father. Agnes arrived five minutes later.

"Now, what's so important we couldn't talk about it over the phone?" she asked, seating herself in the straight-back chair opposite her daughter.

"Why don't we eat first and talk later?"

"Unless what you have to say is short, we'd better not. I still have to visit your father at the hospital and shop for our dinner tonight, so there won't be much time to linger over coffee."

"*Our* dinner?"

Agnes sighed. "I take it you haven't talked to Richard this morning. The three of you are coming to dinner tonight."

Jennifer felt cornered. "But I can't, I'm—"

"*This isn't a request.*"

Her mother rarely gave direct orders when she wanted something, usually finding the time-honored circuitous route Southern women had used for centuries the most effective approach. Since Craig's arrival, she had almost abandoned her usual subtle maneuvering. "What's going on?"

"Nothing special. I just decided the family should spend some time together so that Craig could get to know everyone a little better, and they could get to know him."

Jennifer didn't believe her for a minute. "But—"

"Now what is it you wanted to talk to me about?"

Still reeling from her last encounter with Craig, she considered flatly refusing the dinner invitation. In the end it was the look of determination on her mother's face that made her change her mind. She leaned back in her chair, dismissing one problem to concentrate on another. "I want your permission to sell great-grandmother's diamond ring . . . and the emerald necklace."

Agnes blinked in surprise. She laid the napkin she'd been about to put on her lap back on the table. "Why would you want to do something like that?"

"I have to raise money—a great deal of money—as soon as possible."

"Are you in some kind of trouble?"

How could she answer honestly and not break her word to Richard? "I know it's unfair, but I can't tell you why I need the money."

Agnes leaned intimately across the small table as if they were two spies exchanging information. "The hell you can't," she whispered harshly. "You would never ask to sell that ring and necklace if there wasn't something terribly wrong. Now you've involved me this much, and by God, you're going to involve me all the way."

"I promised Richard—"

"The hell with Richard."

Jennifer's eyes flew open. "What did you say?" she gasped.

"You've been a dupe for that man entirely too long." All remaining traces of the genteel Southern lady disappeared and were replaced by an intense, aggressive shrewdness. "Now I want you to tell me why you need that kind of money, and I want you to tell me right now."

Jennifer stared at Agnes, torn between her loyalty to her husband and the vehement demand by her mother for information. She should have known better than to bring Agnes yet another problem when her life was in such turmoil already. But there was no way to back out now. Surely Richard would understand when she explained the circumstances. "Richard's father is going to lose the farm if he can't come up with $250,000 in three weeks. He's involved with a loan shark over some gambling debt he couldn't pay."

Agnes waved away an approaching waiter. "Tom Martindale involved with a loan shark? That's the most ludicrous thing I've ever heard."

"Richard said it only happened this once and that his father has sworn it will never happen again." Her voice dropped to a whisper. "He told me the frustration of having me for a daughter-in-law finally drove Tom to the breaking point."

"And just what's that supposed to mean?"

"It seems Tom has always been jealous of Mitchell Farm and wanted a chance to—"

Agnes looked at her daughter and shook her head sadly. "Jennifer, you've spent so much time the past ten years protecting yourself from pain that you're like an ostrich with its head in the sand. It's long past time you stood up straight and took a good look around you. If you'd been paying attention, you'd know that Tom Martindale is incapable of what you're describing. He's proud of his farm and the horses he raises—and rightfully so. But more important—and something you should have figured out for yourself—Tom has sense enough to know that five times the amount he supposedly owes that loan shark is a drop in the bucket when it comes to making the kind of changes that would be necessary to redirect his farm.''

Jennifer felt the truthful sting of Agnes's words as powerfully as if they had been individual physical blows. Somewhere in her intellect she had known everything Agnes told her, and yet she'd never questioned Richard's story. She'd accepted whatever tales he fed her whether they made sense or not. She recoiled at her gullibility. How long had she been allowing herself to be so blatantly manipulated? ''But why would he make up something like that?'' she said, unaware she had spoken aloud until Agnes answered her.

''It's time you started questioning a lot of the things Richard tells you,'' Agnes said gently.

''What are you trying to say?''

''Richard isn't the man you think he is.''

Jennifer frowned in puzzlement. Where had she heard that statement before? *Craig.* ''What did Craig say to you?'' she demanded, unreasonably furious that he would talk to Agnes about her. The look of genuine perplexity that came to Agnes's face told Jennifer she had jumped to the wrong conclusion.

''What has Craig got to do with this?''

''Nothing,'' she said quietly. ''I made a mistake.''

Agnes studied her daughter. ''There's something between you two, isn't there?''

''What do you mean?''

''I saw the way you looked at each other that first day.''

''I was just stunned to see someone who looked so much like Dad.''

"All right," she said, obviously going along with Jennifer's reply for the sake of avoiding an argument. "That takes care of you. Now what about Craig?"

"You'll have to ask him."

Agnes leaned back in her chair and wearily rubbed her forehead. "I feel as if there's a wind blowing all around me that's changing everything so much I'll never be able to put it right again."

Jennifer searched for words of reassurance, but they eluded her.

THAT EVENING, as Craig was in the bathroom preparing for Agnes's impromptu family dinner, he glanced at the red slash across his flank that was reflected in the bathroom mirror. Other than the tenderness around the incision and a need for more sleep than he was accustomed to getting, there were no lingering effects from the surgery. He splashed after-shave on his face and ran a comb through his damp hair before wrapping a towel around his hips for the short walk back to his bedroom. He met Kyle in the hallway.

"Wow—that's some scar," Kyle said openly staring at Craig's side.

Craig smiled at the awe in Kyle's voice. "The truly amazing thing is how fast I'm recovering."

"Probably because you were in such good shape to start with. What do you do—lift weights?"

Craig rarely thought about his body; he took the natural leanness and subtly defined muscles on his arms and legs for granted. But he sensed Kyle would be disappointed if he told him he only worked out to make up for the long hours of sitting in his office, so he hedged. "There's a gym in the building where I work."

Craig was unsure how to handle the case of hero worship Kyle seemed to be developing. He was uncomfortable on a pedestal and far preferred his brother's friendship. Opening the door to his room, he called to Kyle, "Tell your mom I'll be down to help her as soon as I get dressed."

Kyle nodded and headed for the stairs, beating an invisible set of drums and singing a song Craig didn't recognize. When he was gone, Craig entered the bedroom. The first thing he noticed was that the suit he had taken out to wear that night had been pressed and now hung on the closet door. Only one person could be responsible—Agnes. Craig shook his head and sighed. She was the archetypal mother fighting to keep her family together with every means at her disposal. He couldn't help but feel sorry for her. She was in a no-win situation. Regardless of her efforts, her two oldest sons would never be the friends she wanted them to be.

The gift he had come to Kentucky to give his father had not turned out to be as simple and clear cut as he had thought it would be. Instead of melding into the strong family unit he had expected to find, Craig felt as if he could become an instrument of destruction. As he pondered the evening ahead, he dressed in his lightweight brown suit and pale yellow shirt, never stopping to consider the questions that might arise should anyone notice the expensive cut and quality of his clothing.

AT AGNES'S REQUEST, Craig took over hosting duties and met Andrew and Cybil at the door when they arrived. It was the first time he'd seen either of them since the day after the surgery, when they had stopped by his hospital room for a quick hello. Now he could almost feel the hostility radiating from Andrew, but it was Cybil who put him on the alert. The look she gave him was distinctly predatory.

"I'm so pleased to see you up and around again," she said, her voice low and husky. "A man like you should only be in bed for one reason." She laughed lightly at her witticism. "Well, maybe two. One does need to sleep once in a while."

She swept past him in a cloud of perfume. Andrew nodded curtly and followed his wife. Craig was about to close the door when he saw Jennifer's car turn onto the driveway. He waited for her.

As soon as the Mercedes pulled to a stop, Richard got out of the car and came around to open Jennifer's door. He stared at Craig while they waited for Nicole. As they walked toward the front door, he proprietorially put his hand in the small of Jennifer's back to see what Craig's reaction would be to the possessive gesture.

He needn't have bothered looking for clues to Craig's feelings about Jennifer. A blind man could have seen how much he wanted her. He was disappointed at the lack of subtlety. He had thought Craig a more worthy adversary, certainly not someone who wore his emotions on his sleeve.

The sense of satisfaction at realizing he was in control of the situation did nothing to keep a searing pain from shooting through his stomach. His satisfaction disappeared when the flip side of the coin showed itself. If the relationship between his dear wife and her brother had progressed far enough to allow Craig to look at her without attempted guile, it was possible Jennifer was going to slip from his grasp and be out of his control far too soon to suit his needs. Another wave of fire burned his midsection, and he brought his hand to his face, ostensibly to cover a cough.

He couldn't let her get away from him. At least not yet. Not when there was still a chance she would come up with the money he needed. Nicole distracted him from his thoughts about Craig and Jennifer when she came up beside him and put her hand in his.

"See, Daddy? I was right, wasn't I?" she asked, her voice bubbling with excitement. "Uncle Craig looks just like Grandpa."

Richard gave her hand a gentle squeeze. "Not so loud, Nicole. No need to let people in the next county hear you."

Craig moved aside to let Jennifer pass. She refused to meet his gaze even as she greeted him. Richard and Nicole followed her inside. Craig closed the door and was surprised to find Nicole standing beside him when he turned around. She had a questioning look on her face.

"I give my other uncles a kiss when I see them. Do you want me to give you one, too?"

Out of the corner of his eye Craig saw Richard glare at him. "I'd be honored," he said, bending and accepting her kiss.

"She has this keenly developed sense of fair play," Jennifer said as Nicole skipped across the entrance hall and entered the living room. "She's even careful to give her dolls equal treatment."

Craig glanced up to notice that Richard's anger had been replaced by a shrewd curiosity. "You've done a wonderful job with her," he told Jennifer, unable to keep the intimate tone from his voice.

"Thank you," she said softly before turning to join her daughter.

"How long are you planning to stay in Lexington?" Richard asked when they were alone.

"I haven't decided."

"You're fortunate to have a job with such a flexible time schedule."

"Yes . . . I am."

"You'll have to forgive me. I don't seem to recall just what that job is."

"Probably because I never said."

Richard chuckled appreciatively. "That could very well be the reason."

Craig motioned toward the living room. "Shall we join the others?"

"After you." Richard surreptitiously examined Craig as he passed him. His own wardrobe was one of the things he prided himself on. Well-made clothing distinguished a man, indicated his status the instant he walked into a room and lifted him above the ordinary. Owning expensive clothing himself gave Richard the ability to recognize it on others. He was positive the suit Craig was wearing had been custom-made and had cost him a small fortune. He added the surprising bit of information to the others he was gathering for his and Craig's upcoming battle over Jennifer.

Craig preceded Richard into the living room by five seconds, giving Richard just enough time to witness Andrew's blatantly hostile reaction to his new brother's entrance. A shiver of pleasure helped ease the burning in his stomach. It was heartening to know Craig still had a way to go before he'd walk an easy path with the entire Mitchell clan.

"Richard, why don't you take the bartender duty for tonight?" Agnes said. She took his arm and steered him toward the built-in unit on the far wall. "And please refrain from sneaking any more rum into Kyle's Coke, no matter how persuasive he might be."

Kyle's head snapped up at the mention of his name. "I told you that was an accident," he protested.

Agnes gave him a look that stilled further comment.

Craig crossed the room and sat on the sofa next to Andrew's chair. "Agnes tells me you and Richard will be leaving for Maryland tomorrow morning," he said, trying to engage his brother in neutral conversation. The Preakness, which was the second race in the prestigious Triple Crown, was to be run in Baltimore the next day.

"It's customary for at least one of the owners to be there when a horse is running in an important race," he said with lilting sarcasm.

Craig decided to ignore Andrew's lack of civility. "What do you think of Nightwind's chances?"

Andrew made a show of plucking a piece of lint from his pants. "I usually leave that kind of thing to Jimmy the Greek."

"I happen to think they're fantastic," Kyle interjected. "Nightwind's going to blow them all away."

"Has a filly ever won the Triple Crown?" Craig threw the question out to the room at large.

Before anyone had a chance to reply, Andrew's caustic laugh silenced them. "You must be the first Mitchell in five generations to know so little about horses."

Nicole left Kyle's side to come across the room and sit next to Craig. "Don't worry, Uncle Craig," she said, looking at Andrew as she spoke. "I'll teach you."

Craig glanced to where she had placed her hand protectively on his knee. Her championing of him had unceremoniously dumped him into a land of unicorns and magic. "Thank you, Nicole," he said softly, struggling with unfamiliar emotions. "I can't think of anyone I'd rather have teaching me."

Across the room, unnoticed, Richard listened to the exchange between Nicole and Craig and intensely studied the two of them together. There was a peculiar aura about them, as if they were somehow connected, an interrelated kind of thing, like summer and hayfever. Their eyes... their hair...even their skin color appeared the same. The air around him grew dense and cloying until it grew too heavy to breathe. Two people didn't look that much alike by accident.

It was as if he had been given his own Rosetta stone, which had allowed everything to fall into place. Although he'd never told Jennifer, he'd known for years Nicole wasn't his. In the beginning he'd spent agonizing months during which he suspected every man he met. But finally he'd given up trying to figure out who had fathered Nicole and contented himself that it was him she called Daddy. How incongruous that when he'd stopped caring who Jennifer had slept with, the mystery had been solved.

CHAPTER FIFTEEN

CRAIG STOOD AT THE BACK DOOR, watching Jennifer spoon fresh strawberries over cake. He had thought the wait for them to be together would be relatively easy. After all, he'd figured, hadn't they waited seven years already? What difference would another month or two make? But he'd been wrong. Being around Jennifer and now Nicole and having no right to their time was torture.

His gaze left Jennifer to sweep the small group. The dinner had been worse than he had feared, but not for the reasons he had originally thought. After three glasses of wine, Andrew had become almost civil. Surprisingly, it had been Richard who had caused the discomfort. He'd developed a thunderous mood that had caused even Nicole to shy away from him. When everyone left the dining room to move into the backyard for dessert, Richard had placed himself outside the circle of activity, a scowl on his face, an unending drink in his hand.

The more Craig saw of Richard, the more convinced he was the Wulff Agency would find something on him. It had been his experience that nervous men produced thick files. How he would use the information the agency found was another matter.

Nicole had come by her sense of fair play and loyalty honestly. It would take more than Jennifer's desire to be with him and a skeleton or two rattling in Richard's closet to convince her that she should leave her husband. But

Craig refused to believe it couldn't be done. There was no way he was going back to Oklahoma without her this time.

"What could possibly be so interesting out there?" a silky voice behind him asked.

Craig turned to encounter Cybil holding a tray filled with cups and saucers. "I've always been a sucker for sunsets," he said, moving out of her way.

"I'm a night person myself," she replied, winking as she passed.

Craig couldn't help but smile at Cybil's attempt at worldliness. She had adopted a walk last seen on Marilyn Monroe and affected a style of dress somewhere between Shirley Temple's and Dorothy's in the *The Wizard of Oz*. Her frills and lace were in sharp contrast to Jennifer's classic style, and the comparison made Cybil appear all the more like a caricature.

Out of the corner of his eye he noticed Andrew approaching. His brother's tight control had been replaced by a hesitant saunter. When he stopped, it was evident he had come to say something that made him uncomfortable. After several false starts, the words spilled out.

"With all that's been happening this past week, I haven't had a chance to thank you properly," Andrew told him, "so I figured it was about time I did."

Craig gave him a questioning look. "Thank me for what?"

"For coming back and giving Dad one of your kidneys. For a while there, we were all afraid we were going to lose him."

Coming back? So Andrew remembered their brief meeting seven years earlier. "It's funny how things happen sometimes. I only found out about Frank by chance.

If Nightwind hadn't won the Derby, I probably would never have come back at all.''

"Well, fortunately for all of us, she did," he said sincerely. He tilted his head slightly in acknowledgment of their tentative truce and walked away.

A slow smile formed on Craig's lips. Perhaps there was hope for him and Andrew, after all.

He glanced up as Richard crossed over to Jennifer and engaged her in hushed conversation. The look she responded with changed from worried to argumentative to accepting. She then left him and approached Nicole, who was sitting on Kyle's lap. After a few minutes of conversation, Nicole put her hand in Jennifer's and was taken over to Agnes. Craig realized they were reluctantly getting ready to leave.

Impotence as well as frustration swept over him. To stand by and do nothing while he watched Jennifer respond to orders from Richard galled him. Something primitive stirred inside him—a sense of proprietorship, an urge to demand he and Richard do battle for Jennifer as if she were a prize. The feeling embarrassed him. He was astonished at how thin his veneer of civility was. And he had no doubt that, if he were pushed, the veneer would disappear all together.

Jennifer found her mother, thanked her for dinner and told her that the reason for their early departure was Richard's suddenly developed headache. Agnes glanced over to her son-in-law and smiled knowingly. She gave her daughter a sympathetic hug.

"Are you still planning to attend the competition in Louisville next week?" Agnes asked, slipping her arm through Jennifer's as they walked toward the house.

"I haven't decided for sure. But if I do, I'll make arrangements for Nicole to stay with the Martindales."

"That isn't necessary. You know she's always welcome here."

"You'll have your hands full getting ready for Dad's homecoming."

"If I do get busy, Kyle and Craig can help out. Nicole seems to be quite taken with her new uncle, and he with her. I think it's amazing how well they've hit it off from the very beginning. Nicole is usually much more reserved around strangers."

"You never can tell with her," Jennifer said. They had reached the back door, where Craig stood. It was all Jennifer could do to look at him and keep the longing she felt from her face. All evening she had sensed him watching her, and more than once she had begun to respond to the need to go to him. Only with conscious effort had she managed to keep her distance. Richard's black mood had made her wonder how well she'd succeeded at hiding her feelings.

"Leaving so soon?" Craig asked.

Jennifer avoided looking at him again by concentrating on Nicole. "Headaches and parties don't mix."

"I thought you told me you had stopped having headaches," he said, his voice filled with concern.

Agnes's head snapped up. She looked from Jennifer to Craig and back again, her gaze penetrating.

"*Richard* has the headache," Jennifer quickly interjected, guiding Nicole through the door. The look on her mother's face told her more than she wanted to know. Someday soon Agnes would ask questions they would no longer be able to evade. She hurried Nicole through the rest of her goodbyes and joined Richard on the front porch, where he stood impatiently waiting for them.

The ride home was pervaded by an ominous silence. But instead of being intimidated by the quiet and Richard's mood, Jennifer became angry. Neither she nor Nicole had wanted to leave, and it had been selfish of Richard to demand that they do so. It was time they settled some things between them. First and foremost was the question of the quarter-million dollars.

It took longer than usual to get Nicole to bed when they arrived home. She seemed to have picked up on the tension between her parents and was reluctant to leave them alone. When a final glass of water had been delivered and an amendment covering her new uncle added to her nightly prayers, Jennifer gave her a firm and final goodnight and went down the hall to the family room to join Richard.

She declined his offer of a drink, wanting to be completely clearheaded for their upcoming confrontation, and crossed the room to sit on the couch while she waited for him to refill his glass. "I'd like to talk to you about the money you said your father needs," she began as soon as he had poured his drink.

Richard raised his glass to her. "I'm all ears, my dear."

His slightly slurred speech made her hesitate. He had been drinking all evening, and the effects were beginning to show. Not exactly the best timing for the probing questions she had in mind to ask.

He shuffled across the room to stand in front of her. "I believe you mentioned something about my father and money?" he said, his tone encouraging.

She realized she should never have brought the subject up. He had naturally assumed she was offering help. Her doubts would not be well received. But it was too late to back down. "I just wanted to be sure I heard you right yesterday. You did tell me it was your father who owed $250,000 to a loan shark for a gambling debt, didn't you?"

He gave her a withering look and brought his glass to his lips to take a long swallow of the golden-brown liquid. "Outstanding recall," he said sarcastically. "How do you do it?"

A warning bell sounded in the back of her mind. There was something terribly wrong. She had tried to blame Richard's odd behavior lately on financial pressure, but it was something more. The farm had been through difficult times before, but never once had he been anything but solicitous to her. Recently, it was as if a Mr. Hyde side of his personality had developed. "Perhaps we should wait until tomorrow to discuss this," she said and stood to leave.

Richard placed his hand on her shoulder and roughly forced her back down on the couch. "But I want to talk now."

The warning bell turned into a shiver of fear. In the years they had been together, Richard's touch had always been lovingly administered. "All right," she said, reluctant to challenge him further. "What do you want to talk about?"

"I want to know how you intend to come up with the money... to help my father."

"Is it really your father who's in trouble, Richard?" She paused then added quietly, "Or is it you?"

He glared at her. "What's that supposed to mean?"

"When I told my mother—"

"You *what*?" he shouted.

"I told my mother," she admitted. "I had to. There—"

"You stupid bitch. What right did you have to spread my personal—"

Jennifer recoiled at the venom in his voice. "Please, Richard" she said, desperate to make him understand she

had not betrayed him. "Let me explain what happened."
She reached out to touch him, to try to reason with him.
He flung her arm away.

"The whole damn county probably knows by now."

"She wouldn't do that."

"Oh, is that right?" he sneered. "Pretty good at keeping secrets, is she? Like mother, like daughter?" He
grabbed her wrist.

"Richard, let go. You're hurting me."

"Good. Maybe you'll understand what it feels like to
suffer a little." He slowly twisted her arm.

"What's the matter with you?" she cried. "Why are
you so angry?"

A mirthless laugh echoed off the walls. "Little Miss
Perfect. So pure. So prissy. But underneath beats the heart
of a liar and a whore."

She wrenched her arm from his grasp. "I'm not listening to any more of this. We'll talk tomorrow when you're
sober enough to know what you're saying. I'm going to
bed."

Fury burned in his eyes. "You're not going anywhere," he told her, his voice a threatening growl. When
she ignored him and started to get up, he swung his arm
and struck her across the face with back of his hand. The
blow made a sharp cracking sound, like that of a distant
rifle being shot.

Jennifer fell across the couch. For several seconds she
lay there, too dazed to move. When her head began to
clear, she struggled to a sitting position. She blinked to try
to clear the stars that swam in front of her eyes. Her hand
went to her cheek. The pain in her head was excruciating.

"Try to leave again, and you'll get more of the same,"
he said, staring down at her.

A numbness settled through her, easing the pain and softening the reality of what had just happened. Not even as a child had she been hit. It was almost beyond her comprehension that Richard had actually struck her. She gingerly touched her tongue to the corner of her mouth and realized it was bleeding. She looked at Richard. "If you dare to hit me again," she said with a deadly calmness, "I will—"

"Threats, my dear? How unlike you. But then I've learned lately I really don't know you at all. You're certainly not the woman I thought I was marrying. Who knows what you might be capable of?"

"Enough of the game playing, Richard. You might as well admit the real reason you're upset that my mother knows about the gambling is because it isn't your father who's involved with the loan shark, it's you."

"How clever of you, dear, dear Jennifer. Did you figure that out all by yourself, or did you have help?"

Her head felt ready to explode. "Why did you lie to me?"

His face contorted into a vicious sneer. "Better yet, why did you lie to me?"

"I don't know what you're talking about."

"I'm talking about Nicole," he shouted. "And all the years you tried to make me believe she was mine."

An odd feeling of relief swept over her, freeing her. "How did you find out?" she said softly.

"You weren't as clever as you thought. I've known for years. Only the identity of her true father remained a mystery. Until today."

"You've known for years?"

He walked over to the bar to pour himself another drink. "After we'd been married a while, I began to wonder how you could have conceived one child so easily and not another, even though we never did anything to prevent it. So I paid a visit to the doctor.'' He raised his glass in a salute. ''He told me I'm sterile. Always have been, always will be. Poor Doctor Hargrove. He was terribly embarrassed when he revealed such a startling bit of information. The implications were obvious.''

''Why did you wait until now to say something to me about it?''

''What? And kill the goose while she sat on such a lovely clutch of golden eggs? I may be many things, Jennifer, but stupid isn't one of them.''

''Are you telling me all I've ever meant to you is the money that will be mine someday?'' she asked in a hushed voice.

''Does that hurt your enormous Mitchell pride?''

''Not at all. It's the most wonderful gift you could have given me—my freedom without guilt.'' She struggled to stand, fighting a wave of dizziness.

''Not by a long shot. And you might as well sit back down and make yourself comfortable because I'm not through with you yet.''

She took a step toward the door.

''I'm not kidding, Jennifer,'' he said, his voice deadly serious. ''If you try to leave this room before I tell you that you can go, I'll do whatever necessary to stop you. Only this time I won't hold back. And I'll love every minute of it.''

''You wouldn't.''

''Don't tempt me. Putting you in your place is something I've wanted to do for a long time.''

''How could I have been so blind?''

''You saw exactly what you wanted to see.''

She thought of the loving times they had spent together in the beginning, the tenderness he had shown her and Nicole. It couldn't all have been a lie. "And Nicole?" she asked.

For an instant his eyes changed, showing confusion and uncertainty. "What about Nicole?"

"Do you feel the same toward her?"

He rubbed his hand across his forehead. "Unlike you—she's innocent. I could hardly blame her for any of this."

Jennifer squared her shoulders. "I know now it was wrong not to tell you about Nicole, but all I ever wanted was for you to be able to be her father in every way possible."

Richard came over to her. "How pretty that sounds. But you're not fooling me. I know what you really were after was some way to hide the fact that you'd been sleeping with your own brother."

"Don't be stupid—Craig is no more a brother to me than you are." She ran her hand across her forehead, suddenly weary beyond comprehension. "How did you find out?" she said, not even trying to change his mind or deny his accusation.

"Anyone who bothered to look halfway closely at the two of them together would be able to figure it out. His stamp is all over her."

"I'm sorry I hurt you. I never meant to."

His harsh laugh cut the air. "*Sorry?* You don't know the meaning of the word." With lightning swiftness he clamped his hand around her throat. "But I promise you that by morning you will."

She wrapped both of her hands around his wrist and tried to make him let go. The harder she tried, the tighter his hand clamped down until he was actually choking her. "Let go of me, Richard."

"Say please," he said menacingly, his eyes sparkling with pleasure.

"Please," she managed to gasp.

He released her. When she stepped backward, he raised his hand to hit her again.

"No!" A scream shattered the quiet behind them.

They both turned to find Nicole standing in the doorway, her face contorted in fear, tears glistening on her cheeks. Jennifer shoved Richard aside to go to Nicole. She bent down to take her into her arms. "It's all right," she said over and over again, cradling her daughter's trembling body.

Richard came over to stand beside them. Jennifer recoiled at his nearness. She stood and picked Nicole up in her arms, and he reached out to cradle her tear-stained face. "Don't touch her," Jennifer said, her voice tinged with an icy calm. "We're leaving. I'm taking Nicole to my parents' house. I suggest you don't try to stop us." She looked into his now-ashen face to be sure he understood her.

"Jennifer—don't leave me," he begged. "I'm sorry— I didn't mean what I said. It was the brandy talking, not me."

For long seconds she stared at him. "Then it's the first time in our marriage I've been grateful for your drinking."

"You can't leave me. You're my wife."

"Can't?" Her laughter edged on hysteria. "Just watch me." She headed toward the hall closet to get her purse.

"I'll never give you a divorce," he shouted. "You'll never be free from me."

"I'm free now, Richard," she said, not bothering to close the door behind her.

She was almost off the farm before the flow of tears made it impossible for her to see anything in front of her, and she had to pull over to the side of the road. She crossed her arms over the steering wheel and pressed her face against her elbow as sobs racked her body.

"Mommy?" Nicole tentatively said, frightened by her mother's ongoing storm of emotion.

Jennifer reached for her terrified daughter and held her, trying to reassure her with loving words. They stayed that way until Jennifer felt Nicole relax in her arms. In the end, exhaustion overcame her young body and Jennifer gently placed her back in her seat. Tomorrow she would find out how much Nicole had heard and try to find the words to explain. Maybe by discussing with Nicole what had happened between her and Richard that night, she would begin to understand it herself.

UNABLE TO SLEEP, Craig was wandering through the house when he heard a car coming up the driveway. His first thought was that someone from the hospital had come to tell them Frank had had a setback. Reason immediately told him the idea was ridiculous. If there was trouble, the hospital would use the phone.

Kyle and Agnes were long in bed, and the darkness of the house made it easy to see outside. He looked through an opening in the library curtains and felt a surge of joy when he saw Jennifer get out of her Mercedes. He arrived at the front door just as she was about to use her key. His joy turned to fear when he saw her face. The left side was swollen and discolored. Her eyes were red from crying, and a sliver of blood trailed from the corner of her mouth to her chin. "My God," he breathed, reaching for her. "What happened to you?"

At the desperate concern in his voice her eyes filled with fresh tears. To tell Craig what had happened that night would be to relive it all over again and she couldn't do that—not so soon. She moved out of his embrace. "Nicole is sleeping in the car. Would you help me put her to bed?'' What little strength she had left was rapidly disappearing. She owed whatever remained to her daughter. Not until Nicole was taken care of could she think of herself.

CHAPTER SIXTEEN

CRAIG GENTLY LAID his daughter on the bed in one of the spare bedrooms. Wisps of dark hair clung to her cheek, and he brushed them aside before pulling the blanket over her.

"Thank you," Jennifer whispered.

"She's a beautiful little girl," Craig said, staring down at Nicole, his heart swelling with love.

A tiny smile tugged at Jennifer's bruised mouth. "You better not let her hear you say that. She thinks she's a *big* girl."

"Will she be all right here alone?"

"I'm going to sleep with her tonight in case she wakes up."

Craig studied Jennifer's face in the dim light. With gentle care he touched her chin. "Did Richard do this to you?"

"Please don't ask me any questions tonight. I'm too tired to talk about what happened." He put his arms around her, and she laid her head against his chest. She soon realized by the rapid beating of his heart that Craig's outward calm belied an inner storm. She wasn't being fair to ask him to wait for an explanation. Taking his hand, she led him into the hallway. "Which room is yours?" she asked.

He indicated the one across the hall. When they were inside, Jennifer went over to the bed and sat down. She felt more tired than she ever had in her life. It was as if every ounce of energy had been drained from her, leaving her bone weary. She looked down at her lap. "He knows," she said simply.

"How?"

"When he saw you and Nicole together, he guessed. I didn't try to change his mind."

"And that's why he hit you?" Craig's hands curled into fists at his sides. He had never had any tolerance for men who hit women. Shortly after starting Templeton Enterprises, he had fired one of his top executives when he discovered that the man's wife had sought shelter at a battered women's center. His rage had been terrible then; it was murderous now.

Although he tried to hide his thoughts from her, Jennifer could detect Craig's anger in the tense way he held himself. "I want you to promise me you'll stay away from Richard," she said.

"I can't. Not after what he'd done to you."

From somewhere came the strength she needed to demand he listen to her. "This is my problem, and I want you to let me handle it myself."

"Do you have any idea what you're asking?"

"Yes." But she felt she had no choice. She was afraid of what he might do to Richard in her defense, and she would do anything to protect Craig from the possible consequences, even if it meant denying him the right to champion her. *"Promise me."*

He stared at her. She looked so small and fragile and defeated. The thought of Richard hitting her was almost more than he could stand.

"Please promise me, Craig," she said softly.

He went to the bed and knelt down in front of her. "All right," he said at last, taking her hands in his. "For now, I will stay away."

"Thank you." Her shoulders slumped in relief.

Craig brought her hands to his face, tenderly kissing one palm and then the other. "It seems whenever I'm around you I give you pain, when all I ever wanted was to give you happiness," he said sadly. "None of this would have happened if I had stayed away."

Her eyes filled with tears at the despair in his voice. "Seven years ago you gave me five days of such exquisite happiness that it has lasted me all this time. And you gave me Nicole."

"And I intend to spend the rest of my life—"

She pressed her finger to his lips. "Shhh—" she whispered. "Not yet. It's too soon for us to talk about the future."

He nodded. Now that he knew they would be together, he could wait to tell her of the plans he had been making for the three of them—how they would move to Oklahoma City and find a house in the country where she and Nicole could have their horses; how they would spend the summers at Templeton Ranch and ask Kyle to come to stay with them; and how they would have children and bring them up believing they could do anything they wanted to do with their lives. He sat beside her and held her in his arms until they heard Nicole stir and call out in her sleep.

"I'd better get back," Jennifer said. "If she wakes up, I don't want her to be alone."

Craig walked her across the hall. He held her face between his hands and looked deeply into her eyes. "I love you," he told her and bent to brush a kiss against her lips.

She stood on tiptoe to receive his kiss. "And I love you," she whispered, her heart swelling with the knowledge that she was again free to tell him so.

THE NIGHT PASSED SLOWLY for Craig as he tossed and turned and thought about Richard. Never had he felt such violent anger. He had been bested in business deals by people like Richard and was familiar with the frustration and anger such a situation could create. But nothing he'd experienced before compared to how he felt now. His promise to Jennifer echoed in his mind. It was the only thing that kept him from going to Martindale Farm and finding Richard.

Finally the sun broke the horizon, and he got up to go downstairs. He found Agnes already in the kitchen, up even earlier than usual. She was beating on a piece of dough as if it were a punching bag. "Jennifer and Nicole are here," he said without preamble.

"They are? What are they doing here this early?" She grabbed a towel to wipe flour from her hands.

He made a motion to stop her from going to look for them. "They arrived late last night."

"Last night?"

Craig went over to the cupboard and took down two cups. He filled them with coffee and handed one to Agnes. "Why don't we sit down? I have a feeling you may not want to hear this standing up."

Agnes covered the bread dough she had been kneading with a clean dish towel and followed him to the small kitchen table.

"I think you've already figured out some of what I'm going to tell you, so I'm not going to go into detail unless you stop me to ask questions." He took a sip of the steaming coffee. "I originally found out who I was seven years ago..." he began.

A half hour later he finished telling Agnes his and Jennifer's story.

"So many things make sense now," she said, as much to herself as to Craig. "I'd always thought it strange Nicole had such a Mitchell look about her. And Jennifer's decision to marry Richard came about so suddenly she stunned the entire family. I never liked Richard, not from the first time I saw him twenty years ago when he came over here with a group of Jennifer's friends. There was something sneaky about him then, and he carried that sneakiness with him right through to adulthood. But Jennifer had made up her mind and couldn't be talked into waiting. And it was such a relief to see her getting out again—she'd been hibernating those three years after David died—that I tried to convince myself I'd misjudged him."

"Richard must have worked hard to keep his true character hidden from Jennifer."

"Oh, a more attentive man you've never seen." She got up to refill their coffee cups. "Have you thought about what Jennifer's leaving Richard will mean to the two of you?" she asked, sitting back down.

"I can hardly think of anything else."

"Am I to take that to mean you still have feelings for each other?"

"I know its going to sound overblown, but my life's been empty without her. If she would go, I'd take her and Nicole back to Oklahoma with me today." Craig became thoughtful as he sipped his coffee. "Does it bother you that legally, at least, the world thinks of Jennifer and me as brother and sister?"

"On my list of life's worries, that somewhat startling fact doesn't even make the top one hundred." Agnes smiled. "It will give the people who do the social pages at the newspaper some interesting copy, compared to their usual boring party descriptions." Her smile disappeared. "But I was hoping all that's happened would encourage you to stay here."

Would she never give up hope that he would move back to Lexington permanently? "I have a business in Oklahoma City that I've worked hard to establish, and I have to get back to it before too much longer."

"Don't you think it would be rather cruel to uproot Jennifer now after all she's been through? And all of Nicole's friends are here. With everything that's happened, she would be lost if you took her away now."

"You're a real street fighter, Agnes," he said. He looked up at the sound of Kyle bursting into the room.

"Where's Jennifer?" he asked, heading for the refrigerator. "I saw her car outside, but I can't find her anywhere around the house."

"She's upstairs sleeping," Agnes told him. "So try to keep the noise down to a gentle roar."

"What's she doing sleeping here?"

"Since Richard's going to Baltimore with Andrew this weekend, Jennifer and Nicole have decided to stay with us," Agnes quickly answered.

Craig shook his head. It must have been a special kind of hell to be the youngest in a family. As far as he could tell, Kyle was an averagely mature sixteen-year-old and more than capable of handling adult conversation. Yet everyone treated him as if he were only slightly older than Nicole. "Your sister has left her husband," he stated flatly.

Kyle paused in pouring his glass of milk. "So she finally woke up to what a creep that guy is."

Agnes gave Craig a chastising look. "Now just what is that supposed to mean?" she said to Kyle.

"Richard's been cheating on Jennifer almost since the day they were married."

"How could you possibly know something like that?" Agnes demanded.

"I have my sources."

"It seems everyone has their sources, except me," Jennifer said, coming into the room.

Agnes got up to give her a hug. She caught her breath in a gasp of surprise when she saw her daughter's face. "The bastard!" she exclaimed. "Wait until I get my hands—"

"Not you, too, Mother," Jennifer interrupted with a sigh. "I had enough trouble with Craig wanting to go after Richard last night. Please don't make me go through all that again this morning." She pointedly looked at Kyle. "That means you, too. This is my problem . . . all right?"

The normal playfulness was gone from Kyle's face. "He had no right to hit you."

It hadn't occurred to Craig until that instant how difficult it would be for Kyle to see Jennifer's cut lip and bruised cheek and to be asked not to do anything about it. He intimately identified with the conflicting feelings that were plaguing his youngest brother. "This is something Jennifer wants to handle herself, Kyle. And like it or not, we're going to have to respect her wishes."

Jennifer gave him a grateful look. "And I would appreciate it if you'd all try to control your feelings around Nicole. She's terribly confused about everything that has happened." Jennifer had to pause a minute before she could go on. "Nicole loves Richard . . . and I sincerely feel he loves her, too." She'd been unable to keep a tremor from her voice, and it angered her to be a puppet to her emotions. It was important for her to be strong. Nicole was going to need her full attention and strength if she was going to make it through the next few months without permanent scars. She had spent the sleepless night going over and over the last seven years of her life and had been forced to acknowledge she had been everything her family had accused her of—especially blind and foolish. The clues to Richard's true personality had been there all along. She'd just refused to see them for fear they would disrupt her well-ordered life.

"Why don't I take Nicole to the hospital with me today?" Agnes said.

"They'll never let her in, Mother," Jennifer said gently, knowing how much Agnes wanted to help. "She's still only six. And as far as I know, they haven't changed the rules about visitors in the past week."

"I'll talk to Dr. Vitrale."

"Better yet," Kyle interrupted, "let her come down to the barns with me this afternoon. I was going to watch the race with John and the other grooms. When the television crews came to the farm last week, they did an interview with him that is supposed to be shown today. I think Nicole would get a kick out of watching it with us."

"That sounds like a wonderful idea," Jennifer said. "And while you're gone, I can go back to the house and pick up some things for Nicole and myself."

"Not alone, you don't," Craig said.

"I'll be all right," she told him. "Richard is in Baltimore with Andrew."

"I still don't want you going over there alone."

Jennifer looked from Craig to Kyle to Agnes. She had lived her entire life in the loving cocoon of family. She had been nurtured and sheltered and never made to stand on her own two feet. It was long past time for her to do so. "If I'm gone more than an hour, you can come after me."

Craig saw the determination in her eyes, and although he couldn't understand her reasoning, he backed off on his demand to accompany her. "Where is Nicole now?"

"She's getting dressed in the play clothes she keeps over here."

"Would it be all right if I went up to see her?" Agnes asked.

Jennifer smiled. Normally, her mother would have gone up without asking. Obviously she approved of her daughter's declaration of independence. "I would appreciate your seeing her, and I think Nicole will, too."

As soon as Agnes had left, Kyle made a move to follow. "I think I'll see what's on television," he said, graciously exiting to leave Jennifer and Craig alone.

"He's really a special kid," Craig said when Kyle had gone.

"I seem to remember telling you something like that seven years ago."

Craig stood and came around the table. "We have to talk," he said, taking her into his arms.

At first she held back, unable to openly leave her role as Richard's wife. When she realized what she was doing, she relaxed in his embrace.

The door swung open behind them, and Kyle poked his head through. As soon as he saw Craig and Jennifer together, he flushed a deep red. "Sorry," he stammered. "I didn't mean to—"

"Don't worry about it," Craig answered. "You've just stumbled on something everyone is going to know sooner or later. I'm hopelessly in love with your sister, and as soon as she's free, I intend to ask her to marry me."

"Kind of sudden, wasn't it?" Kyle said obviously surprised.

Jennifer pressed her forehead into Craig's chest. "Tell him I'll explain everything later," she said.

"Never mind," Kyle answered. "I heard."

"Was there a special reason you came back?" Craig asked.

"Oh, yeah. Mom wanted me to punch down her bread dough."

"I'll take care of it," Jennifer said.

"Thanks." He started to leave, then came back. A lopsided grin grew on his face. "By the way, what do you call a brother-in-law who's your brother, too?"

"Impatient," Craig said.

Kyle laughed. "Sounds kind of formal to me." When he left, he closed the door with pointed emphasis.

"Are we alone?" Jennifer said, looking up from Craig's chest.

"For the moment."

"Then kiss me."

Craig's heart skipped a beat. He slowly lowered his head until their lips met. As gently as possible he melded his mouth to hers, touching her swollen lips with his tongue, tasting the sweetness she offered.

She met his tongue with her own, communicating the promise that had started to grow in her that morning. She loved Craig. She had loved him from the day they had first met. She wanted him to feel her love as deeply as the air that filled his lungs. "I want to talk to you, too," she said. "We have a lot to work out between us."

"Are you sure I can't go with you when you go back over to your house this afternoon?"

"I have to do this alone, Craig. Please understand."

"It's going to be more painful than you might think for you to go back there today."

"I know, but it's time I stopped taking the easy way out of everything."

His answer was cut off by the sounds of Nicole thumping down the stairs. Craig released Jennifer and reached for his coffee cup just as Nicole came into the room.

"Kyle said I could watch Nightwind win the Preakness down at the barns with him and John. Is that okay, Mommy?"

"It sounds like great fun to me," she said.

"Do you and Uncle Craig want to come, too?"

"Not this time. We have some things to talk about, so we're going to stay here."

The happiness left Nicole's face. "Are you going to tell him about Daddy?"

"He already knows, Nicole," she said gently. "He was up when we got here, and he helped me put you to bed last night."

Nicole glanced over to Craig. "Can Daddy come to the barns with me and Uncle Kyle?"

Jennifer's heart went out to her daughter. The next year was going to be a sad and confusing time for her. "Daddy is in Baltimore with Uncle Andrew, remember?"

Nicole walked across the room and looked up into her mother's face. "Daddy didn't mean to hurt you, Mommy," she said hopefully, taking Jennifer's hand in hers.

Jennifer lifted Nicole in her arms. A six-year-old was too young to carry such a large burden. "I know he didn't, Nicole."

"Are you mad at him?"

"Yes," she said softly. "And I'm a little bit mad at me, too. But no one is mad at you, Nicole. We love you and we always will."

"Do you love Daddy?"

"No..."

"Will you love him when you're not mad at him anymore?"

"No..."

"Not ever?"

How could she explain about love dying without making Nicole afraid that the people who loved her would stop if she ever did something wrong?

Craig saw the dilemma on Jennifer's face, and when she looked at him with beseeching eyes, he went over to her. "There are lots of kinds of love in the world, Nicole, and it's a good thing to have as many as you can," he told her. "Most of these loves let you give them to lots of people at the same time—like grandpas and grandmas. But when you get married, that kind of love only lets you give it to one person. If you ever stop loving that person, it's important that you let them go so they can find someone else to care for them in that special way."

Although Nicole never looked at Craig, Jennifer could tell she had listened to every word he said.

"Are you going to let Daddy go?" Nicole said softly, a catch in her voice.

"Yes..."

Nicole wrapped her arms around Jennifer's neck and dropped her head to her mother's shoulder. "Do I have to stop loving him, too?" she asked, her voice trembling.

Craig saw the torment in Jennifer's eyes, and he wished there were some way he could carry the burden that would be hers over the next few months. It had never occurred to him how difficult it was going to be to tell Nicole who she really was. He had approached the problem with an arrogance that was embarrassing for him to think about now. He placed his hand on Nicole's back and felt the hiccupping tears shaking her small body. *God, let there be some part of Richard worthy of her love,* he silently prayed. "No one wants you to stop loving your Daddy," he said quietly, as if the words had been torn from him.

Jennifer's eyes filled with tears. She knew what it had cost Craig to reassure Nicole. The desire to claim his daughter as his own came through every time he looked at her. "Thank you," she whispered.

THE TIME ALONE Jennifer and Craig had planned for that afternoon never materialized. After Nightwind won the Preakness, the farm became a spontaneous open house for friends who called and stopped by to give their congratulations on the stunning three-length victory. Kyle and Jennifer acted as hosts until Agnes returned from the hospital. Nicole, too, was caught up in the excitement, much to Jennifer's relief. Although everyone who came by was unfailingly polite and friendly to Craig, no one thought to ask who he was or why he was there.

It was late in the afternoon when Andrew called. He asked to speak to Agnes first and then to Kyle and finally to Jennifer. Craig watched as her expression changed from a smile to a worried frown during the one-sided conversation. When she replaced the receiver, she turned to Nicole. "Would you please check the backyard one more time to make sure we picked up all the glasses?"

"First tell me what Uncle Andrew said."

"He said his knees were shaking so badly he could hardly stand up and that he was going to stay in Baltimore for a few more days. Now get going." Jennifer held her breath until Nicole was gone, afraid she would think to question her about Richard.

"What is it, Jennifer?" Agnes asked as soon as she heard the back door close.

"Richard's in the hospital."

"What happened?"

"It seems he has an ulcer. It started bleeding this morning on the plane. He was taken to the hospital as soon as they landed."

"So that's why he wasn't in the winner's circle with Andrew," Kyle said to no one in particular.

"He refused to let Andrew call me this morning, but now he wants me to fly out there to be with him."

"You're not going to go, are you?" Agnes said.

Jennifer looked over to Craig, who was standing on the outside of the small circle that had formed around her. His expression was blank. Only his eyes revealed his inner thoughts. She waited for him to say something.

"Do whatever you have to do," he finally said.

She had never loved him more than she did at that moment. She turned back to her mother. "No, I'm not going. He doesn't need me. He never did."

CHAPTER SEVENTEEN

THE DAY FOLLOWING THE PREAKNESS turned out to be even more hectic than race day had been. There were inceasing demands for interviews from what seemed to be every newspaper and magazine in the country. Craig and Jennifer tried several times to get away by themselves but were unsuccessful. Finally, ignoring a ringing telephone, Craig took Jennifer by the hand and walked out the front door. They were almost a mile from the house before he brought up the real reason he had sought to escape with her.

"I have to leave Lexington soon," he said, stopping by the roadway.

Despite the warm afternoon, Jennifer felt a chill. "How soon?"

"Tomorrow..." He had been in contact with Henry Keily and learned that all hell had broken loose with the Lambert/Ingersoll merger. It was imperative he get back to take over the negotiations as soon as possible. Dozens of jobs were at stake.

She walked over to the fence and leaned against the railing.

"I want you and Nicole to go with me," he said.

"And you know that I want to go—but I can't right now."

It was the answer he'd expected, but hearing the words spoken out loud was as painful as a blow to his midsection. "I have to get back for business reasons. You know I would stay if I could."

"Yes, I know," she said, lowering her head to rest her cheek against her arm. Already she missed him.

"How long..." He couldn't finish.

She hesitated answering him. There were feelings controlling her that she didn't fully understand. "I've learned something these past few days," she began softly. "I don't like myself very much." She turned to look at him. "A few days ago someone told me I've been living with my head in the sand, and they were right. I've spent the past ten years—one-third of my life—trying to protect myself by hiding. It's time I stopped. Until I get this part of me worked out and learn to stop being such a coward, I won't be any good to anyone."

"Couldn't you work things out with me?"

She reached for his hand. "There's something else I've been thinking about. Have you ever stopped to consider how little time we've actually known each other?"

He shrugged. "I know it sounds corny, but time is irrelevant when I'm with you."

She smiled. "I feel the same way when I'm with you, but it doesn't change the fact that we know very little about each other. I don't even know what kind of music you like or whether you went to college. Are you a football fan? Baseball? Do you squeeze a toothpaste tube from the end or the middle? Are you Republican or Democrat?"

"What are you trying to tell me?"

"I desperately want our relationship to work. To give it the best possible chance, I think we should spend some time getting to know each other before we try to pick up our relationship where we left off."

"Does this mean you're having second thoughts about us?"

She brought his hand to her cheek. "My love for you and Nicole is the only thing I'm sure about anymore."

"Then I don't understand."

"It's more than just a matter of our becoming friends, Craig. I want to find out who I am and to develop pride in myself before I come to you. I refuse to let you settle for anything less than the best I can be."

"You have to know that none of this matters to me. I don't care where you squeeze toothpaste or whether you're Republican or Democrat." He smiled gently. "For all I care, you could even like opera. As far as I'm concerned, only one thing counts and that's how we feel about each other."

She stepped closer and slipped her arms around his waist. What had seemed so vital to her the night before became almost insignificant when they were together. Her good intentions were nothing compared to her need to be with him. It was on the tip of her tongue to tell him to forget everything she'd said when she abruptly thought of the one insurmountable problem they had to face. "We're forgetting Nicole," she said. "This time we have more than ourselves to think about."

Craig closed his eyes and let out a sigh of resignation. "You're right," he admitted.

"I'm afraid we could do irreparable harm to her if we tried to make the transition between you and Richard happen too quickly."

Jennifer had destroyed any possible argument he had hoped to pursue to get her to leave with him. "How long do you think that will take?"

"Much will depend on Richard, I'm afraid. And how willing he's going to be to let the two of us go."

"What do you think the chances are that he'll cooperate?"

"The night we fought, his final words were that he'd never give me a divorce, so I'm not counting on his cooperation at all. But it doesn't matter. Nothing will keep me from divorcing him. I don't care how long it takes."

Craig's heart sank. With the right lawyer, Richard could keep the divorce tied up in court for years. And what if he tried to use Nicole as a bargaining tool? The thought made Craig sick to his stomach. "You said he needed money. Could he be bought off?"

Jennifer smiled sadly. "I don't have anywhere near the amount he'd want. I gave the trust fund from my grandparents to Nicole when she was born, and I won't have access to the one coming from Mom and Dad for another six years."

"How much do you think it would take?"

"Far more than either of us have," she said.

A smile tugged at the corner of Craig's mouth as he brought her closer. Jennifer still thought he was a small-time rancher from an obscure part of Oklahoma. It eased his mounting frustration to realize that at last there was something he could do. "Perhaps Richard won't be as stubborn as you think," he said.

She looked up at him. "Even if he is, I won't let him keep us apart. The minute I feel Nicole is ready, we'll come to you."

"It can't be too soon," he murmured, bending to kiss her. The wait would seem endless, but he knew they would manage. He broke the kiss and looked down at her. "By the way, where *do* you squeeze your toothpaste tube?"

She gave him a sheepish smile. "In the middle."

He shook his head. "I can see we're in trouble."

"You're an end person I suppose."

"Almost compulsively so."

"Now what?"

"I guess we'll just have to get one of those new pump things."

"You'd do that for me?"

"There's nothing I wouldn't do for you," he said, suddenly serious.

An instant of fear flashed through her eyes. "Does that include waiting?"

"I'd wait for you forever."

"I promise it won't take nearly that long," she said, wrapping her arms around his neck and stretching to give him a kiss.

A truck pulled up beside them and stopped. "Excuse me," Kyle said, after sitting there several seconds and being ignored.

Reluctantly Craig lifted his head. "Did you want us?" he asked.

"Not me—Dad. Mom told him she saw you packing, and he said he wants you to come over to the hospital right away."

With a nod of acceptance, Craig took Jennifer's hand and walked over to the truck. He was on his way to the hospital less than ten minutes later.

CRAIG TAPPED LIGHTLY ON THE DOOR to Frank's hospital room before going inside. His father's eyes snapped open, and an immediate frown appeared. "What's this I hear about you leaving? You could at least wait a few days for me to get out of this place and thank you properly for what you've done."

"It's time I got back to work," Craig said, pulling a chair from across the room. "I have a business to run.

And that business is in the middle of a problem they need me to help solve."

"What kind of business?"

"The one I mentioned the day I arrived," Craig hedged, realizing he have given away more than he had intended.

Frank thought for a minute. "Dealing in venture capital, wasn't it?"

"That's it."

"Who's your boss?"

Tired of skirting the truth, Craig decided to admit who and what he was. "I am."

Frank smiled. "I'm glad you finally decided to stop playing games."

Craig was instantly alert. "Oh?"

"Am I the first one in the family you've told about Templeton Enterprises?"

Craig's jaw dropped. Too surprised to speak, he answered by nodding.

"Good."

"And why is that?" he asked, recovering his voice.

"I realize you're not going to be able to keep what you do for a living secret much longer, but I'd like Andrew to have a chance to come around on his own. He has a lesson or two to learn about human nature, and I can't think of a better way for him to learn them than from his older brother. He keeps trying to convince himself the primary reason you came back here was to lay claim to Mitchell Farm. When he's finally forced to come around to admitting he was wrong, it just might make him realize not everyone keeps a dollar sign on his altar of success."

"How did you find out about me?"

Frank's eyes sparkled. "I had you investigated. How else?"

Craig laughed out loud. He had woefully misjudged his father. "Well, at least now you understand why I won't be coming back here to help Andrew run the farm."

"I can't say there isn't a lingering hope that refuses to die, but I've just about managed to convince myself it will be enough knowing you're around. Historically, the Mitchells have always made a big thing out of holidays, and this generation is no different. We'll expect you to come home to help us celebrate them."

"You can count on it," Craig said. Several seconds passed before he spoke again. "I know we've talked about this before, but just out of idle curiosity, what would you have done if I'd decided to take you up on your offer about the farm?"

Frank eyed him, obviously not believing the disclaimer about "idle" curiosity. "Like I said then, we would have found a place for you."

"And what would you have done with Andrew?"

"Eventually he would have come around and accepted that he had to share the running of the farm."

"In other words, it isn't an ironclad rule that the farm has to pass on to the oldest son?"

"Why don't you stop beating around the bush and tell me just what it is you're getting at?"

"You've been looking in the wrong direction for someone to balance Andrew's headlong flight into modernization. Kyle is the person you want to carry on the Mitchell standards. Once he's old enough and confident enough to challenge Andrew's authority, he'll make one hell of an administrator. They might come to blows once in a while, but between them, they'll keep up the tradition and make more money than the farm has ever made—which should keep both of them at least partially happy."

Frank chuckled. "You know, I think you've got something there. It's certainly worth thinking about." He reached for a manila envelope on the table beside the bed. "Now about this Ingersoll/Lambert thing Templeton Enterprises is involved in. If you take advice as well as you give it, I've got some for you. If I were you, I'd pull out of the merger as quickly as I could. Something's not right about it."

Again Craig was too stunned to reply immediately. When he did, he shook his head and said, "I'm going to have to find out who you use for your detective work. He's not only fast; he's thorough."

"His name is Jack Chapman. I've been using him for years. He's the best there is."

Craig chuckled. "Someday I'll tell you a story about Jack Chapman, Dad." He paused, as surprised as Frank at the use of the name *Dad*. He wasn't sure when the mental transformation had taken place, but the familiar term had slipped out without conscious thought.

Frank stared at his son. "I'm sorry you can't stay longer," he said, his voice heavy with emotion. "We have a lot to catch up on."

"I'd like you to come to Oklahoma for a visit. I've decided to open the ranch house again, and there's lots of room for everyone. There are also some people there I'd like you to meet. They're special to me."

"We'll be there as soon as the doctor says I'm fit to travel."

An incredible sense of well-being came over Craig. He wished Max and Wynona were still alive to share in his happiness. He had a feeling they would have liked Frank and Agnes. He no longer felt the destructive bitterness toward his adoptive parents that had eaten at him in the beginning. Freedom from that bitterness had allowed him to understand that Max and Wynona had given to him from the bottom of their hearts until there was no more to give. Even in death, Wynona had thought of him first.

The afternoon wore on in easy conversation between Frank and Craig. In unmeasured steps they came to know and respect and like each other. Finally it was time for Craig to leave. Frank sat up on the edge of the bed and held out his hand. Craig stared at his father's hand for a moment, then ignored it and gave him a hug.

"As soon as the doctor says I can travel, we'll be down there for a visit," Frank promised his departing son.

"I'll be waiting," Craig told him. "And why don't you see if you can't get Andrew to come along? He seems to be thawing toward me, and I think with some effort on both our parts, we just might become friends someday." The invitation had been an afterthought, but sincerely given. When Craig saw how happy it made his father, he was glad he'd remembered to include Andrew.

"I'll be sure and do that."

Craig smiled and waved one last time before heading down the hall.

When he arrived back at the house, he discovered Agnes had prepared a large meal for his last night home. He had hoped for a quiet evening with only family, but the stream of visitors coming to offer congratulations about Nightwind continued into the night.

Long after he had gone to bed, Craig lay awake thinking about himself and Jennifer and Nicole and his ache to have them with him. Not until he was alone did he acknowledge he was paying lip service to his ability to return to Oklahoma and function without them. Reason told him there was no other way for them to handle the situation. But reason went to hell in a hand basket when he thought about the lonely days and nights ahead of him.

He and Jennifer had already lost seven years. To lose any more time was unthinkable.

He rolled to his side just as the bedroom door silently opened. He stared into the darkness, trying to see who had come into his room. Slowly, a form took shape. When he recognized Jennifer he caught his breath; his heartbeat thundered in his ears.

"Craig?" she whispered as she came nearer.

He sat up and held out his hand. "I'm over here," he said. "Is something wrong?"

"Shh—" she admonished, moving to the side of his bed. "I'd prefer the rest of the household not know I decided to pay you a midnight visit." She stood beside him for several seconds before she reached for the sash on her robe. When the satin parted, a narrow strip of bare skin was exposed.

Craig sat frozen, unable to respond immediately with word or touch. His inability to move ceased when she shrugged and the robe fell from her shoulders, revealing the body that had haunted his dreams for seven long years. He stood beside her and took her into his arms. "My God, Jennifer—you're even more beautiful than I remembered." His hands ran the length of her back, stopped to feel the narrowness of her waist and then moved on to gently cup her buttocks. He lifted her slightly to bring her closer to him. He had never been so glad that he always slept naked.

A shuddering sigh escaped Jennifer's lips as she gave herself over to him. Finally the physical torment that had been burning in her loins since the moment she and Craig had seen each other again would find release. She pressed her breasts against the soft matting of hair on his chest and gently nipped with her teeth the skin covering his collarbone. When she tilted her head back to receive his kiss, all subtlety disappeared. Craig ravished her mouth with a kiss that left her weak with wanting him. She met his thrusting tongue boldly, demanding he take further intimacies.

And then the kiss abruptly ended, and he was holding her at arm's length away from him. "I can't make love to you tonight, not the way you want me to," he said, his voice ragged with desire. "Not after what I let happen last time. I have no way to protect you . . ."

Jennifer took his hand from her shoulder and pressed his palm to her lips. She circled the center with her tongue and breathed against the moisture.

"Jennifer—cut it out," he groaned.

"I love you for thinking about me, but it isn't necessary. I've taken care of everything. I even called the doctor today to make sure you—"

"That must have been an interesting conversation."

She gave him a wicked grin. "Oh, it was. Do you want me to tell you about it?"

"Let's save it for another time when we have nothing better to do," he said, bringing her back into his arms. Hungrily Craig resumed the kiss, exploring the velvety recesses of Jennifer's mouth. His hands traveled up her sides to cup her breasts. The nipples hardened at his touch, and he bent to take first one and then the other into his mouth. He bent lower still to pick her up into his arms.

"Stop that," she breathlessly commanded, moving away from him. "I promised Dr. Vitrale we'd be careful."

Craig smiled. He wished he could have listened in on that conversation. Jennifer's innate shyness should have made a call to Vitrale interesting, to say the least. "How careful?"

"Nothing . . . uh . . ." she stumbled over the answer.

"You mean we have to save the kinky stuff for later?" he said, gently teasing her.

She snuggled against him and wrapped her arms around his neck. "Not *all* of it," she whispered suggestively.

He let out a groan. "Not fair, Jennifer."

"Who said anything about being fair?"

He held the sides of her face and made her look at him. "Do you have any idea how hard it's going to be for me to leave tomorrow?" he asked, suddenly serious.

She swallowed. "Or how hard it's going to be for me to watch you go?" She took his hand and sat down on the edge of the bed. "Let's not think about tomorrow or the problems we still have ahead of us. For tonight let's just celebrate that we found each other again."

Craig joined Jennifer on the bed. He lay down and reached for her. She nestled into his side. "Would you like to know what you're going to be doing a year from how?" he said, pressing a kiss to her temple.

She looked up at him, her eyes filled with love. "Does this mean I'm to add fortune-telling to the list of things I don't know about you?" she asked.

"I think crystal ball gazing sounds a little better."

She ran her hand over his shoulder and down the length of his muscular arm. "Tell me... what am I going to be doing a year from now?"

Craig brought his hand to his forehead and closed his eyes in concentration. "I see you in the arms of a man who worships you," he said. "You and this man are at an inn in the country... surrounded by senior citizens... dancing to music neither of you can hum because you don't know the melody. There's a mirrored ball turning overhead that makes it look like there are stars in your hair... and a pair of quarrelsome squirrels outside in the woods." His voice dropped to a sensual whisper. "I'm getting a new image . . . an old fashioned room . . . there's a four poster . . ."

"You remembered everything . . ." she said. It was as though he had given her a marvelous gift.

"As if it were yesterday. I've relived every minute of the weekend we spent together a thousand times."

She kissed him. "We're going to have a wonderful life together."

"With lots of children to keep Nicole company."

"Maybe we'll even start our own dynasty."

"With just one ironclad rule," he said.

"What's that?"

"If one or a dozen of our children wants to become a part of the business, each will have equal shares."

"Business?"

It was time he told her the truth about himself.

When he'd quickly told her the details and she'd recovered from her astonishment, she said, "I think your rule is a wonderful idea."

"I love you," he said, kissing her and reveling in the knowledge that whether they were rich or poor made absolutely no difference to her.

"How is it you always manage to say 'I love you' first?"

He smiled. "Do you want me to take it back?"

Long tension-filled seconds passed before she answered. "Only if you show me instead," she said softly.

He ran his finger down the length of her face. "I wish I could tell you how much it means to me to have you here with me tonight."

"I had to come."

Craig kissed her and gently touched the corner of her mouth with his tongue. The air she exhaled he took into his lungs and released as a pent-up groan of desire. He lowered his head to her breast and traced moist circles around the nipple with his tongue before drawing the turgid peak into his mouth.

Jennifer moved against him, a core of need building inside her. She caressed him, careful not to touch his scar when she ran her hand across the flat plane of his stomach to touch him intimately. She felt a surge of pleasure at his readiness.

Craig gently turned Jennifer to her back and suspended himself over her for several seconds. He then lowered himself to press a kiss to her forehead. He kissed her eyes, her temples, her nose and her lips before moving again to her breasts. A volatile mixture of pleasure and frustration built in Jennifer as she waited for Craig to initiate the final act of lovemaking. It wasn't until he separated her thighs with his hands and moved lower that she understood what he planned to do.

"Craig—no," she gasped, too timid even with him to release the inhibitions of a lifetime. But he ignored her and she was soon beyond all thought of protesting.

What seemed an unbearable anticipation grew until she reached a climax that left her breathless. She was still experiencing waves of delectation when Craig began to enter her. With deep demanding strokes, he brought her back to the peak of the mountain she had just climbed. Again the anticipation grew, building until she was aware of nothing but the sweet promise of release. She called his name and clung to him.

"I've waited so long for you," he told her before covering her mouth with his. He matched the movement of his tongue to the movement of their bodies. He waited for her until neither of them could wait any longer. Together they reached an explosive climax that left them both emotionally drained.

They cuddled each other while their racing hearts slowly resumed normal rhythms. It wasn't until then that Craig realized he had some discomfort in the side where he'd had his surgery. He turned to ease the pain, trying to make the motion as natural as possible to keep Jennifer from knowing what he was doing.

"Is it a dull ache or a sharp pain?" she asked, giving him more room to lie flat.

"Dull and not very bad, considering," he answered, knowing it was useless to try to fool her.

"Are you sure?"

"Give me a few more minutes, and I'll show you."

She smiled as she lay back down beside him, curling into his side and gently placing her leg across his.

He put his arm around her and drew her closer. "Jennifer?"

"Hmmm?"

"Do you like brussels sprouts?"

After several seconds she came up on one elbow and looked at him. "I *hate* brussels sprouts."

"How about cabbage?"

"Red or green?"

"Either."

"Neither."

"What about parsnips?"

"Yuck."

"Carrots?"

"Cooked or raw?"

"Cooked."

"Uh-uh."

"Raw?"

"Great with sour cream and onion dip. Otherwise, rabbit food."

"Leeks?"

"Love them in potato soup."

"What about—"

Jennifer laughed and put her hand over Craig's mouth. "Is this where we get to the kinky part?"

He pressed a kiss to her palm. "I just figured we might as well get a head start on your project."

"Project?"

"You know—getting to know each other better."

A sudden, overwhelming feeling of emptiness came over Jennifer. Her eyes filled with moisture. "Oh, how I'm going to miss you," she said, choking back tears.

Craig pulled her back into his arms and held her tight. They stayed that way until the sky grew light with dawn. Even then he was reluctant to let her go. Despite the optimistic reassurances they mouthed so easily, he knew it would be a long time before they would hold each other again.

EPILOGUE

SIX MONTHS LATER

JENNIFER HANDED THE DRIVER HIS FARE and stepped from the cab. While she waited for him to retrieve her suitcase from the trunk, she shielded her eyes from the sun and gazed across the plaza at Templeton Tower. An immediate private smile formed as her gaze swung upward along the gleaming tinted-glass building. How like Craig to be so modest about his success. It was one of the things—among so many others she had discovered and rediscovered during their hours of long-distance telephone calls this past six months—that she loved about him.

"I hope you enjoy your visit to our city, miss," the driver said as he placed her single suitcase on the sidewalk beside her.

She was tempted to tell him that she was in Oklahoma City for far more than a visit, but she held in check her urge to shout her happiness to the world and let his pleasantry go with a simple "Thank you. I know I will." She waited until the cab pulled from the curb before taking a deep breath and heading across the wide plaza with long eager strides.

How good she felt. Better than she had in years. Not only was she wildly, passionately in love with Craig—she had finally come to like and respect *herself*. The six months she and Craig had been apart had been agonizing for them, but without the self-enforced separation she was sure she would never have been able to find the strength to stand on her own two feet again. With Craig around, even for an occasional weekend, it would have been too easy for her to slip back into her old habits and allow him to do for her what she should have been doing for herself.

When Richard's ulcer was under control and he had returned to Lexington, he had declared himself a changed man and insisted she give him a chance to prove himself. Jennifer had discovered later that Richard's change in attitude had been a result of a quick trip Craig had made to Maryland shortly after returning to Oklahoma. Craig's purchase of Richard's interest in Nightwind had eased Richard's financial strain leaving him free to concentrate on winning his wife back.

Under Richard's constant persistent pressure, it had been tempting for Jennifer to retreat from the confrontations and let the family lawyer handle the negotiations for the divorce. But instead she had forced herself to meet with Richard. After several unproductive sessions, he had finally acknowledged she was no longer the easily manipulated woman he had married, and they were able to move on to the one thing left that mattered to both of them . . . Nicole.

Jennifer had never doubted that Richard truly cared for Nicole, so when he offered to let the divorce go through unopposed in exchange for visiting rights, she had readily agreed.

Although hurt and confused by all that was happening around her, Nicole had slowly begun to accept and then adapt to the drastic changes in her life. In the beginning Craig had called her once a week to visit and allow her to come to know him better. Soon the frequency of the calls increased to twice a week and then three times. At first, their conversations had been awkward, filled with long pauses and hesitant questions, but Craig had persisted and, in the end, they had developed a marvelous rapport.

Nicole still had no idea who Craig really was and, although Jennifer knew he ached to claim her as his own, he realized and accepted that it might be years before he would be able to do so without hurting her.

As Jennifer neared the entrance to Templeton Tower, her thoughts came racing back to the present. It had been so long since she and Craig had seen each other. They'd endured so many lonely nights and frustrating phone calls. Now that she was only minutes away from seeing him again, she felt as if she were walking on air.

CRAIG TOSSED THE PEN he'd been using to gesture with on his desk and leaned back in his chair. His gaze swept over the men sitting around his boardroom. It was almost four o'clock, and they were no closer to a solution to the divestiture problem with Condomar Electronics than they had been at 9:00 A.M. It had taken eight men seven hours to make one lopsided circle in their thinking. Earlier he'd told the roomful of executives that no one would go home that day until they'd come up with an answer. At the time, he'd had every intention to follow through with his threat, but now he had just about decided to tell everyone to leave and that they would try again tomorrow.

He reached up to rub the back of his neck as he listened to Henry Keily and Burke Wharton argue a point they had been over ten times already that day when a strange feeling gripped him. A compelling restlessness nudged at the corners of his mind. It wasn't until he heard Henry ask him if something was wrong that he noticed the room had grown completely quiet and seven pairs of eyes were focused on him.

"I'm fine," Craig said, leaning forward and stretching in an attempt to refocus his attention. "Why don't you give me those figures on the gross earnings again," he told Burke Wharton. He tried to concentrate on the accountant's voice, but the strange feeling returned, only this time twice as strongly.

"Excuse me," Craig finally said when he realized he'd only half heard Burke's statement. "I'm going to go outside to walk around for a minute to see if I can't clear some of the cobwebs. While I'm gone, why don't the rest of you take a breather?"

He grabbed his coat and crossed the room. The instant he opened the door, he knew why he had been unable to concentrate. Jennifer looked up from the magazine she had been reading and gave him a smile that knocked the wind out of him.

"I couldn't wait until next week," she explained softly, fighting the lump that had appeared in her throat.

Craig struggled to regain his emotional balance. The only way he had been able to get through the past half year had been by living his life one day at a time. As each day ended, he told himself he was one day closer to the time he and Jennifer would be together again. To have her show up an entire week early was such a surprise that he was almost too stunned to move.

Intuitively Jennifer understood what was happening to him. She left her chair and crossed the room. "Would it be better if I left and came back next week?" she asked, gently teasing him.

Nothing in Craig's life had felt as wonderful as that moment. His hesitation disappeared, and he reached for her, holding her close, glorying in the feel of her, taking her wonderfully clean smell deep into his lungs while trying to convince himself he wasn't dreaming. When at last he found words, he almost laughed at their ordinariness. "You should have called," he said. "I would have met you."

"I only decided to come a couple of hours ago."

And then he did what he had been wanting to do for six long months. He kissed her. Deeply, passionately and completely, he kissed her, ignoring where they were in his exquisite pleasure to have her in his arms again. Slowly he became aware of a loud noise behind them. He brought his hands up to cradle Jennifer's face. "Excuse me a minute," he said, after giving her a meltingly loving smile. He then released her and turned around. To a man, his formerly weary executives had stood and were applauding. Craig laughed. He reached for Jennifer's hand and led her back into the boardroom beside him. "Gentlemen," he said, "I would like to introduce you to the future Mrs. Templeton . . . Jennifer Martindale."

One by one, the men came forward to shake Jennifer's hand. Last in line was Henry Keily, who ignored Jennifer's outstretched hand and gave her a heartfelt hug.

"I know this is going to upset everyone," Craig said, putting his arm across Jennifer's shoulders. "But I'm calling it a day. Condomar Electronics is going to have to wait until tomorrow for a solution to their problems." His announcement was met with prolonged, insincere groans. Again Craig laughed. "Now get out of here and go home."

It took a minute for ties to be straightened, jackets to be gathered and final congratulations to be expressed as seven men readied themselves to leave, but Jennifer didn't mind. It gave her a special feeling to see her and Craig's happiness reflected in the smiles of others.

As soon as they were alone, Craig took her in his arms again. "You've changed," he said, studying her.

"I have? How?"

"You've lost that wounded, frightened look you used to have in your eyes."

She smiled her pleasure. "I've been trying to tell you that you were going to see a new me when I came to Oklahoma."

"But you never said how exciting this new you was going to be."

"Do you always know exactly the right thing to say?"

Instead of answering, he gave her a deep, lingering kiss. Heat spread throughout her body, not stopping until it reached her toes. When he ended the kiss, he buried his face in the softness of her hair and held her tightly. "Is it really over?" he whispered.

His voice was filled with such an aching poignancy that Jennifer was shocked at the depth of the loneliness he had managed to keep hidden from her. It was the first time he had let her see past the infinitely patient façade and into the suffering he had been going through. Always before he had been careful to hide his feelings and had never failed to show his support for her decision to struggle through her "coming of age" alone. Not once had he even hinted at what the isolation was doing to him. She had thought it impossible to love him more than she already did. How wrong she had been. "Yes . . . it's really over," she answered in a choked whisper.

"I love you," he said, looking deeply into her eyes.

"And I love you. From this day forward, all I want is to be your wife and the mother of your children."

Craig smiled and kissed her lightly on her forehead. "Does this mean you're giving up all thought of making the next Olympic jumping team?"

She gave him a sheepish grin. "Well, I'm sure you wouldn't want me to *stagnate*."

He laughed and held her closer. "How many?"

"What? Olympics?"

"No...children."

She thought for a moment. "How does an even dozen sound?"

"Even for someone like me, that sounds like six too many."

"But think of how much fun we'll have..."

The playfulness left Craig's face. "Perhaps it would be better if we forgot about what *we* want for a while and just concentrated on what's best for Nicole. If there's any possible way it can be done, I want her to come out of this without any permanent scars."

Jennifer knew that no matter how much she reassured Craig, he was not going to believe how well Nicole was doing until he saw her for himself. "Obviously it was a mistake for me to come here alone," she said with an exaggerated sigh. "I should have waited until next week when Nicole was out of school and could come with me. Better yet—maybe Nicole and I should have waited until next month and come with Kyle and Mom and Dad and Andrew. Maybe then you'd believe how well we're all doing."

"*Andrew?* Andrew's coming to Oklahoma?"

"He decided to take you up on your offer to visit."

"Well, I'll be a—"

The conversation was not going in the direction she had intended. Determined to get his attention back on other matters, Jennifer grabbed his lapels and glared at him. "Craig!"

"Yes?"

"Believe it or not, I didn't leave Lexington a week early and travel all this way to talk to you about the rest of the family. Can we please get back to us?"

He gave her a wicked grin. "So tell me—just why *did* you come down here a week early...and all alone?"

Her voice became a seductive whisper. "I think this is one of those situations where showing is better than telling."

He let out a groan. "Something tells me—"

"Yes?" she murmured, wrapping her arms around his neck.

"By the time we're through..."

"Yes?" She snuggled her body provocatively into his.

"We just might turn out to be the parents of a dozen chidren, after all."

She sighed. "Or even more..."

Harlequin Superromance

COMING NEXT MONTH

ATTRACTIVE, SPACE SAVING BOOK RACK

Display your most prized novels on this handsome and sturdy book rack. The hand-rubbed walnut finish will blend into your library decor with quiet elegance, providing a practical organizer for your favorite hard-or soft-covered books.

Only $9.95

Approximately 16" x 8" when assembled

Assembles in seconds!

To order, rush your name, address and zip code, along with a check or money order for $10.70 ($9.95 plus 75¢ postage and handling) (New York residents add appropriate sales tax), payable to *Harlequin Reader Service* to:

In the U.S.

Harlequin Reader Service
Book Rack Offer
901 Fuhrmann Blvd.
P.O. Box 1325
Buffalo, NY 14269-1325

Offer not available in Canada.

BKR-1

Take 4 books & a surprise gift FREE

SPECIAL LIMITED-TIME OFFER

Mail to **Harlequin Reader Service**®

In the U.S.
901 Fuhrmann Blvd.
P.O. Box 1394
Buffalo, N.Y. 14240-1394

In Canada
P.O. Box 609
Fort Erie, Ontario
L2A 9Z9

YES! Please send me 4 free Harlequin American Romance® novels and my free surprise gift. Then send me 4 brand-new novels as they come off the presses. Bill me at the low price of $2.25 each —a 11% saving off the retail price. There are no shipping, handling or other hidden costs. There is no minimum number of books I must purchase. I can always return a shipment and cancel at any time. Even if I never buy another book from Harlequin, the 4 free novels and the surprise gift are mine to keep forever.

Name _____ (PLEASE PRINT)

Address _____ Apt. No.

City _____ State/Prov. _____ Zip/Postal Code

This offer is limited to one order per household and not valid to present subscribers. Price is subject to change.   DOAR-SUB-1RR

Explore love with Harlequin in the Middle
Ages, the Renaissance, in the Regency, the
Victorian and other eras.

Relive within these books the endless ages of
romance, set against authentic historical
backgrounds. Two new historical love stories
published each month.